Readers Love Amanda

The Prince and the Ice King

"I desperately hope we get to see this cast of characters again because it wasn't just our two leads I fell in love with…"

—The Cozy Reading Corner

Stitches

"I loved the first book in the series, and I love this one as well! It's very creative, the characters are all great, and the story has many twists and turns to keep you on your toes!"

—Bayou Book Junkie

The Bard and the Fairy Prince

"A story full of amazing creatures and stunning magic, with lighting and smoke, whirlwinds, elements working their power…all excitingly written, it started with an easygoing pace but accelerated the further the journey came."

—Love Bytes Reviews

Their Dark Reflections

"I thoroughly devoured this book. Amanda Meuwissen has a gift for creating multi-dimensional characters, full of moral ambiguity, and making you fall in love with them. This book is no exception."

—Paranormal Romance Guild

By the Red Moonlight

"(Amanda) creates a new world of every type of paranormal being you can imagine, and she explains not through heavy backstory or exposition, but as the characters are introduced. Well done."

—Maggie Blackbird Reviews

By A<small>MANDA</small> M<small>EUWISSEN</small>

Coming Up for Air
Their Dark Reflections

DREAMSPUN DESIRES
A Model Escort
Interpretive Hearts

MOONLIGHT PROPHECIES
By the Red Moonlight
Blue Moon Rising
Wane on Harvest Moon

TALES FROM THE GEMSTONE KINGDOM
The Prince and the Ice King
Stitches
The Bard and the Fairy Prince
Void Dancer

Published by DSP Publications
After Vertigo

Published by D<small>REAMSPINNER</small> P<small>RESS</small>
www.dreamspinnerpress.com

VOID DANCER

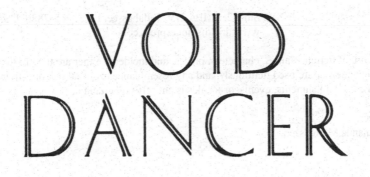

AMANDA MEUWISSEN

DREAMSPINNER
PRESS

Published by
DREAMSPINNER PRESS

5032 Capital Circle SW, Suite 2, PMB# 279, Tallahassee, FL 32305-7886 USA
www.dreamspinnerpress.com

This is a work of fiction. Names, characters, places, and incidents either are the product of author imagination or are used fictitiously, and any resemblance to actual persons, living or dead, business establishments, events, or locales is entirely coincidental.

Void Dancer
© 2023 Amanda Meuwissen

Cover Art
© 2023 by Kris Norris
https://krisnorris.com
coverrequest@krisnorris.com
Cover content is for illustrative purposes only and any person depicted on the cover is a model.

Trade Paperback ISBN: 978-1-64108-557-1
Digital ISBN: 978-1-64108-556-4
Trade Paperback published May 2023
v. 1.0

Printed in the United States of America
∞
This paper meets the requirements of
ANSI/NISO Z39.48-1992 (Permanence of Paper).

CHAPTER 1

CULLEN LANDED with a soft thud of his feet finding purchase in the grass. He'd climbed the rocky crags from the basin of the Lilac Lake to a higher altitude than ever before tonight, but not quite high enough to see over them and take in the lands beyond the Gemstone Kingdoms.

Someday he would, but he was not so foolish as to continue climbing when his footing had faltered and rocks spilled loosely out of place. He'd still descended by a different route to keep things interesting, sneaking toward the outskirts of the residential area and dropping from the cliffs into a citizen's backyard.

The hour was later than he'd anticipated. His father would be wondering why he hadn't come home for dinner. Cullen wouldn't admit the true answer—that his appetite had been sated by a different sort of meal, fed only by the thrill of adventure.

'Twas unbecoming of a prince to creep through the private property of his citizens, but opportunities to do as he pleased would be fewer and farther between once he wed.

Wed. Cullen of House Ametista, the Amethyst Prince, was due to wed very soon. His father had been scrounging up betrothal offers for months, some royal, some noble, some simply from influential families here or in other kingdoms. Cullen had no interest in taking a queen, but he could have a prince consort or fellow king if he so chose. That wasn't the problem. He'd never be free to seek out new lands and people and invention once he was tethered to the throne.

At least the small adventures he could manage by exploring the borders of his kingdom distracted him from the unbearable weight of one day ruling it.

No one noticed him appear out from between two houses, as he headed up the path toward the castle. He nodded at the few passersby he did meet, who recognized him as their prince and bowed their heads.

Cullen loved the Amethyst Kingdom at night, with its dark sky dotted by a blanket of stars, even if he longed to see more of the world outside it. Once he reached high enough on the castle's hill, he could look back and see the glow of the Amethyst itself in the center of the market square far below him, a beautiful pulsing purple, the same color as Cullen's eyes.

Another sign that he was destined to take the throne.

Amethyst did not adhere to strict lineage lines for succession. Sometimes different families, different people could come into power, but whoever ruled found themselves bound to the Amethyst, and from that union their eyes glowed violet evermore. Such a deep connection between the gemstones and who ruled was true for all the Gemstone Kingdoms.

Cullen didn't know what color his father's eyes had been before he became king, but because of it, Cullen had been born with violet eyes from day one, and such was often seen as the Amethyst having made its choice for the next person to rule.

"My prince!" a guard announced upon Cullen's entrance into the castle. "Your father just summoned me to look for you."

"How fortuitous, then, that your job is done," Cullen said glibly, and then felt rude for having projected his annoyance onto someone merely doing their job. "Apologies, Yentriss. As you can see, I am perfectly fine. My father forgets I am no longer a child."

Yentriss was a proud and proper elf, with short dark hair, wearing the simple long-sleeved surcoat and trousers of the city guard. There was little need for guards in their mostly crime-free kingdom, other than running off the occasional highwaymen. Amethyst was the smallest of the Gemstone Kingdoms, made up of only their village that could barely be called a city, with little to no farmland. There were the cliffs, the lake, the forest, and the castle on the tallest hill to look down on it all, but they did not have the sprawling countryside of Sapphire, the massive city and farmlands of Emerald, the glorious expanse of Diamond that filled an entire valley, or the endless caverns of mountainous Ruby. Amethyst could sustain itself with what little they had, but they largely relied on imports, and Cullen shuddered to think what life would be like here if trade were ever cut off.

There was also the nearby tower on an equally impressive hill with its fruitful gardens that had been inherited by Braxton, a young alchemist who Cullen was friends with.

"Pardon my bluntness, Your Highness." Yentriss bowed, posture statuesque and motions controlled. "But while I am not yet a parent myself, I do not believe any are capable of thinking their children more than babes."

Cullen laughed at her adept conclusion. "I believe you may be right. But go on now. Take your leave and head home to that husband of yours. Newlyweds are not meant to keep late nights out of each other's company."

Yentriss bowed once more, with only the faintest of smiles breaching her stately demeanor—a true soldier through and through. "Thank you, Your Highness. But do go easy on your father. He...." Her brow pinched with concern. "He has been troubled of late."

Giving no further explanation, Yentriss left out the castle doors. Troubled? Cullen cringed to think that he had not noticed. Was his father troubled over him and his lack of interest in finding a spouse? Troubled, as Cullen was, about what sort of ruler he might make? But even once wed, that was years away. Much as Cullen dreaded how taking a spouse would seal his fate, he wouldn't ascend to the throne until his father grew feeble or passed on.

The hour was late enough that he saw few servants in the hallways as he moved from the front foyer toward the dining hall, where he expected his father to be. With crystal-filled sconces lighting the halls, the polished stone and white marble of the castle's interior made it brighter than anywhere else in the kingdom at night. Amethyst-colored accents decorated nearly everything else, a constant reminder that Cullen could not escape his namesake.

"Where is that blasted boy?" his father grumbled as Cullen entered the hall, only for the king to keel over in his chair at the head of the table, subjected to a coughing fit he seemed incapable of escaping.

"Father!" Cullen ran to him, coming around the side of the chair to help him upright.

King Charon was a simple man by appearance, average in many ways, in build and temperament, with wavy hair like Cullen's but longer and flaxen tinged with white, a full beard, and a coronet much like Cullen's own when he wore it, in silver with amethyst stones.

He waved Cullen off with one hand yet held on to him with the other. The cough was wet and wracking, one that could not possibly have come upon him suddenly. He must have been hiding it for days. Weeks? Longer?

What else had Cullen been blind to?

"What is the matter, Father? You don't seem well. You should be in bed." Cullen knelt beside Charon's chair once the coughing subsided.

The king had finished by wiping his mouth with a handkerchief, and Cullen could not ignore the red stains upon it. "You should see Luccite. She has brought wondrous healing advancements from Ruby——"

"I have seen her, my son." Charon patted Cullen's hands that clutched the armrest, meeting his gaze with a worn expression—haggard, hollow, like he was far weaker and ailing than Cullen had noticed even an inkling of until now. "She has told me many times that it is high past due for me to tell you the truth."

"My prince, could I perhaps request an audience later?"

"Hm?" Cullen blinked at the young man who had stopped him in the street.

There were adventures of a different kind that Cullen occasionally sought out. He liked a fair face, but one bolstered by a thick, muscled frame, sturdier than his own slender figure, and this man was definitely that. Was it Renault? Sharman? Another? Cullen felt a pang of guilt for not remembering, but a deeper pit of anxiety was swallowing him.

"Apologies, I... I am not myself today," he explained, and then hurried his feet to move past the scowl of disappointment that touched the young man's face.

Cullen's father was dying. He was too young to be dying. Human, yes, so his years would have been shorter than a full-blood elf or a half-elf like Cullen, but he was meant to have decades yet. How could he be dying when Cullen had already lost his mother too soon?

Cullen had barely slept and felt as though he were walking in a fog, moving through the marketplace, past the glow of the Amethyst that seemed to pulse with his own heartbeat. His mother, an elf, had died in battle when he was but a babe, some last bastion of war between the neighboring kingdoms that had ceased with her passing. Cullen didn't remember her, only knew that he reminded his father of her often, having her darker hair and a similarly fair face. Her eyes had been violet, too, as queen, but she had been a warrior first, and a powerful mage.

Cullen knew a little magic, a little of fighting, but was more interested in alchemy and technology like Braxton, and anything else he might learn from other kingdoms. Other than diplomatic envoys for duty's sake, any chance he'd had of visiting them were squashed forever now.

What a horrible, selfish child he was to be thinking more on his own plight than his father's. His father was dying, and Cullen cared more that, sooner than expected, he'd have to bear the weight of a king's crown.

His feet had carried him to the Lilac Lake, so called because of how the crystals around the cliffs made the water look faintly purple in daylight. No one else was around, the air too brisk for beachgoers, and in his solitude, he wanted to scream to the skies, to the magic that had made this realm, to the Amethyst itself, that he was the wrong man. His father should not be taken so soon, for Cullen was not worthy to replace him. How could he ever be worthy...?

"Cullen? Is that you?"

Not in solitude after all, Cullen turned to find Braxton approaching, strolling toward the beach with a regal-looking elf beside him. Braxton was a handsome young human, tall and willowy, with short red hair, blue eyes, and pale skin. His simple tunic had a high collar beneath, with sleeves rolled up as they often were from working tirelessly on experiments. He had a similar enough look and build to Cullen that he could have been one of his human cousins.

The stranger was likewise tall but built sturdier, if not as well-muscled as Cullen would have found most attractive. He was handsome, though, perhaps even paler in skin tone than either of them, with long black hair, dark eyes that held a striking intensity, and wearing red and black brocade that spoke of nobility. A traveler from Diamond perhaps?

Any other day, Cullen would have been eager to meet a newcomer, and despite the ache in his chest, he tried to feign interest now. "A good morning to you, Braxton."

"And you, my friend. Ash, this is Cullen, our Amethyst Prince," Braxton introduced.

"Your Highness." The stranger bowed, his voice having the sort of deep and penetrating timbre that Cullen felt in his bones like the pulse of a drum.

"Cullen." Braxton turned to him, smile brimming with enthusiasm. "This is Ashmedai."

TO CULLEN'S surprise, Braxton and Ashmedai's company banished some of the storm clouds that overcast his heart, both that day and on many to follow it. Ashmedai, too, was a man more interested in alchemy than magic. Perhaps the elves of the Diamond Kingdom had grown too reliant on natural ability and were branching out, for Ashmedai seemed eager to learn about Braxton's experiments.

Alchemy required a cost like innate magic, but it was an even exchange, plainly visible, and therefore less possible to corrupt or push too far. Ashmedai seemed especially interested in that.

"Not to discount the importance of magic, of course," Braxton was saying as they enjoyed tea one afternoon at one of the patio tables outside a marketplace café. "All we know of alchemy and using runes comes from what was originally learned from natural magic, and a combination is still possible and exciting to explore. A true scientist could supersede the lines between life and death if harnessing both correctly."

"I do not believe that should be the goal," Ashmedai said with clear trepidation.

"Only an example, friend," Braxton amended.

Cullen would not put such pursuits past the alchemist. After all, had word not also traveled of an elf so powerful, having taken the Diamond throne, that her people had ceased aging or falling ill?

Before Cullen could bring that up to Ashmedai, the elf asked him, "Do you have magic, Your Highness?"

"Nearly everyone has some," Braxton put in. "It's rarer to have no magic at all."

"True, but with eyes like the Amethyst itself, yours must be unique." Ashmedai remained focused on Cullen.

Indeed, the little magic Cullen could use with ease was tied to the Amethyst, and though he scorned his birthright more of late, he gazed with a sharper penetration of his eyes on his empty teacup. "Shall we see?" he said and picked the teacup up.

Wisps of black-purple shadow emanated from his fingertips, surrounding the teacup in a haze, and then seeped back into him, leaving a reveal of fine lines where cracks in the teacup had been covered up over time.

"One benefit to shadow magic is that it can reveal the truth. How many times did this poor cup break, I wonder, only to be put back together a little weaker than its original form? And how easily can something become hidden...." He plucked one of the remaining pastries from a plate in the center of the table and set it inside the shadow the teapot cast, where it seemed to vanish. "…that otherwise had been in plain sight. Parlor tricks to a full elf, I'm sure." Cullen mustered a smile.

"It is familiar magic to me but very useful," Ashmedai said. "One could even travel by shadows with enough effort." He picked up the same pastry from where it had seemed invisible, then set it down again to likewise vanish. Next, he reached across the table into a shadow cast by a carafe of water and somehow retrieved the same pastry from there instead.

"I am not so adept," Cullen said in astonishment. He had no idea Ashmedai's magic was so like his own. No wonder the elf had decided to visit their kingdom. "Although, if I concentrated more, or was near the Amethyst gemstone, especially if I touched it, my abilities could grow exponentially, as though pulling magic straight from the veil between worlds."

"Veil?" Ashmedai questioned with an odd tremor in his voice.

"Stories of how the demons of old came from a far-off land through the gemstones themselves," Cullen explained, "and then used them to ascend from beings of wild magic to villainous monsters. I am sure you have similar tales in Diamond."

"Of course," Ashmedai said softly.

"They are not just tales, Cullen," Braxton interjected. "The wild magic folk existed. Perhaps you should not talk so boldly about stealing their power." He grinned in exaggerated mocking, and Cullen laughed.

"I have no interest in power; you know that, Brax. Not in any sense of the word," he added quieter, sipping from his teacup before remembering it was empty.

"And what do you have interest in, Your Highness?" Ashmedai asked.

"Ash, please, I have told you repeatedly to call me Cullen." But then he had to pause at the question, because no one else had asked what he would want of life if he could choose a different path.

"Your answer, Cullen?" Ashmedai pressed playfully.

"I don't know. Travel, explore, learn things no one else has."

"You can accomplish the latter without traveling," Braxton groused.

"Because you are a true homebody who would happily live in that tower forever." Cullen nodded toward the tower's hill. "I would see other kingdoms. I would find adventure. What magic do we not yet know of? What advancements in alchemy have the other kingdoms found that we could share with our own people? What peoples themselves have we yet to meet? Could my father's ailment be cured by a trip to Diamond? Perhaps I could sweep him off to salvation and then find other causes to champion like in bard tales."

"With some bawdy romance to cap off the narrative?" Braxton teased.

"As only the best bard songs do. Do you have no interest in romance, Brax?"

"While not a scholarly pursuit, it certainly would be a worthwhile one."

Cullen thought so too. He'd had very little interest in romance or love over lust so far in life, but the mortality recently presented him with his father fading, his own life about to take a turn he could never come back from, made him wonder.

With a glance upward from where his gaze had drifted to the table between them, he saw Braxton's eyes fixated on Ashmedai and realized for the first time that his friend may have found something worth pursuing already. *Good for Brax*, he thought, only to glance over and see Ashmedai fixated on him.

Hopefully *not* fixated on him. Cullen didn't see Ashmedai that way, handsome though he may be. Cullen doubted he could have thought of anyone that way just now. He had yet to meet someone who captured his heart's attention as much as his loins. How could he be free to love someone before he knew the truths of his own soul?

"What about you, Ash?" Cullen asked, hoping to steer the pair toward each other. They were a better match, surely, and Braxton's interest was clear. "Where would your heart's desire lead you?"

The depths of Ashmedai's eyes were something to get lost in, for sometimes they seemed to be a black void that could swallow one whole. He opened his mouth to answer, only for Yentriss to appear out of the throng of marketgoers, with two other guards flanking her.

"Your Highness," she greeted stiffly.

"Yen? What's the matter? Has something happened?" Cullen sat up straighter.

"Cullen," she said, and he already knew her next words, for she never used his given name, "I'm afraid your father has died."

"WHY DIDN'T he tell me sooner?" Cullen lamented as the massive crowd from the funeral began to disperse.

The entirety of the kingdom had attended. Of course they had, for Charon had been a beloved king, ensuring years of prosperity and peace after the death of Cullen's mother and an end to the wars. There were citizens born here like Yentriss and her human husband, Grillo, as well as transients like the healer, Luccite, from Ruby, and even newer residents like the white-haired elf, Daedlys, who had opened a shop in the marketplace.

Their presence did nothing to quell Cullen's anguish, no more so than the presences of Braxton or Ashmedai, who remained at his side.

"We could have traveled to Diamond," Cullen continued. "I might have saved him."

"He was not fit for travel," Braxton said plainly. "You know that."

"He might have been if he had told me when he first knew."

"This Fairy Queen we've heard of hadn't even arrived in Diamond when—"

"I don't care! I could have done something. He gave me but weeks to prepare for this day, and now he's... gone." Just a body shrouded in silk and buried in the dirt beside Cullen's mother. The other graves in the clearing in the wood were well-marked, well-tended to, but the royal ones were ornate, covered in flowers and offerings like monuments to how Cullen would never live up to their legacy.

"Sometimes those we love keep things from us to protect us," Ashmedai said.

"Selfishness," Cullen growled, hands clenched as he glared at his parents' graves. "Nothing but selfishness."

"Cullen," Ashmedai tried again, "your father wished to save you from this grief for as long as he could."

"Only for me to feel more grief now! No. A lie is a lie is a lie. Only charlatans keep the truth to themselves. By sparing me the truth, he merely ensured I would be entrapped here forever." A few of those departing heard the rising ire in Cullen's voice and glanced back at him, and he saw his own miserable selfishness reflected on him like a slap. "I'm sorry, Ash, Brax. I know you both mean well. But can you not understand that I am angry, even in my mourning?"

"Of course we can," Braxton said.

"Once word spreads, who knows what vile opportunists will come to take advantage or invade the weakest of the Gemstone Kingdoms, left in my incapable hands."

Pale hands grasped one of Cullen's as he said that, almost white compared to his own, and cradled his palm with gentle reverence. "To me, my friend," Ashmedai said, as if Cullen were the only man in the world just then, "these hands are far from incapable."

Cullen felt Braxton grasp his other hand, rougher but imparting the same sentiment.

He only wished he could believe them.

DAYS PASSED, but Cullen refused to set a date for his coronation. Surely, someone else would step up to take the burden. Surely, someone else was worthier. No one did step up, however, and no one Cullen pleaded with in secret would answer his summons to take the crown.

Part of him wondered if he should simply run away. It would be less humiliating than abdicating publicly without a successor in the wings.

"Cullen?"

How easily he was snuck up on lately, for his mind was always elsewhere. He turned to see Ashmedai coming toward him from the path into town, where it forked either left into the woods and eventually to the Sapphire Kingdom or right to Braxton's tower.

"Taking a walk?" Ashmedai asked.

Contemplating escape, Cullen thought, but he could not have done so today. He had nothing packed, nothing with him, and would have perished on the road if he'd tried. He knew he was a coward, but he had foolishly believed—hoped, dreamed—that this day would never come.

"Would you perhaps join me for one?" Cullen asked, gesturing back toward town, for a trip into the woods would only stoke the fires of his longing to flee. "I could use the company. My father's absence in the castle makes it too lonely there now."

"I promised Brax…." Ashmedai motioned down the other road, but then shook his head. "Of course, if you need me. Brax will understand."

They spent the day together, and many after it, often without the company of Braxton. Others kept trying to push Cullen to decide on a coronation date, but as Cullen pondered finally admitting to his people that he could not do it and would ask them to vote on a replacement, whether one wanted to be chosen or not, Ashmedai let him forget.

"COME ON, Ash, it's late," Cullen said, tired but reveling in being in the empty market square at night, with only the stars to keep them company, and therefore, no one to push Cullen in a direction he was not yet ready to tread. "What do you want to talk to me about that's so important?"

"I know you've been debating passing the crown to someone else or calling for a vote."

Cullen spun around, still moving slowly backward, nearer to the towering Amethyst at the center of the square. So much for Ashmedai allowing him to forget. "I don't want to talk about that. Not now. I know I have to make a decision—"

"But you're basing that decision off the belief you're not good enough," Ashmedai cut in, causing Cullen to finally stop his momentum. "I simply want you to understand what you won't hear from anyone else. Maybe you won't believe it from me either, but I'm going to say it anyway. You would make an excellent king."

Cullen frowned.

"You *would*. It's your doubt that proves how good a king you could be, because what you want more than anything is to see your people happy. You doubt you can do enough, that you can *be* enough, but that is how I know you will be. You are a remarkable man, Cullen. I have no doubts about that because...."

Oh no, Cullen thought, for Ashmedai's eyes centered on him with raw devotion.

"Because I love you," Ashmedai finished and closed his eyes with the admission.

Damn. Damn, *damn*, because the silence in the aftermath tore at Cullen, knowing once again he was about to fail someone important to him.

"Ash...," he said, voice catching on the words he had to speak, "I'm so sorry, I.... You know I care for you, but...." He pursed his lips because he hated that this was the only truth he could speak.

"You don't feel the same," Ashmedai finished for him, eyes turning wet, and then... flashing with inverted color as though white irises upon black.

Cullen gasped, because it was not only Ashmedai's eyes that shimmered. His skin was shifting, fluctuating through the monochrome spectrum from white to black and every shade between like shadow made manifest, like....

Wild magic.

"I'm sorry." Ashmedai lurched unexpectedly, and there were points on each of his teeth like a terrible beast. "Please, don't be afraid—"

"What are you?" Cullen demanded, though he knew the answer already.

A demon. One of the vile villains from ages past.

"Please." Ashmedai moved toward Cullen with a crunch into cobblestone from massively sprouted claws. "I just wanted—"

"Stay away from me!" Cullen cried, backing toward the Amethyst. He reached blindly behind him, seeking the magic inherent in the gemstone, and pressed a palm to it. "You lied. You tricked us."

"No, I swear—"

"Stay away! I won't let you hurt my people." A pulse of magic surged from Cullen into the gemstone like instinct, calling upon his birthright for the strength to fight the terror before him.

Ashmedai's clothing, his elvish facade, all melted away, revealing him to be a thing of nightmares that Cullen had hoped were no more than stories. He chanted a spell beneath his breath, making it up as he went, a warding, a shockwave that would fling this monster from the kingdom and then erect a barrier to keep it out forever.

What horrible manipulation had it been planning that it had pretended to be a friend?

Cullen felt force push outward from the gemstone, his spell beginning to work, but Ashmedai fought the power trying to expel him and reached for Cullen, the great claws that had also replaced his hands descending toward Cullen's shoulders.

He screamed. Something was wrong, and not only because this creature was trying to tear him from his duty and stop the spell, but because the spell was being twisted. Why? How? Could Cullen not even do *this*?

The Amethyst glowed with multicolored sparks, blinding bright against the shadowy abyss of Ashmedai's true form as he clamped one clawed hand onto Cullen and lunged with the other to touch the gemstone directly.

Pain like nothing Cullen had ever known coursed through him, and Ashmedai was flung backward. Not out of the kingdom, for batlike wings outstretched to catch him as he landed only a few meters away. Claws soon dug into the ground as he leapt up, horns menacingly pointed in Cullen's direction, as were the glow of white on black eyes that were sometimes all white, sometimes black, sometimes not there at all.

The gemstone was turning black too—Cullen could see it in his periphery—because he was being swallowed by it, unable to scream a second time. He'd failed. He'd proven incapable after all. His only solace was that his pain seemed to be swallowed too, and he was becoming numb, fading, dying....

And then, seeing in his last moments Ashmedai the *demon* gazing after him, he realized with a renewal of fresh, agonizing grief, that Ash looked so very... very sorry.

"TRAPPED WITHIN, were you? Then I am your master, for the Amethyst's power is within me. Yield."

"Void beast? Why, he's a void dancer! Aren't you, Voidy my boy?"

"Come now, friend. We'll have you making your own decisions yet. Come play a hand."

"Are you with me or not?"

"Silver and gold...."

"By the abyss, our little boy is growing up!"

"He keeps staring at his reflection, like he can't believe it's real. Or wondering if he's real."

"You know me. Remember...."

Ash.

Janskoller.

Nemirac.

He remembered. He remembered the night he was lost within the Amethyst. He remembered an endless void living inside it for centuries, and then being freed when a young half-elf—half-*demon*—mage stole the Amethyst's power and released him with it.

He'd lived a half-life as a mindless being of shadow, at the mercy of Nemirac's bidding, but the memories had trickled back. Janskoller, warrior bard sworn to protect Nemirac on his journey, had convinced the mage to give the power back. They'd released Cullen. He remembered everything, but now, as he was fading from existence, he clung to the last remnants of feeling grounded, because... he didn't want to go. The part inside of him that was still connected to the Amethyst called to the Ruby too, some residual magic from Nemirac perhaps, lingering in the cavern of the last gemstone he'd tried to drain, and giving Cullen the power to tether himself back to the earth.

Horrible pain prompted a scream that died in his throat as he saw Janskoller and Nemirac vanishing through a distant tunnel. He felt so heavy, so tired.

Cullen, he thought. *I'm... Cullen.*

But the memories were fading again as his body solidified. He was forgetting everything in the trauma of being reborn, and as he tried to cling, all he could remember was a song.

Which song? he wondered as he drifted to sleep, only to wake some time later, seemingly buried alive and unable to remember anything but darkness and shadow, as the melody continued to play in his head.

"Now, here's a tale of a traveling bard known all across the lands...."

"WHO'S SLAIN each beast and bedded well fair maidens and their men," Enzo sang, low beneath his breath, and then continued the song in a jolly hum.

Ever since hearing the bards perform, he hadn't been able to get it out of his head. It had been hours! He hadn't even wanted to partake in the Ruby King's memorial merriment. He'd simply been on his way through the streets to escape the celebration, but after missing Janskoller's previous performance, he hadn't wanted to pass up another chance—especially when Jason, the former bard who'd borne the Janskoller moniker, joined him.

After a few songs, however, Enzo had still wanted to get away, because everywhere else he looked were tables full of people praising and toasting to the lost king. It wasn't that Enzo wouldn't miss him or had wished him to depart this world so soon, but it was difficult being the son of royalty.

When no one knew you existed.

The forbidden caverns were Enzo's favorite places to walk when he needed to clear his head. He knew no one was meant to go this way, especially down by the Ruby gemstone, but even as a bastard child, he'd been taught about the ancient times in the Gemstone Kingdoms. The Ruby was calming for him, with its radiant red light and gentle hum. He honestly didn't know if his father had ever seen it for himself, but Enzo had ventured out to find it when he was but a young lad. Royals were buried beyond these caverns, so perhaps his father had seen it when the last Ruby King died.

Enzo didn't have any magic of his own. Well, maybe he did. He was a farell, and his elven mother had always said his natural way with invention and alchemy was a power all its own. Perhaps that was true. Regardless, while he held enough wariness and reverence for the Ruby to never touch a hand to it, he felt at home in its presence and in some ways wanted to see it now to say his goodbyes to his father there, when he couldn't do so inside the castle where the king's body was being prepared for burial. Only other royals and nobles were allowed there, and he didn't count.

The Ruby seemed brighter than usual, Enzo thought, when he exited the tunnels into its cavern. There was something almost wrong in the air, and when he glanced around, using his torch to brighten areas cast in shadow, he discovered another torch, tossed aside from the path, long since burnt out.

Someone else had been here.

Walking slowly onward, Enzo checked for other signs. There were footprints in the dust, more than one set—although one set looked a bit... beastlike, which set him on edge, since he was no fighter and didn't have any weapons with him. There were vines as well, as if they'd grown up from out of the stone and then dropped lifelessly across the path. He even saw scorch marks like bolts of lightning had struck here when there was no opening in this cavern to the skies above.

"What on earth?" he said aloud.

A groan alerted him to the far side of the Ruby, and he thrust the torch out in front of him like a shield.

"Who goes there? I promise I have nothing worth stealing if you be thieves."

No one replied at first, but then came a shifting of rocks, like pebbles falling, and another groan. Whoever it was sounded injured.

"Hello?" Enzo hurried around the Ruby, giving it a wide berth, and cast the light from his torch every which direction, hoping to find the groaning's source. "Are you all right? Please, I mean no harm if—"

A hand shot up from out of a pile of loose smaller rocks, tumbling them toward the Ruby's base, and Enzo dashed toward it with a drop to his knees.

"Hang on! I can help!"

He couldn't risk setting his torch down and having it go out. There was some light in the tunnels, but with so little understanding of what had gone on here, he didn't want to risk a dim walk back. That left him with only one hand to dig the stranger out, but he did so quickly, never so thankful that his dwarven hands were large and meaty and used to such tasks.

The rocks only covered half the man and were thankfully not very heavy, as if he had simply collapsed there and disturbed a few rocks to roll onto him. Once he was dug free and better rolled onto his back to blink upward, Enzo saw that he was a half-elf—and a beautiful one, if a bit dirty from his surroundings.

He had pale skin and brown hair that curled around his ears and fell into strikingly violet eyes. He was clean-shaven and fair, wearing a violet and dark brown tunic with a deep purple cloak, like some noble who'd been besieged by highwaymen. Perhaps that was exactly what had happened.

"Tell me your name, friend, if there's breath in you still." Enzo helped the man to sit up.

He coughed, clinging to Enzo gratefully. "It's... um...."

"Take a moment." Enzo rubbed the man's back, carefully checking for signs of breaks or torn clothing that might indicate other wounds. He seemed to only be dusty and a bit winded, which Enzo hoped was the worst of it. "There we are. Now, try again. What's your name?"

"It's... Cullen?" he said, as though unsure.

"And tell me, fair Cullen, what else is there to know about you and how you became buried in these caves?"

Cullen looked at Enzo squarely, but his violet eyes blinked with uncertainty, and a terrible dread began to fill his expression. "I don't remember."

CHAPTER 2

PANIC SETTLED as Cullen realized his inability to focus on facts beyond his own name was not a mere haze from having woken in rubble, but deeply rooted.

He couldn't remember.

He couldn't remember anything.

"Calm yourself!" the young farell said, grasping Cullen's shoulder strongly.

His kind voice, however filled with concern, shook Cullen from the vortex of dread he'd nearly succumbed to. Even in the dim lighting of the cave, the torchlight in the farell's other hand, mingling with the red illumination from the Ruby, was enough to reveal how handsome he was.

Powerfully built, the farell was nearly as wide as he was tall. Well, not quite that pronounced, since his elven half added a bit of trimness to his form not seen in most dwarves, but his broad chest and rippling arm muscles spoke of a laborer who it was no wonder had been able to dig Cullen free with one hand.

His skin was a deep bronze. Everything about him seemed to be bronze-colored and radiant, like well-oiled armor. Half his longish hair was pulled back into a braid, the rest falling free to his shoulders with two smaller braids framing him behind the ears, all only a shade darker than his skin. It matched the golden-bronze sheen of his eyes and contrasted against his white teeth when he smiled. He didn't bear a beard like most full dwarves, just the scruff of rough stubble. He wore a red and brown tunic over a crisp white shirt buttoned high. His ears were larger than a human's, but as a farell, they came to the barest of points, as though inviting one to trace them with a fingertip.

"Cullen?" he pressed. "Are you all right?"

"I... I think so." Cullen allowed his handsome savior to heft him to his feet, and he found that he could stand well enough on his own. The farell came up to the middle of Cullen's chest with them standing.

"I'm Enzo, by the way," he introduced himself finally. "Enzario, but Enzo to my friends. Anything coming back to you yet now that you've found your feet?"

Cullen shook his head.

"No idea how you got here? Where you're from? Where you were staying or headed?"

"No. Nothing but my name."

"Not to worry." Enzo patted Cullen's arm, and his large dwarf-like hands brought an added comfort. Cullen had always liked large hands like those. Hadn't he? Had he? "For now, why don't we get you out of these caves, hm? You can stay with me until your memories return. I'm sure it's only a bonk on the head, and your mind will clear in time. Can you walk all right?"

Cullen tried a few cautious footfalls on the uneven ground, and while it wasn't ideal terrain, he managed without stumbling. "I believe so." He followed Enzo as the kind farell began to lead them around the Ruby toward a tunnel exit that did indeed seem familiar, but Cullen could not place why.

The Ruby was familiar too, and he knew it was the central gemstone of this kingdom, but the details of when he had last seen it eluded him. It seemed to hum and pulse and… call to him somehow, like it spoke a language few understood, but he could almost… hear….

Numbness filled Cullen's hands, and he glanced at them with a wiggle of his fingers. Dark tendrils seemed to coil outward from within his skin, but after a nervous shake, the strange vision of moving shadows faded. Must have been a trick of the light. Or were shadows normal within his palms…?

"Watch your footing. It's a bit steep from this point on."

Cullen focused on Enzo leading the way, but it wasn't easy when his own body felt oddly foreign to him. He was both cold and yet overheated, tired and yet revitalized, numb and yet aware of every shift in air or rustle of cloth against his skin. He pulled his indigo cloak tighter around him and thought its fabric felt familiar, but he also mused that it seemed like it had been forever since he'd last known the sensation of it against him.

"Talk to me, fair Cullen. Let me know you're still with me, and not in danger of swooning against the stones."

"I'm all right. But also not? I would say I don't feel like myself, but I don't know what myself should feel like. You call me fair?"

"Because you are," Enzo said with the stretch of a smile as he glanced back. "I'm afraid I don't have a looking glass on me to show you, but I promise you are quite fair. Violet eyes, pale skin, wavy dark hair. If you were not smudged and dirty from your ordeal, one might think you a prince."

Cullen stopped. He hadn't been paying attention, but they were deep in the tunnels now, following a narrow path that made him feel short of breath. He hurried to catch up to the retreating light and clutched the back of Enzo's tunic. "Forgive me. Perhaps I am not as steady as I thought."

"No worries, friend. Here." Enzo reached back and moved Cullen's hand from gripping fabric to holding more firmly across the top of his shoulder. The way went easier from there, and Cullen tried to breathe shallowly.

"What about you?" Cullen asked. "Why were you in the caves?"

"The presence of the Ruby soothes me."

"You needed to be soothed this night. Day? Night…?"

"Night," Enzo said with a chuckle. "We need not talk about it, but… the Ruby King passed away. I sought to mourn him on my own in the company of the gemstone."

"I'm sorry," Cullen said. "You needn't tend to me if you are in mourning. I'm sure I can find accommodations—"

"Nonsense. You remember naught but your name. I'll see you through this, fair Cullen."

Again, he called him fair, and Cullen felt his cheeks flush at the constant ease with which the compliment was given. He doubted he could so easily title his savior as handsome Enzo. Or could he? Robust Enzo? Manly? Thick…?

Cullen cleared his throat against his straying thoughts, feeling the very muscles he was admiring under the cup of his hand.

"Thank you."

"My pleasure. I would rather help a lost soul than mourn one, to be honest. Ah, here we are now. You'll breathe easier the rest of the trip."

They had reached another mouth in the tunnels, and as they exited, it opened to a spacious cavern far larger than any Cullen could have imagined, for the entirety of the Ruby Kingdom lay before them.

Roads of all kinds led into the city like the tunnel they were leaving, and around the central city were villages dotting the distance. Where they were coming from would lead directly into the city proper, but toward a descending slope, for they were high up currently, looking down on a spectacular sight.

Shops and homes were built into the rockface, many stacked atop one another, with ladders or staircases connecting them, even all the way to the top of the cavern, which was twice as high as they stood now. Skylights allowed both for the collection of rainwater and reflected distant sunlight down into the depths of the caves—or would have. Moon and starlight shone down now. Plant life grew despite the uniqueness of the surroundings, and buildings were either painted brightly or left to their natural reddish stone.

Lanterns, forges, and mirror-lights brightly lit the landscape, and it was clear that some sort of celebration was being had, for most of the streets near the center of the city were filled with tables bursting with revelers or people dancing and sharing songs. In the very center was where all the roads led to, an archway of twisted stone with benches all around as though it were most often used as a stage.

As disoriented as Cullen felt, the breathtaking view made him smile.

Until an explosion rocked the entirety of the cavern, flames and smoke billowing up from an area among the partygoers, farthest across from them near the rockface wall—which was when Cullen noticed the castle, so smoothly built into the stone, its spires and windows looked like natural formations.

Enzo yanked Cullen to his side to keep him steady as his footing teetered in the aftermath, the torch, no longer necessary, rolling away from them down the path and snuffing out. "No…. They've done it."

"Who?" Cullen questioned, mind awhirl with all he had seen and was struggling to comprehend. "Done what? What's happening?"

Enzo's kind and handsome face was marred now by a pained scowl as he said, "Rebellion. Come, fair Cullen. The streets will not be as safe as I'd hoped."

DAMN THEM. Damn their ambitions.

And damn, *damn* Vanek.

"Hurry!" Enzo kept hold of the fair half-elf's hand as he guided them down the steep terrain from the tunnels toward the city, and finally into the throng of people running in terror after the explosion.

How many had been hurt or killed where it was set off, and to what purpose? Had they even weighed the possibility of casualties, or merely chosen a target close to the castle? Fools, selfish and cruel, every last one of them, for not caring if the very people they touted wanting to save got caught in the crossfire.

What was worse was Enzo knew, he *knew* Vanek used his invention to cause it.

"Where are we going?" Cullen asked, feet occasionally catching on the rocks, but Enzo could not risk slowing their pace. There were too many people, too much chaos, and if they stopped their momentum, they might stumble and become trampled before they reached safe harbor.

"Almost there. Stay close." In truth, Enzo's home was still several streets away, but thankfully ground level, unlike the homes stacked atop his. He couldn't spot city guards. They must all be hurrying toward the blast site.

Tables had been overturned, food and drink spilled into sticky sludge in the streets, and while many had reached their homes by the time Enzo and Cullen truly neared Enzo's, others were choosing a different goal over shelter.

"This way. We can use the alley to   " But before Enzo could turn the corner he'd intended, he caught sight of three large brutes down the alley, towering over a young and clearly half-inebriated couple.

Flattening himself and Cullen back a step, Enzo kept them around the wall, watching and waiting for their chance. Opportunistic thieves, it seemed. Why had Vanek not listened to Enzo that no matter how justified a cause, the vilest of people would always take advantage to do evil in the wake of good intentions?

"Please! We're being attacked or pillaged or something!" the young man cried, human and unsteady in his steps, but keeping his companion held close behind him. She was an elf, clearer of eyes but clearly frightened.

"Indeed, ya are, mate," the shortest yet broadest of the brutes said. Enzo knew that voice. *Rufus.* Half dwarf, half human, and full slimy snake. "Ya didn't even need to spend a cent on meal and drink tonight, did ya?"

"Please!" the woman tried. There was nowhere for the couple to go, not even back down the other end of the alley once Rufus and his ruffians finished surrounding them. "Aren't we all at risk from whatever's happened?"

"Only the wealthy, miss," Rufus leered. "And you look heavy of purse indeed."

He was clearly not looking at her *purse* when he said that.

"Enzo…," Cullen whispered.

Enzo knew they had to do something, but he had nothing but one empty hand and another clinging to a fair and frail-looking amnesiac.

Wait! There, just inside the alley leaning against the wall was a hammer! They were outside Dorff's blacksmith shop! That man always had extra tools lying about, and with a hammer, Enzo knew he could swing true.

Summoning his resolve to make up for whatever role he'd played in tonight's madness, Enzo hushed Cullen behind him, released his grip on the half-elf—

"And just when I was trying to take a piss too," a newcomer's voice echoed down the alley from the other end.

Out of the darkness came a man, human with tanned skin, brown hair to his shoulders, a neatly trimmed but full beard, and lively green eyes. He was large, thick with muscle beneath his tunic, and wore a floppy black cap tilted to one side, as well as a weapons belt that appeared to have been added in a hurry, for the rest of his simple ensemble was not quite right for battle. Still, he seemed ready for one, given the resolve in his gaze.

"First the earth moves, which usually only happens in my bedchamber, mind you, then a gaggle of idiots stumbles across my path. Good thing I had time to recover my accessories. Such a lovely night, though. I really hate it being sullied." He drew a short sword and axe from the belt, one in each hand, fierce and formidable-looking and….

Janskoller? 'Twas the bard himself! And he was clearly no mere entertainer.

"Nothing sullied, mate," Rufus said with a raise of his hands.

"Misunderstanding," lied another.

"Just clearing a path for these fine folks," intoned the third, and as one they moved to the side to allow the young couple past, who spared a grateful glance at the bard before fleeing.

"One would hope," Janskoller said. "Scurry along now. Wouldn't want to catch you being so neighborly with anyone else." He resheathed his weapons and turned his back on the brutes, but Enzo saw Rufus pick up the hammer he himself had been about to snatch.

"Jan!" a different voice cried before Enzo could, and the next eruption down the alley was a bolt of lightning.

Cracks of brilliant force and thunderous sound struck near the feet of all three brutes, making them dance a hapless jig before racing from the alley to free themselves of the onslaught, thankfully not noticing Enzo and Cullen.

Enzo also recognized the beautiful young half-elf who joined Janskoller, with radiantly dark skin, long braided silver hair, and eyes that glowed gold. Nemirac, the Fairy Prince. Ruby's streets were full of gorgeous noble types tonight.

"Enzo...." Cullen's voice sounded shakier as he tugged Enzo's sleeve. Tucked behind him as he was, Cullen couldn't see any of the commotion but had surely heard it. He looked deeply troubled and cringed with an obvious pain in his head.

"At least you didn't wipe them off the face of the earth this time," Janskoller was heard.

"Perhaps I should have," answered Nemirac. "Now, let us catch up to my mother and the kings."

"No rest for the wicked, eh, love?" Janskoller chuckled.

"Not wicked like us, anyway."

Then they were gone, and long gone were Rufus and the brutes who'd tempted their wrath.

"I wouldn't have been nearly as powerful an opponent as those two," Enzo muttered. "And what a curious elf the prince is. I've never seen a man so wholly silver and gold."

"Ah!" Cullen doubled over, clutching his head.

"Cullen?" Enzo tried to reach for his shoulders, only possible at his stature because the half-elf was hunched. "It's only a little farther. Are you remembering something?"

Cullen looked more pained trying to answer.

"Come on," Enzo urged him. "We're almost there. Then you can rest." Gripping Cullen's hand anew, Enzo pulled him along, even with Cullen in a daze and gritting his teeth with every fresh gallop forward.

A little farther was true this time, for once down the alley, Enzo's home was across the street from the front of Dorff's shop. There, finally, was Enzo's door—with a crossbow bolt pinning a note to its surface that bore a single unmistakable rune.

Ash, like a flag with a broken banner.

Enzo tore it from the bolt in a rage and stormed inside, nearly forgetting the half-elf he dragged behind him. Once he ushered Cullen ahead of him, he slammed the door shut in their wake.

Damn the Ashen. Damn Vanek.

And damn Enzo too.

CHAPTER 3

THOSE VOICES. Why had Cullen known them?

Shutters were thrown closed and curtains drawn, causing a mild clatter and rustling around him as Enzo hurried about his home as though sealing it against a siege. Cullen tried to take stock of where he was, to ground himself in his surroundings.

A simple and lovingly cluttered abode proved to belong to his savior, appearing as one open room, with three doors besides the main entrance, two ajar and a sturdier one tightly closed. Ruby was known for technological advancements, Cullen could remember that much, but he could not recall ever seeing such easily accessible plumbing. The sink in the kitchen did not appear to even require a pump. There were a few dishes stacked beside it in need of washing: one plate befitting each meal of the day, one teacup, and one glass for water.

The kitchen also had a pantry, an ice box, and cupboards aplenty. Its small table—the only visible dining table—could seat four and had what looked like schematics spread over it, writing utensils, and a triangle like a builder might have used. The only other furniture was a padded rocking chair with a standing lamp beside it and an end table, the latter of which held a stack of books.

There *was* another table, Cullen eventually saw, a shorter one that in another house might have had a chaise or sofa behind it. Positioned near a hearth, it was so covered and surrounded by metal and stone and crystals stacked or otherwise fused together that there had clearly been dubbed not enough room for additional furnishings.

"You're an inventor? An... alchemist?" Cullen cringed as another spike of pain tore through him.

"Inventor, alchemist, all the above," Enzo answered absently, spinning in place once he'd finished flitting about the main room to close off any possible view inside.

Cullen had known an inventor once, an alchemist, hadn't he? Had he? Another man who wore many hats....

And those voices from the alley, he'd known them, hadn't he? Had he…?

"He's a lover, and a soldier, who lives the tales he tells."

"Jan… for…."

"Janskoller?" Enzo approached him.

"Jan… skoller?" Cullen repeated.

"The bard. Did you hear him perform perhaps?"

"I…." Again, Cullen cringed as a spike of pain assaulted him. Every time he was close to remembering something, his head ached in the attempt to capture it.

"Don't force yourself." Enzo took Cullen's hand in both of his, rough workman's hands that emitted the most wonderful warmth. Before Cullen could blink the haze from his eyes, his savior was saving him again, leading him to the table and sitting him in one of the chairs. "Much is happening this night. Rest." They were closer to eye level with Cullen sitting, and the bronze eyes of Enzo were as warm as his hands that Cullen gripped tightly when they started to pull away.

Enzo smiled. What a handsome, rugged young farell with an inquisitive, kind face.

Stampeding feet and a ruckus of voices rushed past them outside, signaling continued exodus from the recent explosion.

Enzo's expression fell as he looked to the door. "I feared something like this might happen."

"What?" Cullen hoped to lessen the aches in his head with anything other than his own memories. "Rebellion, you said, but why? In what way? I thought… is Ruby not an open kingdom, one that allows people of all races and creeds and inclinations to live as they are? Free with magic. Free with… love." That was the version of the mountainous kingdom Cullen remembered, though he could not say if he had ever walked its rocky paths before.

"A point of concern for you, fair Cullen?" Enzo's smile renewed.

Cullen chuckled, but then realized, that much he remembered too. "I suppose so. I know I never craved the company of women."

"Then you are in good company now." Enzo's warm eyes widened after he said it, and he cleared his throat. "What I should say, um… is yes, all true of Ruby. But there is one great equalizer that is not so equal when some have more and others none. Coin."

A storm of frantic knocks on Enzo's door further interrupted them, and both jerked their heads toward the din.

"Blast, I forgot to lock—"

The door opened just as Enzo dashed forward to intercept, and in barreled a dwarf, swiftly swinging the door closed behind him as though used to crossing this threshold. "There you are," he announced with a scowl. "By the stone, Enzo, where were you? Did you not receive the summons?"

He was thickly built like Enzo, with ruddy skin, long black hair in a single braid, and the start of a proper dwarf beard plaited into three separate braids with the longest in the center.

Or was he a farell? While not as tall as Enzo, his stern face was pretty behind his beard, and his ears came to similar points.

"I received it." Enzo stepped between them, blocking Cullen before the other farell could notice him. It seemed Enzo had stuffed the paper he tore from the door into his pocket, for he pulled it out now and hurled it forward. "I promised you nothing, Vanek. How dare you—"

"Be sensible," Vanek broke in. "You know the importance of our plight."

"I will not be part of this, I told you!"

"Are you not the most obvious example of how we are scorned? The Ashen need you."

Ashen? Like the rune on the paper.

Ash….

Cullen's hands felt numb like before, and he clenched them into trembling fists.

"You stole the plans from me, didn't you?" Enzo hissed. "After I told you I couldn't go through with it, that altering my design would be too destructive, too unpredictable?"

"It worked exactly as intended."

"With how many dead and injured?"

"Enzo, I need you—"

"No! I cannot condone what you did."

"Fine," Vanek snarled, throwing his hands up and pacing enough away from Enzo that Cullen saw him clearly again, "but do not pretend like doing nothing is better." His eyes snapped to Cullen suddenly, narrowing in suspicion. "Who is that? You let me speak freely in the presence of some stranger? Looks like one of those damned royals visiting and eating our hard-earned fare."

Enzo spun around as though having forgotten Cullen, his face marred with panic. "In that old outfit, smudged and tattered? He's just a friend who drank too much," he said, clearly lying for Cullen's sake, since neither knew the true answer. "Now go." He swung back to face Vanek. "I will not be tied up in this."

"You will be," Vanek said, more a threat than a promise to Cullen's ears. "You know you can't stay silent forever." His piercing blue eyes were as icy as a lake in winter, and he shot one last glance at Cullen before departing.

"I'm sorry, friend." Enzo latched the lock at Vanek's exit, though which friend his words were meant for was unclear. "Pay no mind to all that, fair Cullen. Here you are wrapped up in your own mystery and have to hear yet another one you cannot possibly understand."

"Your friend... caused the explosion?" Cullen dared ask.

Enzo sighed and pulled one of the other chairs out to sit, which was when Cullen realized how low the chairs and table were for his own longer legs, crossed at the ankles to avoid his knees hitting his sternum. "Perhaps it is folly to tell you, but your eyes seem kind, and I could use someone to confess my sins to, should you be willing to listen."

Cullen nodded, for Enzo's eyes were kind too, causing him to innately trust the farell and want to be trusted in return.

"I knew the king was ailing," Enzo said, "but his death came unexpectedly fast. That suddenness made me fear those who wished to overthrow the monarchy might act, and so they did. There has been much unrest between the classes in Ruby of late. Those who live near the inner ring and then toward the castle are wealthier, nobles, merchants, or those born or married into families with close ties to the same.

"Those in the outer loop, like a horseshoe the farther you get from the castle, the edge of which we are in now, are not as fortunate. There have always been problems; resources and aid reaching these streets in less volume and with less frequency than others. As well as more crime and fewer guards to protect against it. But the divide has grown wider, especially in the past decade.

"My own mother...." Enzo's eyes grew distant and watery at the mention. "She passed away from illness that an elven woman in wealthier districts might have been able to heal with proper help."

"I... also lost my parents," Cullen said as a gentler stir of memory cleared some of the fog from his mind. "I remember the pain of no longer having them with me, yet nothing of them at my side. Not their faces... nor their touch."

A hand came down upon Cullen's on the table. "A sad connecting thread between us, friend. I am sorry. Though perhaps this means you will remember more soon."

"Perhaps." Cullen tried to smile and quelled the urge to reach after Enzo when the farell pulled his hand away again. "You mentioned sins to confess? An invention used without permission?"

Again, Enzo sighed. "My true goal was safer mining, a controlled explosion that would then implode to reduce blast radius and avoid cave-ins. Often the only jobs available for those less fortunate are the dangerous ones in the deepest mines, where important ores and building materials can be found. Naturally, in the process of trying to control an explosion, one usually first learns how to make it worse.

"Vanek and I are... were friends. We are friends! I... we haven't agreed on much of anything for some time. When I explained what my experiments had wrought, his first thought was to use it for revolution. That symbol, the rune for Ash, is a calling card used by the Ashen, those who consider themselves forgotten and more often caught up in the ash and soot and dust of the stone. They use the rune to recruit like minds and pass information."

A resistance, Cullen deduced.

"Vanek wanted me to be part of it, but I am no revolutionary. Through invention, certainly, but to help people, to make lives easier, not to.... I could never forgive myself if something I made caused the death of someone undeserving, and now, it seems that may have already happened."

"He stole your invention, your plans for it?"

At last, the grief that had been twisting the otherwise handsome and ruggedly stubbled face of Cullen's savior turned to a snarl of fury. "I trusted him, but he cares more for the cause than the people it affects." Almost as instantly, Enzo's anger melted to a smooth expression of empathy, and his hand came back upon Cullen's. "I am sorry, here I go thrusting this upon you, when it is doubtful you are even from Ruby or part of our plight. Your outfit *is* a bit noble. Maybe you came with the traveling delegations. An attendant to one of the royals?"

"I...." The pain was there, so close to the surface that Cullen flinched before it could impale his thoughts, yet he tried to push past it, to remember.

Janskoller.

Someone... someone named Ash.

And....

"Ah!" Noise inside Cullen's mind struck like a gong and curled him in two, his hand yanking free from beneath Enzo's kind touch to twist in his hair and press with the base of his palm upon his temple.

When the throbbing lessened, he felt the weight of Enzo's hand upon the base of his skull, and then gently stroking down his neck, only to start again with rhythmic pets. He focused on that and the hushing and mumbled comforts from Enzo until the pain subsided enough for him to sit upright once more.

"Rest," Enzo said. "Surely, the memories will come on their own. Are you hungry?"

Cullen wouldn't have thought it, but at the question he realized how famished he was. For all he knew, it had been ages since he last ate. He nodded.

Enzo hopped down from his chair, and watching him scurry to the kitchen cabinets, Cullen realized how charming, how alluring he found Enzo's girth in contrast to his diminutive height. He was tall for a dwarf, even tall for a farell, but the thick, square nature of his figure was a captivating example of manly form in motion.

He hurried about the kitchen almost as swiftly as he'd shut the shades and curtains, and again, Cullen took better stock of the house. The counters and cabinets were all built to be accessible at Enzo's height, and while the ceiling was not so low that Cullen needed to duck, he might need to kneel to wash a dish.

Such a silly, domestic thought to entertain. Had he ever washed a dish? He had to have, hadn't he? Had he?

"Blast," Enzo muttered, like he had at the forgotten lock on the door, meaty hands planting on his hips as he turned to Cullen. "I'm afraid my cupboards are a bit bare. I have a bad habit of forgetting the organic part of my life in favor of the technological. Not to worry! There's sure to be food on tables that didn't get toppled to the ground."

"You're not going back out there." Cullen readied to leap to his feet, even if it would have been awkward with how his legs were curled beneath his chair.

Enzo paused midstride to the door. "I'll be all right. I could use a nibble myself, and in truth, I need to find out which target was hit, how much damage was caused, and who might have been hurt. I'll protect myself." He glanced around, shuffled toward the low table covered in materials, and retrieved a simple two-headed smithing hammer from behind it. "No better weapon for a blacksmith, inventor, and alchemist like myself." He feigned a grin Cullen didn't trust, for he saw the pain in Enzo's eyes, the guilt and sorrow over what he might find.

Cullen didn't want him to go, in worry for Enzo's sake, but selfishly too, not wanting to be alone.

"Here, fair Cullen," Enzo spoke softer, approaching with his free hand outstretched.

Cullen took it, and the ease with which Enzo lefted him upright sent a tingling thrill through him. He had no doubts that Enzo could bodily lift him off his feet and carry him like a bride over a threshold.

Enzo led him deeper into the house and gestured into the room of the first ajar door, where a latrine, sink, and bathtub could be seen.

"My washroom. Use as you please. My bedchamber there." He gestured through the second ajar door, and inside was a low to the ground but large bed covered in pillows and blankets made of furs and soft-looking fabrics. Even Cullen's long legs wouldn't dangle over its edge. "Rest if you like. Please! My bed is yours for as long as you stay with me."

Cullen smirked and nearly made an inappropriate comment, as if it once would have been natural for him to do so in the company of a man he found attractive.

"Oh! And this is my workshop." Enzo indicated the closed, heavier door. "Not off-limits by any means, but there may be some tripping hazards inside, so be careful if you explore.

"Now, wash, rest up, whatever you desire, fair Cullen. I won't be long." With a parting squeeze of Cullen's hand, Enzo released him and headed back toward the exit. "Lock the door behind me if you decide to lie down, but hopefully the worst is behind us." Unlike Vanek's parting pierce of an icy glare, after unlatching the door and pulling it open, Enzo looked back with a warm smile before leaving.

Holding a hammer was a good look on him, and Cullen stood still a moment, envisioning the young farell's sleeves rolled up, muscles rippling and tendons straining beneath his skin as he used the hammer upon an anvil to shape some new part for an unknowable invention.

The thoughts stoked Cullen's already piqued curiosity about the workshop, and having been given permission to enter, he turned his attention there first. He was tired, grimy, and would need the latrine soon, but that could wait.

The workshop door was indeed heavy, but not locked, and he pushed it open, at first concerned that there was too little light. Then, upon entering, the crystals of various colors lining the walls and ceiling pulsed brighter. Cullen gaped at however that had been accomplished, for clearly the crystals knew someone had entered and brightened to light his way.

Perhaps it was some alchemy attached to the rune beneath Cullen's feet, for it was the symbol for Torch, like the stick figure of a man with one leg stepping outward, that he had tread upon when entering.

The workshop was like a whole other house, as large as the main room, but deceptively smaller from the excess of materials and contraptions piled upon shelves, the floor, and various tables. The mess by the hearth was clearly spillover.

The center of the workshop was less untidy, where an anvil rested like Cullen had envisioned, a forge not currently lit, hammers of varying sizes and other smithing tools, and a more neatly organized table. Cullen assumed the items upon it were successful experiments and inventions, for they had their own honored placements, including small placards beside each one.

There was a lantern dubbed the Ever-Burning Torch. Even natural crystals that glowed, once mined or removed from a direct power or magic source, would eventually dim. Perhaps this did not. Inside the lantern was a beautiful clear crystal like a diamond that glowed with a constant soothing light.

Another item was an orb that seemed almost like a puzzle box for a child to decipher, for it had gears and obvious fissures where differently colored materials connected. Its placard said Dragon's Gland. That didn't make Cullen think of a puzzle box or toy. Was it the device Vanek had stolen the plans to? If so, Cullen certainly had no wish to touch it.

Then there was a hammer, similar to the smithing hammer Enzo had taken, but larger, and its double-sided head was a bronze or golden color rather than steel. It had many runes etched into it, both the head and handle, some Cullen couldn't name, and its placard called it the Gemstone Maul. There were no gems in it, merely the runes, its golden head, and a dark wood handle.

A few other smaller items rested upon the table, the last being a pendant on a heavy chain. The pendant itself was shaped like a diamond with four even points. It was silver with an engraving like a family crest. First was a shield, within it two crossed hammers, and coiled around the heads and handles of the hammers was an ouroboros, but not a normal snake. This was a dragon, for it had wings that outstretched behind each hammer's head.

There was no placard there, but into the table had been crudely carved *Father's*.

Enzo mentioned his mother's death and implied his father, too, had passed, but not how or when. Had he? If Enzo's mother was an elf, then his father would be the dwarven half. Feeling it wrong to touch any of the treasured items, and with curiosity assuaged for now, Cullen left the workshop, noticing as he shut the door that the crystals returned to dim at his departure.

Hunger and thirst were his next concerns, but while he waited for Enzo, secondary was to relieve himself. He headed into the washroom, again marveling at the ingenuity of the plumbing. Was this merely something an Inventor had, or was all of Ruby likewise advanced? They must be, for Cullen was able to flush the waste away when he was finished and wash his hands with a mere on and off of the tap.

He could use a soak too, and given his benefactor had permitted him to wash and rest, he decided to take up that offer and turned on the tap of the bathtub, filling it with water that poured forth already steaming hot. Incredible. While the tub filled, Cullen stripped off his cloak and hung it on the hook on the back of the door. A closet in the washroom had robes, as well as pieces of cloth he could use to wash and dry himself.

Enzo had said to lock the door if Cullen decided to rest. Perhaps he should do so now. Pausing in undoing the ties of his tunic, he met his own eyes for the first time in the mirror above the sink. Enzo had described him—violet eyes, pale skin, wavy dark hair, and a fair face like a prince. That was the visage Cullen saw in his reflection, but it seemed a foreign thing, much as he knew this was him.

"I'm… Cullen," he said aloud. *Was* he Cullen? Was he this half-elf man with this collection of features and figure? Why, then, did another image stir in his mind like an overlapping of black and purple shadow?

Tendrils seeped from his hands like he'd noticed in the caves, black and purple indeed, coiling out of his skin, around his fingers and up his arms. This was… normal, wasn't it? This was—

"Ah!" Pain clanged in his head like a gong again, right there on either side of his ears, and it seemed the whole world trembled. Cullen's reflection shook, cringing as he cringed, and then… snarling with an angry, terrifying aura, as the shadows consumed and changed him entirely.

Overtaking his own rediscovered face was a hulking, monstrous head upon an equally hulking torso, eyes glowing within an otherwise formless face, that gave way to a gaping maw, filled with rows upon rows of shadow-like fangs.

He roared, and it was a roar, a howl, a bellow for retribution, only to feel all strength within him fade as the shadows that had become him suctioned within him and disappeared again with such force that he could only teeter before he collapsed to the floor.

CHAPTER 4

ENZO HAD been so frazzled and desperate to get back on the streets and learn the outcome of his folly that he hadn't thought to grab a knapsack to carry the food and drink he found among the turned-over banquet. Thankfully, a sack with fruit was one of the first items he discovered upon a not yet toppled table, which he used to also fill with bread, cheese, and a couple unopened bottles of spirits.

He'd chosen his path with care, heading toward the source of the destruction, while any stragglers he met were swiftly galloping the opposite direction. He soon neared the central square, or rather hexagon, where the many streets through Ruby converged. It was larger than the residential square where Enzo had been earlier and seen Janskoller perform. Janskoller had performed here recently as well, though there was no salvaged food or drink to be found, no merrymaking bards, dancers, or other revelers. All these tables had been upended, wine and beer flooding the square like the spillage of blood in battle.

Here too was where Enzo finally spotted city guards.

They were standing watch over the Royal Road that led to the castle. They must have feared a second assault, which was smart, but Vanck and the Ashen would not attack the same night. They would allow this slight to linger in the minds of the people at least until morning.

Ducking down an empty alley, Enzo hurried for one of the side streets that spanned parallel to the Royal Road. It was the nearest he could get to the castle without risking questions from the guards. The alley and surrounding streets were eerily quiet after the ruckus from earlier, all that joy in celebrating the passing king. It wasn't that the Ashen hated him, but in their eyes, he had never done enough to change their plight.

Honestly, Enzo agreed with that much. Once, the king had seemed very likely to change things for the better in Ruby, but after Enzo's mother died, so too had the king's resolve to do anything but blindly rule. He hadn't even sent letters to Enzo after that.

He. Him. The king. Enzo almost never thought of him by name.

Amdal Dragonbane.

"Dragonbane didn't have a queen? No fellow king or consort either?"

Enzo stopped, flattening himself to the side of the last building before the road hooked left. He'd hoped for this, that the otherwise quiet of the streets would mean an easier time overhearing anyone on the Royal Road and nearer to the castle. He knew this voice too—the beautiful dark-skinned half-elf who'd been with Janskoller—Prince Nemirac.

"His Majesty had a queen once," said another familiar voice, for this next man had spoken on behalf of the Ruby King for what seemed like years—the High Advisor, above the Forgemaster, Master of Caves and Mines, and any other lower-ranking officials in Ruby: Tyraag Kragvold, acting Regent until a new family line was chosen. "She passed many years ago during the birth of the king's first child, who also did not survive. He has no other offspring or living kin."

Enzo fought the grimace those words evoked. He didn't exist because he wasn't the right sort of offspring to claim. Perhaps tradition and the people in power would have overlooked the king choosing an elf as his second wife—perhaps, but not one so lowborn. And therefore, Enzo was lowborn too.

"If I may, Your Highness," Tyraag continued with a catch in his voice like speaking through venom, "while I understand the bard is your... companion, he is not performing currently, and such proceedings are generally only overseen by those of appropriate status."

"Excuse me?" Nemirac answered.

"My love," Janskoller spoke up. "I do believe this dwarf is calling me gutter trash."

"N-not at all!" Tyraag attempted to assuage the growing static in the air—and quite literally, for Enzo thought he felt the hairs on his arms begin to prickle like when a storm raged above the mountains. He risked a peek around the building, and though sound carried well, there was a gap dropping to rocky abyss, separating him from the Royal Road by a dozen meters or more.

Janskoller and Nemirac were not alone with Tyraag. They were at the end of the road, which opened into the Royal Square, a higher-end marketplace and courtyard of sorts that went right up to the castle gates. The damage from the explosion could be seen nearby, left of the castle, where there were many destroyed tables from celebration in this part of the city too. And not only nobles, merchants, or others among the wealthy had attended here, but all sorts, for a king's death was one of the few times when status could be forgotten—for a night.

Guards were carrying wounded to hastily set-up cots, where healers and alchemists were treating those in need. And right there amongst them were the visiting royals offering the same unfettered help. Had Vanek even thought to come here and see how his most hated of targets were doing their part?

The Emerald and Sapphire kings were arranging more cots, making room for others rescued from the debris. They were both handsome, regal humans, in colors matching their kingdoms. Reardon of Emerald had auburn hair and a kind, youthful face, while John, called Jack, of Sapphire was still young-looking, but his hair was pure white and wavy to his shoulders.

The Fairy Queen and her Prince Consort were tending to wounds and wrapping them in bandages. She was a radiant elf, dark of skin and hair, in all indigo, with an antlered crown. Her husband matched her finery, but was a human with flaxen hair, blue eyes, and a pale complexion, like the sun and moon in their contrast.

The Shadow King and his consort were entertaining wounded children to keep their tears dry—or had been, until Janskoller and Nemirac were overheard.

Ashmedai, the Shadow King, had the most immediately ominous presence among the others. Tallest for certain, but while not as broad as Janskoller, he carried darkness in his wake, and all who knew of him knew his appearance was a guise. There were monstrous features hiding behind his glamour of an elf with pale skin and long black hair, dressed in red and black brocade, with unknown power that could subdue anyone who faced him.

Oddly enough, Enzo thought, aside from the red hair, the Shadow King's consort looked a bit like Cullen.

"May I ask, Lord Kragvold, what it is you *are* implying?" Ashmedai demanded.

A dwarf among powerful men twice his height, with Ashmedai's voice carrying weight in its reverberation, Tyraag seemed very small indeed, and Enzo took some enjoyment in the man's quaking. He had never spoken to the High Advisor, but he could not say he cared for him much.

Tyraag wore a long, high-collared burgundy coat over a dark gray tunic, with a white cravat. While his head was bald, he had an impressive beard nearly to his waist, with braids made of either end of his equally long mustache, all dark auburn with liberal gray. His eyebrows almost seemed to connect to his remaining sideburns, making his scowl more prominent. Every part of him that could be decorated with gold or other coveted minerals from the mines was thus ornamented, even with baubles at the ends of his braids.

"Would you have Prince Nemirac dismiss his consort?" Ashmedai pressed when Tyraag held his tongue. "And if you would do so, would you too have me dismiss mine, simply because he was not born of richer blood?"

Enzo leaned so heavily forward, the corner of the building dug into his shoulder. Saying *richer* rather than royal blood was like a reminder that Ashmedai was a demon—or rather, a being of wild magic, once corrupted—and that he could likely devour Tyraag in one swoop.

The guards didn't seem to know how to react to the advisor being challenged, and all the royals were watching now, waiting on Tyraag's response, as were the consorts in question.

"Would you dismiss everyone of lower stock?" Ashmedai went on. "Perhaps toss some of the wounded into the crags?"

"Your Majesty…." Tyraag bowed, no doubt more to avoid the Shadow King's looming stare than out of deference. Then again, he must know the power vacuum left by the Ruby King's death would not be fixed by war breaking out with the recently recovered kingdoms. "Forgive me. I merely speak the traditions of my people."

Enzo huffed and then retreated behind the wall when he saw the Fairy Queen's head turn his direction. Pure elven ears were sharp, after all. Although, if rumor be true, she was wild magic born like Ashmedai.

"It is in my experience that hosts cater to the traditions of their guests," spoke Jack, the Sapphire King, who sounded closer with each word, moving toward Tyraag as well. "Or is that not the way in Ruby?"

"Of course, Majesties. I meant no offense, only to ensure that retribution for this attack is handled swiftly by those in power to protect those who are not. I assure you that is all I ever hope for."

Lies, Enzo thought with a clench of his teeth. Perhaps Tyraag did believe that, but it was rarely seen in practice.

"As one would hope," answered Ashmedai. "So let us all do what we can. It is a miracle there were no deaths tonight, despite the many wounded. All should recover, and we should work first to ensure that before we set loose upon your kingdom to find those responsible. After all, that would be most prudent in protecting those without power, would you not agree?"

Tyraag's silence proved he cared more about finding someone to punish than helping the injured, but eventually, he said, "At your leisure, Majesties. I am but a humble Regent, not by choice but circumstance, until our people decide on a new royal line. I acquiesce, always, to those who bear a crown."

As if that was the only test of worth—power, wealth, status. Enzo hated it, and he thought, too, the visiting royals must feel the same given several had consorts of no noble birth. Could even the Fairy Queen and Shadow King be called royal? As beings of wild magic, they were something else entirely, but had ruled their kingdoms for a thousand years.

Once more, Enzo attempted to sneak a peek, but his quick glance proved that not only was the Fairy Queen still looking his direction, but Ashmedai had turned as well.

He darted back down the way he had come from. He'd learned what he needed—several injuries but no deaths, and the blast had missed the castle itself. Whether that was intentional, he could not say. Regardless, he suspected this was only the beginning. The king's funeral would be soon, and the Ashen would not care how kind the other royals were being if they could make a larger statement before the Ruby crown passed on.

Enzo had nearly let it slip to Cullen that he was part of the current line. He needed to be careful. Sweet and trustworthy though the fair half-elf might seem, he was a stranger to both Enzo and himself. No one knew that Enzo was in fact Enzario Dragonbane.

No one but Vanek.

Returning to the central square, Enzo slowed his steps so as not to draw attention from the guards still blocking the Royal Road. Although it was not the guards whose eyes Enzo felt upon him, but a presence seemingly from the shadows cast by the pillars. He paused just shy of moving through one of those shadows and could have sworn the darkness itself watched him.

Clinging tighter to his scavenged bag of food and drink, Enzo neared his other hand to the hammer latched on his belt. Surely, he was imagining things, the hour growing late, with all manner of folly and danger about, but just as he'd felt the weight of eyes on him, so too did he feel when they retreated. The darkness seemed less thick, as though whatever had been lurking there had dubbed him no true threat.

Enzo covered the remaining distance home in a blink. He gasped and wheezed upon reaching his door—only to have a hand grip his arm before he could open it.

Whirling about with hammer drawn in a sweep of his arm, he readied to defend—

"Calm yourself, tinkerer," spoke one of his neighbors.

"Jason." Enzo sighed, nearly having attacked a poor old man with a cane. "Forgive me. I am on edge tonight."

"Aren't we all? But a young man like you shouldn't get involved. You *aren't* involved, I trust?"

His not-so-subtle question of whether Enzo had joined the Ashen was clear. Jason was a good sort, a former bard, who Enzo had seen perform beside Janskoller this night. He might have even been a little starstruck if he hadn't lived next to Jason for so many years.

Jason was also a farell and lived in a single-story home. His wife had passed away several years ago, both having been like grandparents to Enzo in his youth, especially after his mother died. Jason wore a beard in three long braids, like Vanek's, but as white as the hair on his head, atop which rested a floppy cap.

"Not willingly, I assure you," Enzo said and rehooked the hammer to his belt.

Jason leaned upon his cane, fixing Enzo with a penetrating stare. "You know, it is quite rare for the royal line to be broken by lack of heirs."

Enzo fought goosepimples that threatened to break over him, not for the first time wondering if Jason knew the secret of his lineage.

"In fact, I don't think it's happened since the Ruby Queen of old refused to bear a child, having married a man she didn't love after her true lover left her. Though I can't remember where I heard that tale…." He looked off as if contemplating memories long forgotten.

Enzo smiled, and the song that had been in his head not long ago returned. "It's the story of the original Janskoller, Jason. Everyone from Ruby knows it   including you who performed it earlier.

"He once seduced the Ruby Queen who'd sworn to love no more,
And when he left her bed at last, she wept and went to war.

"I remember being a boy when *you* were Janskoller—"

"Shh!" Jason hushed him, and then tipped his hat with a wink. "You'll spoil an ancient secret. The point, tinkerer, is that broken hearts come in all forms, but a true leader puts their people above themselves. Hopefully, the right kind will rise to lead us next. Until then, try not to get caught up in all this trouble, hmm?"

Enzo certainly didn't want to, though he still wondered if Jason knew more than he said.

"As payment for my wisdom, I'll confiscate one of these." Jason reached into Enzo's bag, producing one of the bottles of spirits.

"How did you—?"

"Good evening, tinkerer."

Enzo huffed as Jason hobbled away.

Definitely a bard.

After retreating inside, Enzo rested against his closed door. His house was as quiet as the streets, broken only by the buzz of running water. Cullen must have decided to take a bath.

With the washroom door open…?

And water spilling out of it!

"Cullen!" Enzo dropped the bag, barely registering the clink of the remaining bottle hitting the floor that thankfully didn't break before he dashed forward with a renewed burst of strength.

The half-elf lay sprawled upon the washroom floor, nose and mouth nearly sunk into the water filling the room from the overflowed tub.

Enzo dropped to his knees, rolling Cullen onto his back, and checked first that he was breathing. Cullen's breaths were shallow but there, the pulse of his heart slow. With that knowledge, Enzo leapt up to turn off the bathtub's tap, then quickly pulled the latch behind it, opening the grate in the washroom floor to drain the water into the central plumbing. Thank the skies for floors made of stone, though any damage to the home was hardly Enzo's first concern.

"Cullen," he said gently, returning to the crumpled and shivering young man. The water that had spilled had cooled upon the stone, and Cullen was freezing. "Please, fair elf, rouse for me and let me know what ails you."

Hefting Cullen into his lap, Enzo found him to be incredibly lightweight for all his long limbs. He was easy to cradle close and stroke the side of his face until enchanting violet eyes fluttered open. Thank the skies again. If Enzo had taken longer to return, Cullen might have drowned in ten centimeters of water.

"There we are." Enzo tightened his hold on Cullen's torso. "Stay awake for me now. What happened? Do you remember?"

"I…." Cullen trailed off, eyes distant as he searched his mind for an answer, but as had happened so often, he flinched and gritted his teeth against some wave of pain.

"It's all right. Let us focus on keeping you well. You're trembling. I'm going to reheat the bath for you." Enzo hefted Cullen once more, this time to rest him against the wall. Cullen seemed disoriented, more than before, but when Enzo hushed him and petted the backs of his fingers down the half-elf's dampened cheek, Cullen calmed.

Moving swiftly, Enzo drained some of the overflowed tub, then flipped another switch, this one activating alternating Sun and Torch runes on the flooring that emanated heat to rewarm the water better than actual fire.

Cullen was conscious but still looking about himself as if in a daze, which made it easier to help him undress with objective care. Well, perhaps not entirely objective, for the half-elf's bared body was as ravishing as his face, all pale, blemish-free skin, and delicately muscled. His dark hair was oddly fine down his legs but certainly thicker between them. Not that Enzo allowed his gaze to drift there any more than he needed to.

Lifting Cullen into the bath was his true test, not because of the effort to heft him, but because the brush of soft skin begged to be caressed, which was hardly a decent thought to entertain of a weakened man who needed Enzo's help. But oh, he was the most beautiful thing, bare or otherwise, that Enzo had ever seen or touched.

Cullen was too bewildered to appear bashful, but he smiled at Enzo upon sinking into the water. By the time Enzo retrieved soaps and oils from the washroom closet, the distantness in Cullen's eyes had cleared.

"I'm sorry," he said, hugging his knees to his chest.

"Needing aid is never worth an apology, fair Cullen," Enzo said, setting the supplies on a ledge in the stone, easily within Cullen's reach. "Perhaps I won't be letting you bathe alone for the time being. Not that I'll be participating! Or watching!" He ducked his head as he felt his cheeks warm like the water. When he dared flick his eyes back to the fair half-elf, Cullen was smiling again.

The steam from the water made the waves of his dark hair flatten to his face and lengthen, some long enough to stretch down his neck nearly to his shoulders, while shorter strands across his forehead teased the tips of his eyelashes. And oh, those eyes. They nearly seemed to glow with their violet color, especially with a violet crystal casting light into the room from the wall behind him.

"Hold tight just one moment." Enzo held Cullen's gaze before turning away. "Let me see if I can find you something clean and dry to wear, though bear in mind, I'm afraid any trousers of mine are going to be about knee-length on you."

After returning from his bedchamber with soft simple trousers and a similarly plain tunic, Enzo did watch the bathing a little from the corners of his eyes—the delicate way Cullen washed his hair and scrubbed the dirt from his porcelain skin. He helped Cullen from the bath eventually too, but politely kept his gaze turned away while Cullen dried and dressed. The shirt was too wide but long enough, with the trousers cinched as tight as Cullen could make them, which did indeed hang only to his knees.

"I-I have slippers!" Enzo announced, hurrying into the main room to find them beside his armchair. They were fur-lined and the right size for Cullen, and he met him at the washroom doorway for Cullen to slip into them. "The stone can get rather cold at night. There you are."

And my, yes, he was.

Somehow, seeing Cullen in Enzo's clothing was even more enticing than seeing bared skin.

"SH-SHALL WE get some food in you now?" Enzo seemed to stutter, overexcited or nervous or.... Cullen could not say for sure what, but he found the occasional trip of Enzo's tongue endearing. He was such a kind man, having saved Cullen yet again, aiding him in whatever ways he could, even by helping him in and out of the bath.

Roused and revitalized now, Cullen could better dwell on how this sweet farell had gathered him in powerful arms like some knight from a bard song, the warm skin of his hands having brushed Cullen's lower back and beneath his thighs when he deftly laid him in the water. Cullen mourned a little that it had not been the same connection to lift him out again, but his own feet standing and Enzo taking his hand to steady him.

"Food, and then you should rest. No memories yet?" Enzo asked as they traipsed to the dining table.

Cullen dared not try to remember or risk another spike of pain, but letting his mind go blank and hoping the memories flitted in on their own brought forth the vague sense of shadows in his reflection.

What had he seen before he passed out? He did not want to recall nor relive that dread.

"I don't think so," he said, as true as he could speak. "Your inventions in the workshop looked quite fascinating." Enzo was a better topic, for Cullen could still say no more than his name, and all that lay beyond it seemed shrouded in some unknown guilt and fear.

"You explored?" Enzo retrieved a sack from near the door, and then pushed the clutter of papers out of the way to begin setting the table with the provisions he'd brought. While simple enough, bread, cheese, and an apple sounded like ambrosia to Cullen's empty stomach. "Please pardon whatever mess you found."

"An inventor's prerogative," Cullen said. He felt a little useless sitting there, being catered to, as Enzo retrieved clean plates and cups, poured from a bottle within his sack into one of them, and began slicing the fare to fill Cullen's plate. "I was curious about the pendant. It didn't appear to have any special properties or a placard like the rest."

Tension rippled across Enzo's shoulders, only to ease off as he mustered a strained smile. "I forgot that was in there. Just an old family heirloom."

Cullen sensed more was left unsaid, but it hardly seemed polite to question one's savior.

"The good news is the visiting royals are aiding the injured," Enzo continued, "and no deaths were reported. The bad news is what might come next."

"You believe the Ashen will strike again?"

"Most certainly."

"Using your invention? That orb, the... Dragon's Gland?"

Enzo paused, looking pained by the name's mention. "Vanek is clever enough that the plans were all he needed to make another."

"Won't it take him time to make more after using one?"

"Yes, but he doesn't need more right away. I designed the Dragon's Gland to be reusable. It isn't destroyed from one blast. The one in the workshop is the proper design." He finished with the bread, cheese, and fruit, and once he sat with his own plate filled, Cullen allowed himself to eat. Enzo, in contrast, went first for a sip of spirits from his cup. "That one would implode after its explosion to contain the blast and collect the rubble in a neat pile. But what Vanek made could take down whole city blocks, entire sections of the castle, or worse. It was lucky this time that mostly unremarkable walls were destroyed."

"What are you going to do?" Cullen asked.

"I have no idea." Enzo's gaze drifted down, and he seemed to notice something beneath the table. He hopped from his chair to retrieve it, which proved to be the crumpled note he'd thrown at Vanek

Most of the home was lit by colored crystals in the stone, but there were some torches and candles. Enzo retrieved a candle from the kitchen, and then spread out the note with the blank side facing up. Careful not to set it ablaze, he lowered the flame near the paper, dragging it across and down every square bit of space. Moments later, previously unseen words appeared as if brought forth by magic.

"I suppose I didn't need to go out to learn where they'd hit," Enzo said with a sigh. "It seems Vanek did intend to miss the castle with this first strike. Still, I needed to see the rest for myself."

From Cullen's view, the words were upside down, but he could read enough to see that they detailed the where, when, and why of the attack to all who might aid them or ensure others loyal to their plight were not nearby when the explosion occurred.

"I know what you're thinking," Enzo said, almost as if speaking to the paper. "Why not turn them in? I know the identities of several members, including their leader."

"Vanek. But he is your friend."

Enzo's brow scrunched like he was trying to stay tears, and Cullen wondered if they had been more than friends once. Enzo downed his remaining spirits, before realizing he'd never poured any for Cullen. "What a terrible host I'm being!" He amended by filling Cullen's cup, and then his own again.

"My thanks." Cullen took his first gulp greedily and immediately went back for another.

"A trim, beautiful half-elf who can also hold his liquor?" Enzo chuckled. "Yet another fine surprise from you, fair Cullen."

"You are too flattering when I have given you many not so fine surprises tonight."

"Given all else that's happened, I am honestly glad to not be spending the night alone." Perhaps it was the spirits that made Enzo less stuttery in his admissions, though that too was charming.

"Since I cannot tell you much about me," Cullen said, "what else is there to know about Enzo the inventor?"

However late it might have been, they chatted while enjoying their meal and most of the bottle of spirits, allowing Cullen to learn about his savior. Enzo was an only child, with few close friends but many acquaintances, since he tended to spend most of his time in his workshop. This home had been his mother's, who moved to Ruby when she was a young woman, supposedly having fled from an arranged marriage, but Enzo guessed that to be a story, and the simpler truth was she wanted adventure, though nothing had turned out the way she'd hoped.

"I keep a picture above the hearth." Enzo pointed at it, but there didn't appear to be anything there. "Blast, must have fallen again." He went to it, using a stool near the hearth to reach the top of the mantel where a framed picture had indeed fallen forward. He brought it to the table and handed it to Cullen.

The picture showed a beautiful young elf as well as the child version of Enzo, fairer of face without his stubble, and hair not yet long enough to be braided. His mother was darker skinned, with brown hair and eyes, and a lovely face. Her smile was very much like Enzo's.

Very much like Enzo's, because the picture was crystal clear, as if Cullen could reach right through it and touch the people portrayed there.

"What an odd portrait." Cullen dared not touch it directly, even over glass. "I can't see the lines of the paint at all."

"It's a photograph," Enzo said.

"A… what?"

Enzo's nose twitched, and he blinked a few times before saying again, "A photograph. A photo? From a camera?" When Cullen continued to stare blankly, Enzo went off again, digging through some of his clutter around the shorter table by the hearth and retrieving what looked like a box with a circular protrusion sticking out the front, covered in a rounded pane of glass. The top popped up and caused a few smaller crystals to light up. "There aren't many portable ones like mine, but surely whichever kingdom you're from has some. And it isn't difficult to enlarge a photo after it's taken. The invention originated in Ruby, but I would swear the technology has spread... oh! Perhaps that's the answer!"

"Hm?" Cullen pulled his attention from the intriguing device that had somehow created the picture framed like a still plucked from memory and returned to Enzo's brightened face.

"The cursed kingdoms that have opened," Enzo said, setting the camera on the table, where Cullen set the picture. "I nearly forgot. Perhaps you're from the Mystic Valley or the Frozen Kingdom. Or even the Shadow Lands!"

Cullen didn't recognize any of those places.

Did he?

"Sorry, I mean Diamond, Sapphire, or the Amethyst Kingdom, as they were once called. They've been closed off for centuries. That could explain your predicament."

Amethyst.

Ame... tista....

Cullen's hands went numb, and he tightened them into fists, not wanting to look at them until the numbness went away. When he finally felt like he could, he blessedly saw no signs of shadows.

Like in the mirror....

He closed his eyes. He didn't want to remember. He didn't want to remember!

"All will be well." Enzo's warm hands came down upon his, and Cullen opened his eyes to see glorious bronze, like a sunrise beating back the darkness. "It's late. You should rest. Please. I have work I should get to anyway."

"Work? But...."

"Sleep, fair Cullen. I'll be fine."

Like every time before, the loss of Enzo's hands when they pulled away made Cullen want to clutch them back to him. But he knew Enzo was right. Cullen needed rest. Maybe in the light of a new day, his mind would quiet and clear, and he would not fear the shadows as much.

He hoped.

Without argument, he finished another sip from his cup and then retired to Enzo's bedchamber, where he hoped no dreams of his yet unknown past would follow him.

IF CULLEN did dream, he remembered nothing come morning, waking to light brightening outside the bedchamber window, where he knew mirrors filled the street corners to illuminate the Ruby Kingdom. He also woke to the sounds of shuffling in the kitchen.

Cullen could not say if Enzo had slept, but his clothes had been cleaned and laid on the bedchamber bureau for him to change into, there was breakfast waiting, and Enzo seemed invigorated.

He also had the Dragon's Gland out and set upon the kitchen table amidst the food.

"Good mor—"

Something struck the door, almost like a knock, before Cullen could finish his greeting. Enzo opened it, seeming to have expected what he found, which was another note marked with the rune for Ash.

Not appearing at all disturbed, Enzo immediately set about laying it flat on the table and using a candle to reveal its message like the one last night.

"What does it say?" Cullen asked, taking his same seat from before.

"A meeting place and time to discuss next steps."

"Do you know what you're going to do?"

"Yes." Enzo looked across the table at Cullen, and whatever work he had gotten up to during the night had clearly led him to a decision. "*We* are going to attend."

CHAPTER 5

IT WAS a terrible idea to bring Cullen to the Ashen's meeting, but surely it would have been worse to have left him alone. The poor thing had nearly drowned last night, passed out on Enzo's bathroom floor, and he still had no memory of what happened before Enzo found him in the caves, or who he was beyond his name. Enzo owed it to him to keep him close.

And close they remained upon arriving at the Bottom of the Barrel tavern, an establishment farther from the castle than almost any other, built into the very bow of the horseshoe of the poorest streets. It was the perfect meeting place, since Enzo doubted he'd seen a city guard within a dozen blocks of it since he was a child.

Salacia "Sally" Draftborn was the proprietor, having inherited the tavern from her parents, a rowdy dwarf with a glass eye and a steel tongue. She tolerated bar fights so long as no spirits or ale was ever spilt. Blood was less hassle on the tables and floors, apparently, and cost less to replace.

Cullen had no weapons, and all Enzo had was his smithing hammer—and the Dragon's Gland, but that was for other purposes today. Enzo didn't wish to fear the people they passed on the streets, nor those in attendance once they entered the tavern—impressively packed for before noon after a night of previous celebrating. But then, perhaps none of these people had joined in, since they were responsible for the explosion that ended it.

All he needed for entry was the note bearing the Ashen's rune, but he told Cullen to wear the hood of his cloak low to hide his face since they couldn't be sure of the ramifications of anyone recognizing him. Cullen's finer clothing garnered a few flicks of interest anyway when the intricate stitching of his tunic peeked out of his cloak. Many more people had joined the Ashen than Enzo had last seen.

All the tables had been claimed, but two spots at the bar remained empty, which Enzo hurried toward, with Cullen's hand clasped in his own to lead him. The bar was built for dwarves, so while it was a high top for Enzo, Cullen's feet touched the ground when they sat.

"Enzo the tinkerer!" greeted the man in the stool beside Enzo. It wasn't only Jason who called him that but everyone from the slums. "'Bout time. I was beginning to think you weren't part of the cause, sad affair that'd be if it true."

"Dorff...." Enzo recognized his dwarven neighbor, the blacksmith whose hammer he'd almost used as a weapon last night since he'd been without his own. "Well, um... I...."

"As well you should be part of this! Just 'cause we live closest to the nicer streets don't make us highborn. My daughter got accosted just the same by... someone or another. A noble to be sure. Can't recall his face, she said, but remembers fine clothing. Brutes, terrorizing babes!"

Enzo held his tongue from saying he'd seen plenty of babes on the cots by the castle after the Ashen's attack.

"I should thank you again for fixing my anvil." Dorff nudged him, clearly on at least his second ale. "Can't eat if I can't work!"

"I wouldn't have the maul I'm working on if you hadn't forged the frame. Besides, I'm always happy to help those in need."

"Why you're here too, I'd wager. That's Enzo the tinkerer for you, always coming up with new baubles to ease the people's plight."

Again, Enzo held his tongue. He did always help when he could, but he'd never wanted it to be through the use of destructive invention. He wanted to create, to build, to provide.

"What's with your friend?" Dorff asked, nudging him again in indication of Cullen hiding in his hood.

"Um... he's shy."

Sally herself poured and passed them mugs of ale, other help delivering drinks to the tables, and while it might be gratis for the Ashen's meeting, Enzo was quick to add coin to a nearby jar.

"Are all these people...?" Cullen didn't finish his thought and kept his voice low.

"So it would seem," Enzo whispered back.

The tavern smelled of ale and broth for stew later, but without the undercurrent of sweat, blood, piss, and bile that Enzo remembered from even less than a year ago when he and Vanek frequented this place often. The Ashen were serious indeed, even if some of the occupants were questionable.

There were dwarves, elves, farells, humans, half elves, and half dwarves all. The only necessary connecting thread between them was where and to what status they had been born.

"Three cheers for the Ruby King!" a voice cut through the din.

"Oy, oy, oy!" answered overlapping cries, and almost every mug raised high.

"Quite the celebration we had in his honor, eh?" the voice continued, and Vanek appeared in the center of the tavern upon a tabletop for all to see.

He was handsome with his rich black braided hair and beard, and the piercing blue of his eyes like sharply cut sapphires. He could command any room he sought to control, but he hadn't been able to control the will of Enzo's heart, and for that, Enzo was still sorry.

How could one remain true friends with a lover they'd discarded?

Cullen tugged his hood back slightly to better see, and the height of his cheekbones, his delicate nose, and sharp curve of his chin filled Enzo's belly with more heat than Vanek had ever conjured. He felt guilt for that too, but he couldn't help the sort of face and figure that roused his loins.

"Quite the celebration for all those visiting *royals* too, I dare say."

A few boos and laughs filtered through the crowd.

"I hear they've sent a few from their delegations back home," Vanek went on, "and good riddance, but Their *Majesties* and whichever bed partners they've claimed remain. They say it's to keep a protective watch over Ruby until after the king's funeral and a new line has ascended. But wouldn't you know... the king's funeral is being postponed."

"What?" Enzo gasped.

"They're launching an investigation as we speak, claiming the explosion was too well timed to not have been part of something premeditated."

Enzo's belly grew cold, and he stared in disbelief at Vanek's apparent glee in commanding the crowd with this news. Did they think the king murdered?

"All a convenient excuse to have the demons in their midst hunt us down, to have strangers to our kingdom dictate justice. I don't know which is worse, another rich Ruby line or a foreign takeover, but I know a good royal when I see one, and it is no royal at all!"

Cheers rang out, and Enzo's stomach felt colder and low like it was sinking to his toes.

"Seems they're forcing our hand, aren't they?" Vanek called over the crowd to quiet them. "We can't sit idly by and wait. We need to strike again, soon, as planned, and that means our next target is either… the guest quarters of the castle!"

Cheers again, as though everyone would gladly see the visiting royals bloody and buried.

"Or!" Vanek paused for effect with a wicked grin. "The temporary tomb where the king's body is being kept!"

"No!" Enzo leapt from his stool. His voice carried loud enough that the next cheers rose and swiftly fell, all eyes turning to him. The crowd parted, creating a pathway between him and Vanek. Enzo hadn't meant to confront his friend this way, but he couldn't stay silent. "Please. You can't do that."

"And why not, *friend*?" Vanek said with biting scorn. "The king is gone. He'll feel no sting from rubble. Would you have our kingdom taken over by royals who were cursed, who are demons, who know nothing of our lands? Or perhaps the High Advisor is preferable, as all is poised for? Either way, our plight remains the same or worsens. We need to strike again and in a way they cannot ignore."

Poised for Tyraag? Enzo had not considered the High Advisor vying for the throne, but he did have a strong noble line, with a wife and three children to succeed him.

Surely the visiting royals had no interest in a takeover. They'd stayed to help, that was all, but no one in this tavern would believe that.

"Then let me present an alternative target," Enzo said boldly. "In private."

Dissenting murmurs rose all around, but Vanek was the voice of this revolution, and when he raised his hands to call for quiet, they listened. "All have a say here, unlike with those in power. I will listen to our resident inventor, but our plans only change if your alternative is of equal value to the cause." He dropped down from the table and motioned for Enzo to follow him into the back.

Almost immediately, the crowd returned to drinking and talking among themselves, but this time, many a wary glance was cast upon Enzo when he darted through their ranks leading a tall, hooded figure behind him. Enzo knew most of these people and had fixed plumbing, lighting, and tools for most of them. Barmaids and other help who worked for Sally, miners aplenty, Dorff and other working class, as well as Rufus and the very ruffians Janskoller and Nemirac had confronted. The Ashen accepted any who'd aid them, regardless of motivation or character.

One such brutish human guarded the back room where Vanek waited.

"I believe you said *privately*," Vanek sneered with a withering look at Cullen.

Enzo turned to him in apology. "I'll be swift, I swear, but…."

Cullen nodded when Enzo trailed off. He peered out of his hood at Vanek and the brute, then slinked away back to the bar.

Vanek led Enzo into the room, where the brute remained in the doorway to keep others out. A bottle of spirits rather than ale and several cups rested on the table, but when Vanek made to pour some, Enzo waved the offer away. Neither sat.

"Before we speak, I must know… did the Ashen murder the king?" Enzo asked.

"Of course not." Vanek glared with enough contempt that Enzo believed him even before he said, "If anyone did, it was Tyraag, who didn't realize other royals would be present to oversee the aftermath. He didn't call for investigation, you see. The Emerald King did, and the others backed him, suspicious of foul play because of our attack.

"And good, because not only does it postpone the funeral, it gives us more targets to make an example out of."

"Then target something that makes a statement without good people getting hurt," Enzo pleaded. "Don't use your creation from my plans, use the real thing, the one that can be controlled." He pulled out the original Dragon's Gland and set it on the table. "Destroy the statue of the Dragonbane progenitor in front of the castle using that."

"You're helping?" Vanek looked at the orb as though suspecting a trick.

"Only because I know you won't stop, but I won't let you use my invention to harm innocents."

"Enzo…." Vanek's bombastic front gave way to the gentler soul Enzo knew was in him. "You know that was never the goal."

"It was still an outcome. Use my original invention to reduce collateral damage and on a safer target that still sends a message. Please."

Vanek was quiet at first, not yet reaching to claim the orb. "Only if you come with me."

"Vanek…."

"Help plant the orb. Then you can ensure I keep my end of the bargain, keep an eye on all the… riffraff in our ranks you turn your nose up at. Or are you too busy babysitting your *friend*." He jutted his chin in indication of Cullen. "I miss you, and not only for that brilliant mind or all it could mean for the Ashen." He reached for one of Enzo's braids and tugged it gently like he used to.

It pained Enzo that he had to pull out of reach. "I will participate to ensure the plan is followed through safely. That is all."

Vanek sighed. Then he stretched his smile, as if to say he wasn't giving up yet, and whispered in Enzo's ear, "For now… Your Highness."

CULLEN LIKED the din. It drowned out the buzz from his muddied thoughts.

He'd been able to reclaim his previous stool, tucked into the corner of the bar, where his mug of ale waited. He gulped from it to ease his nerves at being alone in such a crowded space. He gulped from Enzo's forgotten mug too. When both were empty, the dwarven woman behind the counter refilled them. She was middle-aged with a heavily painted but beautiful face and long ginger curls messily tied up. There was something strange about her left eye, and the corset over her dress did wonders for her ample bosom, both of which she seemed to appreciate Cullen not staring at.

"Thank you, madam," Cullen said, head low to keep hidden in his hood, "but I'm afraid I haven't any coin like my friend to add to your jar."

"Enzo's an odd duck, but a good man," she said with a nod, "and you not having any coin may be to your benefit, young… elf?" She eyed him—or at least the right one seemed to peruse him—trying to see past the cloth covering his ears, but she must have seen enough of his face to guess he was part elf with his thin nose and fair face. "If you had a purse on you, boyo, it'd be empty before you left that stool again. Watch yourself," she finished in a hiss, and Cullen couldn't be sure if she meant those words as threat or warning.

He pulled both mugs closer and kept his head bowed, waiting for when Enzo would rejoin him. Calming as the noise in the tavern may be, the presence of so many others was still overwhelming. He didn't think anyone was looking at him unkindly, but he wondered how quickly that might change. The dwarf a stool down was definitely curious.

He should have stayed in Enzo's clothes.

"Demons! The whole lot!" one voice rose above the clamor.

"No, no, the Emerald King was but a poof prince before he wed. He's human."

"Wed to the Ice King! Who knows what true form that monster has? And the Fairy Queen's a right witch herself. Definitely a demon."

"Also married to a *human*."

"Who's lived a thousand years! Something's off about that son too. Looks nothing like either of 'em. Where'd he get silver hair and gold eyes, eh? Demon's blood is where!"

"And tamed by Janskoller the bard. Also, human again. You're mad, Rufus. Or drunk," snorted the voice of reason.

"Janskoller the *traitor*, you might say. Ain't he supposed to be on our side? And he's off gallivanting with those royals. He attacked me and my boys with his little princeling just for trying to pilfer a purse. As if that bard's never nicked a purse before! And don't get me started on the Shadow King. Bloody creature from the abyss, they say, that Ashmedai of Amethyst."

Ashmedai.

Ash....

"Do you have magic, Your Highness?" asked a voice.

No. There was no voice. Not *that* voice.

"...if I concentrated more, or was near the Amethyst gemstone, especially if I touched it, my abilities could grow exponentially, as though pulling magic straight from the veil between worlds."

Cullen tried to take another drink, but wisps of black-purple shadow coiled out from his fingertips and wrapped around both mugs.

No! He was not near the Amethyst. That was leagues away, in a whole other kingdom. And yet... he could feel it. He could feel a pulse from the Amethyst's power with the beat of his own heart.

"What about you, Ash? Where would your heart's desire lead you?"

The black-purple swirls were not merely wisps but encasing Cullen and becoming the whole of his hands, turning them to shadows themselves like massive claws.

"You all right there, lad?" the nearby dwarf asked.

"To me, my friend, these hands are far from incapable."

Nearly upending both mugs, Cullen yanked his hands inside his cloak to hide them and clenched his eyes shut. He didn't want to remember. He didn't want to remember!

"Cullen, are you—?"

Cullen pushed from the bar, upsetting his stool, and bolted for the exit.

"Cullen!"

He had to push people out of his way, bodily with his shoulder, for he kept his changed hands to his chest, and any protests that followed him were a senseless babble.

It hurt. It *hurt*.

Didn't it?

He felt as if his mouth was stretching wider, and he tongued what pricked like fangs as he pushed outside into the bright light of day, too bright, even within the shadows of his hood. Fangs. So many fangs. Like in the mirror. Oh *skies*, he remembered what he'd seen in the mirror. What he looked like. What he was.

Demon.

Void beast.

Voidy...?

"Some fancy clothes hiding beneath that cloak, I think," called the same voice he'd heard inside—Rufus, having followed him out. "Stitching on the cloak ain't half bad either. You lost, little rich boy?"

No. Not now. Cullen could barely see, let alone know which direction those taunts came from. He needed Rufus to get away from him, for he knew not what he might do.

Defend.

Protect.

Consume.

"Oy! I'm talking to you!" A hand clamped down on Cullen's wrist, and he readied a roar.

"Stop! Remove your hand from him at once! Now!"

All was an endless void. He needed to fill it. He had to or become trapped within the darkness forever.

"Enzo the savior now, is it? You wish to protect little rich boy like all those royals you love?"

"I *said*... remove your hand."

Rufus's grip released Cullen, and with its departure left some of his bloodlust. Oh, but he could still taste on the air what consuming Rufus might have felt like.

"Lower your hammer, tinkerer," Rufus's voice faded with a grumble as he left. "Can't believe you'd choose some highborn over your own kind."

Cullen was aware only of the wall he leaned against and the shadows pulsing over his skin and hazing his vision in violet.

"Cullen?" Enzo's voice preceded a tender touch on Cullen's shoulder. He didn't want Enzo to see him like this, and yet, with how he was hunched, trying to keep his hands, his whole form hidden within his cloak, he welcomed that Enzo was able to reach high enough to brush his palm against Cullen's cheek.

Enzo gasped. Did the shadows burn him? Were they freezing? Both? Regardless, his touch grew firmer, and he tilted Cullen's head down to see up into his hood. What might have been a roar came out after all, but as a pained whimper.

"Fair Cullen... what is happening?" Enzo's eyes were the same beacons of bronze light leading Cullen out of the darkness, and though he must have seen Cullen's fiercer face for how the shadows had overtaken him, any fear lasted but a moment, replaced by a resolve to help.

"Enzo..." Cullen clutched Enzo's cloak with shaking shadowy claws, his voice like an echo in a cavern. "*I think... something is wrong with me.*"

CHAPTER 6

CULLEN'S SURROUNDINGS became a blur as Enzo led him through the streets. The shadows refused to return within him like they had the other times this strangeness enveloped him, leaving him in a daze, and yet terrified that someone might see the monster hiding in his cloak. He dared not look out of his hood and risk that happening, blindly following Enzo's lead.

Occasional views outside the fabric struck Cullen's senses anyway. He had noticed the increasing decay of the streets on their way to the tavern, how Enzo was on the apparent edge of the horseshoe, and therefore, his home, his neighborhood appeared cozy and clean. But the closer they'd gotten to the bow, farthest from the castle, the worse conditions had become.

Seeing it backward, supposedly getting better as they went, Cullen thought the decay they were leaving behind more prominent. Crumbled buildings where the stone had caved in, but not been fixed. People living on the streets or beneath the overhang of some partial hollow. The dirty and tattered clothing of those they passed, scrounging for food, some even brushing off spoiled fare from last night's celebrating that had long since been trampled on. The jeering and watchful eyes of criminals who would pounce once they saw an opening. The whines of injured without recourse for aid, or children without the essentials they needed to thrive.

In his own contained abyss, Cullen saw more clearly the one these people tried to carve their way out of. Yes, there were fewer signs of it as they neared Enzo's home, but then he saw why after a quick glance behind them.

They'd stepped through an invisible barrier at the edge of the horseshoe, some wall of illusion that blocked the view into the conditions of those worse streets unless you were in them. Cullen hadn't noticed before, but the mere crossing of a street, even a magical one, didn't erase the plight on the other side.

He breathed deep upon entering Enzo's house. The haze seemed to have lifted, the shadows fading like mist from his skin and allowing him to pull his hood back without fear. "It really is awful for many of the people here, isn't it?" he said, thankful to no longer hear an echo in his voice. "There's even a glamour spell to hide it. Who would do that?"

Enzo finished closing the door before joining him with a wide-eyed perusal of his form. Yet again there was no fear, only intrigue and a desire to help. "The Ashen were created for good reason, even if I don't agree with most of their methods or everyone who aids them. That glamour has been there for years now. Some official or another put the spell in permanently as part of a beautification initiative, because it's easier to pretend something doesn't exist if you can't see it." He took Cullen's hand, grasping skin this time, not over the safety of fabric as Cullen had insisted on during their trek, and sat him down at the kitchen table. "You are you again."

"Whoever that is," Cullen muttered.

"You still remember nothing?"

"I… started to remember some things."

"Tell me." Enzo hurried to pour them both some water. Having his eyes elsewhere made it easier for Cullen to answer.

"The Amethyst. I think I share some of its magic."

"Violet eyes." Enzo nodded.

"When others speak of the kings, the other royals, I…." In the attempt to recall the memories that had surfaced, Cullen felt the familiar spike of pain and winced as he tried to push past it.

"The Shadow King?" Enzo rejoined him, thrusting one of the cups of water into Cullen's hands. "Ashmedai?"

Wisps of black-purple shadow returned, first from Cullen's palms, as if in answer to the question and that familiar name.

"I could seek an audience!" Enzo declared. "He might—"

"No!" Cullen shoved the cup away from himself, if only to deny the shadows their desire to throttle whatever they held closest. They slithered back inside him, and it *hurt*.

Didn't it?

Did it?

Did he feel anything at all?

"I don't remember enough. I… I don't—"

"The Shadow King might!" Again, Enzo's hands came down upon Cullen's without fear. "Any of the royals might. They could help you."

"Please...." Cullen shook his head. He was tempted to pull free of Enzo's hold, but his bronze and burly savior was a balm to what unraveled within him. "I am not ready to face all that I am." Everything was so close to the surface, but so were the shadows—shadows that were hungry, angry, and wanted nothing more than to fill the void at their core.

"I understand," Enzo said, his warm, thick hands squeezing Cullen's in assurance. "May I still try to help you find your way back to yourself? If magic is at work here, perhaps I can learn something through my own methods."

"Like what?"

ENZO'S MOTHER had always said his affinity for alchemy, invention, and tinkering was its own sort of magic, and of course it was, for one needed magic to activate runes, even if only a tiny amount. Then again, Enzo's mother had also said his curiosity toward his affinity was a curse—jokingly! Although the char marks still present on the stone in his bedchamber begged the question of how serious she might have been.

His bedchamber was the only place he'd been able to tinker in when he was a boy. His current workshop had been his mother's bedchamber, the actual master suite. He could have taken it over when she passed away. Instead, he'd kept his own room and transformed hers, often speaking to her when he was in there, promising to not char any new walls.

He *was* curious, and maybe to a fault, especially with an unknown entity in his home.

Cullen looked like a half-elf, but Enzo had never seen nor heard of anyone becoming living shadow before. That's what Cullen had looked like within his cloak until their return. Malleable black-purple mist in the shape of a man. His features had almost, *almost* been Cullen's, but within his mouth when he spoke, with its edges stretched unnaturally wide, were rows upon rows of merciless fangs.

Demon whispered the answer in Enzo's mind. He'd heard plenty about King Ashmedai, that in his homeland of the Dark Kingdom all manner of monsters resided, and the king himself bore fangs and fierce eyes and wielded shadow magic no normal mortal could defend against. Shadows....

Like the darkness that had seemed to watch Enzo when he hurried from the blast site.

So much might be answered by the royals, but if they be trustworthy, why had Cullen been cast out? What role had they played? He could not have deserved such a fate, no matter who he was. He was a gentle soul that did not wish to burden another. And he was so very beautiful. Even his shadow form held its appeal, not frightening to Enzo the way another might have been frightened. True monsters could take any form, for evil was in a person's heart, not their visage.

Enzo brought Cullen into his workshop, cleared away the clutter from one of the tables, and motioned for the half-elf to sit. Cullen had removed his cloak if a bit reluctantly. Without it he could not hide himself should the shadows resurface, but Enzo kept his attitude jovial to impress upon Cullen that he need not hide at all.

While Cullen waited patiently, Enzo gathered an armful of crystals, water, and his mortar and pestle. He chose an amethyst crystal first and began to crush it within the mortar, slowly adding water once the shards became a sparkling powder.

"These are dormant crystals," he explained to Cullen's curious stares. "Certain ones evoke different elements and power when active, just like how the gemstones are tied to elements and magical effects. Forge fire for the Ruby, ice for the Sapphire, and so on. Most people think a dormant crystal useless, but I've found that they can serve their own purposes."

He tilted the finished product toward Cullen, where inside the mortar was now a glimmering violet paste.

"It becomes like paint that when used to draw a rune can enhance that power without using an active crystal's magic. Nothing wasted. I know it doesn't look like much, but I'll show you. Um… take off your tunic, please."

Cullen's eyes darted to Enzo's, but he seemed more concerned about what his inner nature might do than any embarrassment over bared skin. Enzo reminded himself that he shouldn't feel embarrassed either. Cullen had already been naked in his presence, and this was an experiment, methodical and chaste. The beautiful curves that defined Cullen's arms and chest and abdominals, all covered in pale skin like ivory silk, should not affect a true scientist's motivation.

"A-and if you could, uh… spread your legs for me so I can get closer?" Enzo's voice cracked on the end of the entirely necessary request.

He needed to get at Cullen's chest, and the most direct access with him sat upon the table was by parting his thighs for Enzo to step between them.

Cullen did as told, legs wide, in just trousers and boots. The height of the table meant Enzo still had to reach up to begin drawing, closer in eyeline with Cullen's navel. The half-elf smelled like bath oils from last night and a hint of earthy musk like wet moss on stones after a storm.

A faint gasp left Cullen at Enzo's fingers beginning to paint, using the amethyst paste to create the rune for Man, like an M or gateway door.

"I should know some of this," Cullen said, his violet eyes not unlike the glittering substance Enzo painted with. "Alchemy, runes, magic. But I can't remember how any of it works."

"Persons with a lot of magic," Enzo explained, partially to distract himself from the soft texture he was being allowed to touch, "can manifest runes naturally to call upon power without using too much of their own reserves. A powerful mage could draw a rune in the air to cast a spell, for example, with no tools or paint. While not as powerful, someone less magically inclined like me can still draw and activate a rune for a desired result. Sometimes the right materials can enhance that outcome without more natural magic being present.

"Crystals, ores, combinations of different runes, can all have different effects. I used amethyst since whatever happens to you is shadow based, and as you noted, the Amethyst gemstone is the source of such magic. I'm drawing the rune for Man to cast a sort of scanning spell to determine your magical affinity. There we are. Now, to activate the spell, I just need—"

The instant he tapped the rune to trigger it, a flash of violet light exploded in his face, and he went airborne.

"Enzo!"

He slammed into the wall of his workshop and crumpled to the floor.

"I'm fine!" Enzo coughed through the winded pressure on his lungs, accepting assistance from Cullen, suddenly beside him. He had to weigh more than Cullen from sheer density and girth, yet Cullen had no trouble hefting him. "Fine, see? Wouldn't be the first time I sailed across this room. Sorry, Mother," he mumbled to the ceiling. "No new scorch marks is always a win, though."

Cullen huffed the laugh Enzo had hoped to evoke, but his brow scrunched when he said, "I'm sorry."

"Not your fault. You weren't what threw me. Just a byproduct." Enzo's eyeline wasn't much higher than Cullen's chest when they stood, and he tried to keep from obviously inhaling more of that musk.

The rune remained on Cullen's chest but looked like it had been scorched. Not to ashes, such as how a nonmagical person might have caused the spell to react. The color still glittered violet yet seemed like it had overheated, having produced something in answer to the spell that was more than a simple rune could handle.

"One experiment down merely means we move to another." Enzo led Cullen back to the table. "Let's call that first test our control, explosive though it may have been." He cleaned out the mortar to start over, crushing a ruby crystal next to create a new paste.

"People with more natural magic affinity do not require runes to cast spells?" Cullen asked.

"Correct, but using them can help magic stretch further, and many magically inclined people have unique abilities that don't require any cost at all, with or without runes."

"Do you have a unique ability?"

"My mother said for me it was this." Enzo indicated his workshop. "And perhaps it is. She had an affinity for lightning. If water ever grew scarce when I was a boy, I would swear, she'd look skyward, and a storm would brew over the mountains." The memory made Enzo smile. He'd often heard that lightning was common magic for elves. "There's a very potent power in lightning when it comes to invention. That's how I got the Ever-Burning Torch to work." He nodded at his lantern with its core always faintly glowing after imbuing it with, well, lightning in a bottle. "Ingenuity and forging play their roles as well. After all, my father... um, sorry, we should focus on you."

Enzo had gotten so caught up in his explanation, he'd nearly confessed his lineage again. Anyone from the current royal line had a strong connection to the Ruby gemstone and all its power, but Cullen didn't need to know that.

After brushing away the scorched amethyst residue from Cullen's chest, Enzo replaced the rune for Man with one painted in ruby paste instead. He and Cullen shared an expectant look before he tapped it like the other one to activate it.

The rune pulsed—and then faded as though not having been activated at all.

"Huh." Enzo leaned up close to inspect the rune, finding it just as he had painted it, not scorched like the first but as if silent of any reaction.

Cullen moaned, and Enzo startled, at first unsure what he had done. When he glanced downward, he discovered his free hand braced on Cullen's thigh.

"S-sorry!" He snatched his hand away. "I-I'll… uh… try another. Crystal, I mean!"

His cheeks burned as he turned away, escaping once more from between Cullen's thighs, though he thought his fair, mysterious friend might be smiling more than timid of the mistaken touch.

Enzo fetched a damp cloth to wipe the paint from Cullen's chest this time, given it was not so easily brushed away. Then he moved on to the next crystal—sapphire.

"Your father also had magic?" Cullen asked while Enzo worked. "Affinity with forge fire, I believe you were going to say?"

"Um, quite common among dwarves," Enzo tried to dismiss.

"He must have been rather adept, your mother too, for both their abilities to manifest in you so splendidly as an inventor."

"Enough that I created something that threatens the very city at my own friend's hand," Enzo scoffed, and then frowned at his snippy retort when Cullen was only being kind. "I'm sorry."

"You and Vanek were quite… close once?"

"We'd been good friends since childhood," Enzo said, finding that at least this topic made it easier to step back between Cullen's legs and paint the next rune. "But Vanek wanted more. I thought, because I loved him as a friend, perhaps I could give him what he sought if I simply tried hard enough. Maybe deeper affection like what he wanted from me could grow in time. But it never did. I don't love him the way he loves me, and it pains me to see the longing in his eyes that I can never fulfill. I only made things worse between us by being untrue to myself."

Again, Enzo tapped the rune upon completion, and it glowed briefly and then dimmed like the ruby.

"Cullen?"

"Hm?" The fair elf's eyes seemed distant, not having noticed another experiment came and went. "It just struck me as sad, what it must be like for a friend to love you when you can't love them back."

"Yes, but we aren't able to control who we love."

"No, I suppose we're not."

Enzo hovered too close, looking up from Cullen's navel while those violet eyes gazed down on him, the beautiful man's legs spread again to invite Enzo closer. "L let me try another. Crystal! Obviously." Enzo cleared his throat and stepped back.

He went through the same process with emerald and diamond-like crystals to cover all the colors, all the kingdoms and their inherent magics. None reacted like the amethyst had, but Enzo couldn't formulate enough of a hypothesis on what was happening to Cullen or who he might be based on a single explosion.

"I have another idea." He made a new batch of amethyst paint and drew the rune for Man like before, but before activating it, he made more ruby paint as well and drew beside it the rune for Sun, often used for fire and the Ruby Kingdom.

No explosion occurred, but when Enzo tapped the runes in tandem, they glowed—and remained glowing until Enzo smeared them to lose their shapes.

"What does it mean?" Cullen asked.

"If I were to call upon your innate affinity correctly, normally, the rune would rise from you like a beacon and then disappear. The amethyst-painted rune exploded, all other crystals failed to react at all, and now this...." A wild idea occurred to Enzo, and he darted from the table to find a larger mortar. He could create two separate batches in his smaller one, but not the five he needed.

Sectioning the larger mortar into five even areas, Enzo mixed new paint for each of the colors, then drew on Cullen again. Positioned like the five points of a star, he painted the rune for Ash, often used for shadow, in amethyst at the bottom left. Centered but higher went the rune for Earth in emerald. Back down, right of Ash, went Sun in ruby. Up halfway and leftward went Storm in diamond. Then across rightward was Ice in sapphire. All the base elements in each of their matching gemstone colors.

Finally, between them in the center that had been left empty, Enzo painted the rune for Man, only this time, each portion of the symbol was done in a different color, so that all were used before it was complete.

If he was right, he'd have his answer. If not, well....

He hoped he didn't become a final scorch mark on the stones.

The glow Enzo's activating touch created seemed as if it might explode after all, but then, something far more miraculous happened.

Each of the symbols rose from Cullen's chest, colored elemental runes one by one disappearing inside the rune for Man and making the part of its lines that glowed that color brighter. When all that remained was Man itself, the colors blended and yet remained distinct, like some prismatic, cosmic star. When it finally dimmed, its particles dispersed like fairy dust.

Enzo had never seen anything so beautiful, other than Cullen's fair face.

"You *are* wild magic," he gasped. "You've touched the veil between worlds. Who are you?"

WHAT ARE you? Cullen heard, and fear gripped him at the final rune's dazzling retreat.

"Please... don't send me away."

"Away?" Enzo's look of awe that Cullen had taken for terror gave way to an unexpected grin. He gripped Cullen's hands, marring him with rainbow smudges from the remnants of differently colored paint. "Fair Cullen, you are the most treasured guest I could imagine hosting within these walls. You're either one of the wild magic folk yourself like the Fairy Queen and Shadow King are said to be, or you've connected with that power in a way few others ever have. You are a remarkable man."

"I have no doubts about that," rang another voice in Cullen's head, and he winced and clenched his eyes shut, and no—no, no, no!

"Cullen!"

He roared.

Because....

Because.

He thrust the startled farell away from him, sending Enzo soaring through the air and across the workshop like he had when the rune exploded between them. Enzo landed on his back on the floor, equally as winded and gasping, and his handsome face with rough stubble and a bronze glowing complexion like the sun itself was too bright to look upon.

He needed to snuff it out. To smother it.

All must be consumed like he had been consumed.

"Cullen, stop!"

Not Cullen! He was the void, the darkest pits of shadows at the depths of the Amethyst where no light would ever touch. Where no light *could* touch. He would draw everything to him to ease the pain and consume it all.

He crossed the distance between him and Enzo like a hawk in a dive after its prey. He too could fly, float, *descend*, and so he did, monstrous claws falling upon Enzo's shoulders to keep him pinned. Black-purple tendrils licked out from his body in ravenous hunger, and Enzo hissed as the shadows pressed divots into his skin and wrapped around his throat.

Because....

"I love you."

A drop of water fell upon Enzo's cheek, dark like something from a swamp, but where it landed, it seemed to sizzle and freeze like an entombed snowflake meeting the summer sun.

"Cullen...." Enzo said softly, not choking, for the shadows around his throat had yet to squeeze. They rested there, like the claws resting upon Enzo's shoulders without tearing his tunic or breaking the skin.

He didn't want to do any of those things, did he? *Did he?* He didn't want to consume. He wanted....

He... wanted....

Enzo reached for him, and thick, hearty fingers pressed to his cheek and cupped his chin. His eyes must be glowing like violet embers, mouth a maw of vicious fangs again, body distorted and expression fierce, and yet.... Enzo's touch came tenderly.

"It's all right," Enzo said, and oh, how Cullen wanted to believe him.

The shadows like coiling tendrils remained, along with the sense that he was both hot and cold at once. Surely, it must pain Enzo to touch him, yet he didn't look pained. He smiled, as Cullen's claws became hands again, still black-purple and shimmering.

Instead of squeezing, the tendrils around Enzo's neck *caressed*.

"Ah!"

"*I'm sorry!*" Cullen's voice echoed like it had outside the tavern.

"N-no, it's, um...." The tendrils dragged farther down Enzo's neck and chest as if of their own accord, and Enzo shuddered. "Oh...."

Cullen's body had felt weightless when he leapt—*flew*—from the workshop table, as if he didn't have a lower half, just the wisp of a spirit form tapering to nothing. He very much felt his lower half now, and Enzo's, for something pushed up against Cullen's stomach with how low he hunkered over Enzo's body like a beast that had pounced.

"I-it doesn't... hurt," Enzo said, and the way his cheeks darkened proved how much he meant that. "Y-you don't... want to hurt me. I know you don't. You... ohhhhh!" A wilder howl left Enzo, low and guttural and lusty with want, which Cullen knew he had caused without trying to. Without *consciously* trying to, but his shadow tendrils had a mind of their own and still wanted to consume, one way or another.

Cullen's body was its normal shape, but he was still made of shadow, and parts of his undulating self wrapped all around Enzo to cradle him closer. The hardness pressing into Cullen's stomach coaxed an answering response from him, and he wanted to thrust downward, to envelop this handsome, sun-like creature and rut until the darkness in him cleared away like storm clouds.

"C-Cullen... please, it...."

"*Hurts?*"

"No," Enzo said like a laugh. "B-but I don't... know... if you understand what you're doing." His mouth dropped open with a longer moan and arch of his neck, and Cullen realized he'd thrust downward after all, his own hard cock, however made of shadow, finding Enzo's, and rutting like he wanted.

"*Yes... yes*," Cullen said, both in answer and in honor of the sensations building between them. It felt like fire and ice colliding, like he knew his shadows must feel upon Enzo. He felt. He *felt*. And he didn't want to stop feeling yet.

"C-Cullen...."

"*Yes... handsome Enzo?*"

Enzo laughed, face rosy and eyes darkening. "M-maybe...."

Cullen kissed him, and his shadows pulsed forth with such a great wave of desire, different than the hunger he'd thought he felt before, that Enzo squirmed up against him in obvious pleasure and feverishly kissed him back.

Cullen did want to consume. Enzo's lips. His body. His very being. He wanted it all.

So he never had to remember the void.

The sound of the front door slamming open was such a thunderous interruption that Cullen nearly let loose another ravenous roar when his lips tore from Enzo's.

"Enzo!" Vanek's voice cried in frustration. "Where on earth did you flee to?"

CHAPTER 7

DREAD FILLED Enzo's belly as Cullen, a shadow being of invigorating touch, snarled with renewed ferocity in the stretch of his mouth and fangs within. His eyes sparkled with menacing light, and his form began to grow and grow, towering in its added bulk, yet without lower mass to form legs—or other things— as he floated off Enzo with intent to attack.

"No!" Enzo grabbed after Cullen to hold him still.

He hissed, wrenching his hands back again. Only now did the graze through translucent yet not truly translucent skin cause him pain. The first touch when this creature descended had surprised him and almost hurt, the intensity so great that someone with thinner skin might have shrieked. But Enzo was callused and roughened from years of diligent work. The hot/cold balance at that magnitude, like the center of the sun on a bitter winter morn, had made Enzo want to arch closer.

Now, his fingertips were left smooth like having been burnt on ice or a coal fire.

"Cullen!" He reached again anyway, gritting his teeth past the sting of angry black-purple wisps that rose from Cullen like steam. "Please! He's my friend. You don't want to hurt him or anyone. *Please*." The pain of clinging to Cullen's broadened shoulders was growing more difficult to weather. Enzo would need to let go soon or risk his hands blistering open, but if he released Cullen, he knew not what fate Vanek might suffer. "Fair Cullen," he said softer, "please. Whoever you are, you are not a monster."

Violet eyes like the sparkle of amethysts to be excavated snapped from the workshop door to Enzo. This larger version of Cullen had less shape to his head and features, truly like a beast or spirit, like some entity that had crawled from the other side of the veil, through the Amethyst gemstone itself, and was stripped of its nature of a kind, curious, beautiful half-elf who deserved more than his torment.

That man was still within him, and he reformed before Enzo's eyes, at first a shadow self, but with legs again, that floated down to hover over Enzo, thighs spread to straddle him with a far more pleasing touch. Then the wisps, like arcs of black-purple flames, retreated too, and the flux of light and dark across Cullen's skin found its stability in pale ivory, dark wavy brown hair, and violet eyes with a mortal soul behind them that begged forgiveness.

Their arousals had both dwindled, but Enzo could feel Cullen against him, the press of his hips and squeeze of his thighs. Cullen reached down, and while Enzo would have leaned up into any touch offered his cheek, what Cullen grasped were Enzo's hands. He pulled them from where Enzo still held tight to Cullen's shoulders and turned them palm up to frown at the reddened and bubbled skin.

Enzo marveled at how the wounds were both as if from flame and frostbite, but it was the press of Cullen's palms to his, fingers lacing to connect them like lovers entwining, that renewed a pleasured gasp. It should have hurt, his skin still tender, but something new passed between them, and Enzo arched upward again, feeling the singularly thrilling sensation that Cullen stirred in him.

Shadows returned at Cullen's palms, seeping out from between their connected hands, but these tendrils did not burn or sting or pain Enzo. The soothing, exhilarating relief was like soaking in a mineral hot spring, with a beloved's touch drifting down between his—

"Enzo, will you answer… oh." Vanek's voice ended in an exhalation of discontent.

From his angle, he couldn't see the shadows, which quickly retreated into Cullen. All Vanek saw was a shirtless half-elf, sprawled atop Enzo with their hips aligned and hands clasped.

"V-Vanek—" Enzo tried.

"I see you are previously engaged." Vanek managed to keep the sneer from his lips, though it came through clear in his voice. "Do come out when you're finished." He left with a slam of the workshop door, and all the guilt Enzo felt at not being able to return his friend's affections churned in him anew.

He wished he could ease Vanek's suffering, but he did not wish he loved him. He wished only for a love he could return and that Vanek would find the same.

"Are you all right?" Cullen asked, bringing Enzo back to sparkling violet eyes.

Slowly, Cullen released Enzo's hands, where no pain remained. Enzo turned his hands to look at them, and not only were his wounds healed, but every callus, every roughened edge he'd earned through tinkering and experiments gone wrong were gone, like all had been smoothed away to reveal brand-new skin.

"Huh."

"Enzo?" Cullen prompted.

"I'm fine. Even when it hurt, it wasn't terrible, and I know you didn't mean to."

"Intent doesn't excuse outcome. I'm so sorry."

His words, however much Enzo wished to sooth the sweet half-elf, endeared Cullen to him even more. He truly was remarkable, wholly unique, powerful, and still the fairest face Enzo had ever had so close to his own.

Gently, softer than the hungry eruption they'd displayed when Cullen was made of shadow, Enzo kissed him. He needed Cullen to know he was forgiven, and the press of their lips seemed like the right language.

Cullen's mouth was different as his normal self, not as malleable or with a zing in its touch like a shock from a discharge of lightning. Cullen kissed back with an exploring press, and a bold lick of his tongue delved between Enzo's lips, making them both shudder.

"We'll solve this," Enzo promised. "We'll find out who you are."

Cullen nodded, and though Enzo would have preferred a different end to their entanglement, he had a guest to tend to.

He and Cullen left the workshop as straightened and dusted off as they could manage, with Cullen's tunic back on and any mussed hair smoothed. Vanek sat at the table with a glass he'd filled with the bottle of spirits from last night.

"You ran off before I could announce our renewed plans," Vanek began without meeting Enzo's gaze. As Enzo sat beside him and Cullen beside Enzo, Vanek pulled the Dragon's Gland from his pocket and set it on the table. "We act tonight."

"Tonight?" Enzo sputtered. "No, that's too soon. I'm helping my friend."

"Helping," Vanek huffed with a flick of daggered eyes on Cullen. "Right."

"Vanek...."

"Your inventions for the wealthier side of this kingdom keep you fed and housed, but do you remember how many don't have homes like yours?" Vanek slammed his mug down hard enough to rattle it when he let go. "How many are forced to work in the mines dangerously long hours just to feed their families? How many only had their first true meal in weeks because the king's death opened the coffers to everyone, when no other time would that ever happen?

"Maybe your *friend* can convince you there is no time to waste if he has so much more sway over your attention. You promised you would aid me."

"You did?" Cullen asked.

"Yes, using the true Dragon's Gland." Enzo indicated the device. "On a high-profile but safer target to prevent injury. There's a statue of the first of the Dragonbane clan in the Royal Square. It would send the Ashen's message without anyone having to get hurt."

"Will its destruction make a difference?"

Enzo glanced at Vanek, who had always been so certain of this path. "Perhaps, if we can make it clear to those in power, both our own leaders and the visiting royals, that this unrest is for a reason, and something must be done."

"Then you're with me?" Vanek pressed.

If only he meant the question for the mission alone.

"He is," Cullen answered, and Enzo's attention snapped to him. Cullen's resolve matched Vanek's own, as he stared down the leader of the Ashen without waver. "And so am I."

"WHY, CULLEN?" Enzo demanded once Vanek left.

"Because it needs to be done, but I won't let you go alone."

In truth, Cullen was terrified of the mission going wrong and the unknowns of what might happen to Enzo if it did. Something needed to be done to fix the woes of those he had seen in the forgotten streets of this city, but he also selfishly wondered what might happen to him without Enzo around, just as he selfishly didn't want Enzo to be alone with Vanek.

"If you feel yourself losing control again…." Enzo broached the subject they had yet to address.

Whatever Cullen was, he was dangerous, and guilt tore at him for how he had hurt the man working so hard to help him. He'd felt so hungry. So empty. But Enzo filled the void, and when the promise of that had been interrupted, Cullen had given over to the beast inside him, ready to devour Vanek whole.

And in that unthinking madness, he'd almost devoured Enzo too.

Whoever you are, you are not a monster.

Cullen wanted to believe that so badly.

"You can pull me back," Cullen said. He honestly wasn't sure if that were true, but he knew Enzo made him feel calm like nothing else could.

Not even....

Cullen cringed as a flash of purple—no, amethyst, *Amethyst*—flickered behind his eyes, painfully bright amidst a dark night sky. There, silhouetted by that violet glow, was a creature more terrifying than what Cullen could become, but with wings, horns, and larger claws that reached—

"Can I?" asked a tender voice, as that black-purple nightmare gave way to warm bronze. Enzo was right there, holding Cullen's face, his chair scooted closer as they sat together at the table. "Perhaps I can." He smiled and stroked his large palm across Cullen's cheek.

"Perhaps you can indeed," Cullen said. He pushed his own chair back, but not wanting to lose the connection of Enzo's hand, he held it there with his own, as he crouched between them on the floor.

Enzo's face darkened almost to a ruby glow, his thighs parting without question to allow Cullen closer. The parallel to how they'd been in the workshop made Cullen bolder, but there was so much more he wanted than to paint upon skin.

Their heights were nearly aligned with Enzo sitting and Cullen on his knees. Cullen gathered Enzo close, tugged to the edge of his chair, and held him tight to his chest. He licked between Enzo's lips as brazenly as before. This was familiar in a way that didn't cause a spike of pain in his temples.

Heat. Passion without distraction. Passion without... attachment, but that was where this felt different. He didn't think he'd ever encapsulated someone in his arms who he wanted body and soul. Enzo called to him, to the very depths of his being, in a way that did not require memory to make sense, and oh, Cullen wanted him.

He kissed Enzo harder, wet, and suctioned firm with tongues tangling, while his arms held tighter around Enzo's shoulders. He could feel Enzo squirming as he roused in his trousers, his hardness pushing against Cullen's stomach once more, ripened by eagerness. Cullen pressed closer, and Enzo whimpered between their mouths.

With appetite parallel to what his shadow self wished sated, but better, so much better, Cullen untwined his arms from trapping Enzo's at his sides. He reached for spread legs instead and hoisted them beneath the knees.

"Cullen!" Enzo yelped, but Cullen was watchful of the teetering chair, assured of its stability before he began to push the front flap of Enzo's tunic aside and yanked the undershirt free of his trousers. Next was to untie the trousers themselves. "Skies... *yes*...." Enzo muttered permission Cullen had neglected to ask for.

He paused, with Enzo's feet nearly resting on his shoulders. The rosiness in Enzo's cheeks seemed to have moved to the tip of his nose, like he'd had one too many ales, drunk on the promise of what Cullen intended.

"It seems... you may be remembering some things," Enzo said with a breathy laugh.

"Yes." Cullen chuckled with him. "Some things are close at hand indeed."

Like the heavy curve at the end of Enzo's cock that bobbed against his stomach when Cullen finally dragged the trousers down and hefted Enzo closer. He leaned forward to get at the wet spot left behind by that tempting bounce and lapped at Enzo's stomach with a long lick. The dusting of bronze hair was much like Enzo's stubble, but like an arrow from beneath his navel that spread wider at the point of destination.

Similar hairs adorned his chest where Cullen had Enzo's undershirt rucked high, soft like silk threads, signs of his elven half, while the dwarf in him had provided the muscle, powerful and broad in his thickness.

And not only thick in his arms, torso, and thighs.

If ever Cullen had wanted to devour a cock in one swallow, it was this one, a true meal spread before him and framed in bronze.

He descended with a voraciousness that formed a purr, a *growl* in his throat, that surely would have echoed like his shadow self's voice if released into the open air.

Enzo squeaked, the sound catching in his throat with similar inability, as he melted into the chair beneath him. It teetered again, but Cullen had hold of it. He'd locked his knees around its legs, still cradling Enzo's knees over his shoulders, as he buried his nose in the soft arrow of curls and milked Enzo's gently curved cock.

"Oh!" Enzo managed the moan he'd squeaked before, eyelids fluttering, with Cullen's gaze locked on his reactions as he sucked harder, barely popping off or pausing for breath, save to offer a greedy lick at the excess of pre-release.

He massaged Enzo's thighs—with hands that became black-purple vapor.

"*Oh*! Yessss…!" Enzo writhed from the return of the shadows' contrasts, the power in them tempered enough to be pleasant, *pleasurable*, not painful.

Cullen sucked harder, sliding one shadowed hand lower to tug and fondle Enzo's sac.

"C-Cullen…!" he warned, and it was with violet in his vision and a tongue that seemed to stretch longer than a normal one that Cullen felt Enzo spill down his throat.

It wasn't the taste that invigorated him, much as he enjoyed that too, but a thrum within the release like he'd devoured some potent pulse of *life*.

The haze over his vision cleared, and when he pulled from Enzo, he tongued his own teeth to be certain they'd never formed fangs. All seemed well, though there was the barest redness to a swath of Enzo's skin on his inner thigh where Cullen had squeezed too tightly.

Enzo hardly looked like he minded. The tip of his nose was even redder now, as were the apples of his cheeks, and his gaze was heavy-lidded with a look… with a look that Cullen wasn't certain he'd ever seen directed at him in a way that he wanted to see again. And *again*.

And only from Enzo.

He cleared his throat of the thickness coating it. Licked his lips. Lowered Enzo's legs to allow him to sit normally again—or as much as one could with their trousers at their knees—and gently ran one of his no longer shadow-made hands over the red mark he'd left behind. The other swiped through remnants of release and lapped it from his fingers.

"That… felt like a part of me I remember," Cullen said.

"O-oh?" Enzo sputtered laughter that summoned more color to his handsome face.

"Yes." Cullen sat back, allowing Enzo to right himself and tuck his cock away. "Do not doubt for a moment that I was very aware of what I was doing and how much I enjoyed that."

Enzo ducked his head, as if that were the main portion of the past few minutes to be embarrassed by. "You are a wonder, fair Cullen, to even want someone like me."

"Like you, *handsome* Enzo?" Cullen made a point to call him that now if he be so blind to his own allure. "Why wouldn't I? Every bit of you is precious metal glittering in a dark cavern and leading me toward riches."

Enzo's eyes widened, expression slackening to something akin to awe. "You must have been a poet. Or a wooing prince like I first guessed."

Cullen's smile faltered, and again he saw the vision of a monster behind his eyes with wings and horns and claws greater than his own.

Ash.

Ash.

"It doesn't matter!" Enzo's voice cleared Cullen's thoughts, anchoring him in the present. His thick, beautiful hands grasped Cullen's, and it felt so right to be there, knelt before Enzo and tucked between his thighs. "Whatever the truth, whatever you were expelled from, running from, or escaped, if it be any of those things, you can be who or whatever you want to be now."

"Like a revolutionary for a kingdom I don't even know if I've been to before?" Cullen smirked.

"Apparently. But… are you certain—"

"I'm coming with you. And we should prepare. There is much to consider before tonight."

"What about…?" Enzo nodded between them, and if he hadn't called attention to the tent in Cullen's trousers, Cullen might not have realized how hard he was. He had so very much enjoyed relieving Enzo of that problem.

"Tempting as reciprocation may be…." Cullen ran a thumb along the edges of Enzo's lips. "I don't believe there's time for everything I want of you."

"A-and what might that be?"

This too felt familiar, like Cullen had flirted and teased and propositioned others before. He must have. But there was a sense of having rushed with them, of never having truly savored a partner or cared if he experienced them again.

He wanted very much to taste more of Enzo, and not only *taste*.

Lifting as tall as he could on his knees, Cullen slithered both hands up beneath Enzo's undershirt and tunic that were still twisted out of place and leaned close enough to speak against his lips. "To climb into my savior's lap… and impale myself upon your glorious *cock*."

Enzo shivered with a charming huff of disbelief, and then smiled in satisfied wonder.

"When our task is over perhaps?" Cullen asked.

"Yes!" Enzo answered eagerly. "That… would be a boon worth cherishing."

CHAPTER 8

IT HAD been morning when they went to the Ashen's meeting, and Enzo's experiments had pushed them into the height of midday. Now, the hour grew late, and the streets were darkening again. A new note on Enzo's door informed them of all Vanek hadn't stayed to explain—where to meet, when, and who would oversee what. The Dragon's Gland remained with Enzo, for he would be the one to plant it.

And Cullen would accompany him.

Cullen... who had mouthed Enzo's cock like a man born to bring another pleasure and promised to sheathe Enzo inside him later.

Enzo's cheeks had never felt so ablaze, especially since... that was something he'd never experienced before. Clearly, Cullen had, but when Enzo was with Vanek, it was always the other way around, with Enzo the one... impaled.

Not that he hadn't enjoyed it! But Vanek had presumed how their encounters would go, always taking charge. Cullen's boldness had made Enzo wonder if he'd be the same, and then Enzo had been too stunned by the whispered promise upon his lips to admit his inexperience or that Vanek was the only man he'd ever been with.

Enzo needed to focus. There were far more pressing concerns ahead than how they might celebrate after their task was done.

He just hoped what he was about to take part in would be worth it.

"Ready?" Cullen asked with more confidence than Enzo thought the fair elf felt, for he knew his own resolve was largely feigned too. Cullen stood near the door wearing his violet cloak, as Enzo exited his workshop with the Dragon's Gland, the Ever-Burning Torch, and an extra cloak and tunic slung over his arm—black and a little less noble-looking.

"Almost. First, you need a change."

IT WAS silly, practically childish, ridiculous really, that the blush remained in Enzo's cheeks simply from seeing Cullen in more of his clothes.

"I was so disoriented that first night," Cullen spoke quietly as they hurried toward the Royal Road, "traversing tunnels and foreign pathways, with a mad dash through streets to reach your home. It's different seeing the city at night with our steps sure and slow."

"Perhaps because tonight our goal is different," Enzo said.

Cullen looked good in black. They both wore their hoods up, but neither should have seemed too conspicuous, since Cullen still wore brown trousers, with Enzo in his customary red beneath his own brown cloak. The streets weren't deserted like they'd been when Enzo slipped out the previous night to check on the destruction. Those who were out in the late hour, however, seemed to move quickly, as if sensing the worst was not yet over.

The Ever-Burning Torch guided their way more brightly than lit streetlamps or natural crystals in the stone. Normally, Enzo didn't take it out of the house. It was still a prototype, meant to replace torches in the mines, where gas pockets could cause unexpected explosions, but it could be used for more than just light.

Word had spread and was relayed in the Ashen's note that the Royal Road was open, though a few of the injured remained at the makeshift medical camp beyond for further treatment. That bolstered Enzo in his task, for only the true Dragon's Gland could prevent those previous victims from being hurt anew.

The guards at the Royal Road eyed him and Cullen as they passed, but neither tried to stop them. As expected, and yet still a relief, the courtyard was crowded like on any normal night. Different than those who'd elsewhere been moving quickly, the people here were in a world all their own.

Aside from the injured on cots, nobles, merchants, and others mostly in finery were going about their evenings unaffected. The castle was not the only destination down the Royal Road, for there were shops, taverns, a theater, and all in attendance were pretending those cots didn't exist.

Which Enzo reminded himself was part of the reason for their quest.

"That's Chadwick's Pub there." He pointed out the well-lit tavern, devoid of the rowdy atmosphere from Bottom of the Barrel, where an intricately carved pipe adorned each of the double doors. "Best ale in the city. And, of course, there's the Central Theater...." He was making a point to play tour guide so as not to draw unwanted attention, as they gathered between the tavern and theater, where Enzo was meant to meet Vanek.

"Does Chadwick's really have the best ale in the city?" Cullen whispered.

"No idea. Never been inside." Enzo pointed at various landmarks as they talked. "Though I did sell them some of my motion lights."

"Motion lights?"

"My mother acquired our home when she still had money," Enzo explained, "something that had been dwindling before she passed. My inventions were how I survived after she was gone. Simpler things, like crystals connected to Torch runes that only activate when someone enters a room, are a luxury the wealthy are willing to pay well for."

"Like in your workshop?"

"Exactly. It's how I fund my more important inventions." He turned to Cullen more seriously. "I'm going to leave the Ever-Burning Torch with you. If you run into trouble and need to make a quick getaway, all you need do is disrupt one of the runes on the side and point the lantern toward whoever you need out of your way. They won't be hurt. It'll just be a bit of a lightshow."

"All right...." Cullen sounded uncertain, but before Enzo could reassure him, he noticed several members of the Ashen among the crowd.

That was the plan, for the Ashen to blend in as nobles and merchants, waiting for the chaos of the explosion to leave the message Vanek had decided on. Once people were fleeing, not knowing the explosion would become self-contained, the Ashen would act.

Of course, at the moment, all Enzo saw was Rufus, dressed in what was obviously a stolen surcoat, picking the pockets of anyone who got too close to him.

"Opportunist snake," he muttered. "Vanek's standards need to improve greatly if the Ashen are to accomplish anything good."

"Oh?" Vanek's voice caused Enzo to whirl around, as the other farell appeared out of the darkness behind them as if *he* had been made of shadow.

He too was mostly in black, with the hood of his cloak up. One thing Enzo could never deny was how handsome Vanek was, with his thick beard that had grown in when they were barely sixteen, sapphire eyes, and a proud, confident smile.

"Here I thought my standards were right on course. At least where it mattered." Vanek eyed Enzo with open interest and then sneered when his gaze drifted to Cullen. "You know I still haven't gotten a name for your friend."

"Cullen," Cullen answered.

"Of what? From where?"

"Never you mind." Enzo stepped between them. "He's going to be helping keep watch just like your riffraff, so I am allowed mine. Not that he's... I mean... I didn't *mean*...."

Vanek laughed, making Enzo feel like a right fool, but at least Cullen was smiling when he glanced back at him in apology.

"Here." Enzo handed him the lantern, lowering his voice so Vanek wouldn't catch their parting words. "In mere minutes this will be over, and then we can return home."

"For a boon worth cherishing?" Cullen's eyes glittered within the dark of his hood.

Enzo's cheeks set freshly aflame, and he hoped his answering smile was affirming.

He walked casually beside Vanek across the courtyard to where the Dragonbane statue stood. It was towering, the height of ten men—well, ten dwarven men—and looked very much like Enzo's father, though it was an ancestor from ages past. A long single-braided beard and thick mustache framed a stern face, his powerful and strong-looking figure in kingly armor, with a helm that bore what looked like wings up either side. He held a hammer high as if in victory, a large maul that it was said he'd used to drive the last of the dragons from these caverns. Maybe that was true, but the Dragonbane progenitor had never been king. He was a warrior, and Enzo's father's father had used that story as reason for their family to be chosen as the next royal line at the time.

Not *their* family. Not Enzo's. Not really. Not when he'd never been recognized.

"Are you ready?" Vanek asked as they neared the statue's base. "The eyes of our people are on us, and all others are completely clueless. We're simply admiring a statue in remembrance of the lost king."

Indeed.

Set the orb's timer, Enzo thought, reaching into his pocket to palm the Dragon's Gland. *Plant it at the base of the statue. Walk away.* The rest was up to the others, and once the explosion shook the courtyard, Enzo's part would be over, and he and Cullen could be alone.

"You're smitten with him, aren't you?"

Enzo snapped his attention to Vanek, who had an unreadable expression, as their strides came to a halt.

"Are you really blushing over that skinny elf?"

He should have known Vanek would notice. "You used to encourage my crushes."

"Is that what it is between you two? A crush?" Vanek turned inward to speak with Enzo toe-to-toe. "Who is he?"

How could Enzo answer when even he didn't know?

"You're hiding something. Tell me."

Again, Enzo said nothing.

"I am the one person who knows you truly, and you won't even tell me how you met this man? Unless of course… you've confessed your lineage to him?"

"No!" Enzo hissed, and then glanced around, not that their voices were loud enough nor anyone near enough to have overheard. "I… found him in the caves the night the king died."

"*What*?"

"He doesn't remember who he is. I'm just trying to help him."

"He's a complete stranger? What do you even know about this elf?"

Enzo wasn't about to tell Vanek anything about Cullen's other form. "Enzo…."

"He's kind."

"Everyone is kind without a past. *You're* kind despite yours. Too kind. I'm allowed to not want to see you get hurt." He stepped closer, and Enzo felt Vanek's breath on his lips. "Just like I'm allowed to miss you."

"I miss you too," Enzo confessed. "I miss my friend."

Vanek sagged, leaning away again, and Enzo risked a glance at where Cullen waited on the other side of the courtyard. "At least you know me to rebuff me. Don't pretend like you know him when all you have is a name."

Enzo had more than a name. He… well. He didn't have much more than a name, and some of what he did know would be terrifying to others, but he knew the heart of Cullen. The goodness there, didn't he? What he was feeling toward the fair half-elf was more than passing infatuation or lust.

Even if he'd only known him for a day.

He'd only known him for a *day*....

"Enzo," Vanek growled, but now wasn't the time to dwell.

"We have a job to do," Enzo said and pulled the Dragon's Gland from his pocket. "Let's do it."

SOMETHING WAS wrong. Enzo and Vanek had reached the statue, but they paused, talking closely met. *Very* closely met. So close that Cullen's hand clenched around the handle of the lantern as he thought, in the midst of it, Vanek might kiss Enzo.

He didn't, he leaned away, and Enzo's eyes found Cullen's.

They were talking about him.

They were friends and had been more. Surely, Vanek was worried and clearly jealous. And really, what was Cullen to Enzo but an enigma to solve, a stranger with dangerous powers he couldn't control?

Cullen tried not to think on it, to focus instead on being part of something that could enact change for people who needed it. As Enzo said, this would be over in minutes, but the impact might mean more, and when it was done, they'd be back at Enzo's home to celebrate.

Where Cullen hoped that all he remembered about his past was other ways to make Enzo moan.

For now, he was another set of eyes, meant to watch for guards catching wise to something amiss or too many people getting close to the statue. The explosion would eventually implode and avoid a larger blast, but that didn't mean it was foolproof against causing injury to passersby.

He scanned the courtyard and especially near the medical camp. Enzo had said the visiting royals were there yesterday, and honestly, Cullen had been wary of seeing them, and yet... he didn't spot any now.

Would he recognize them? Would they recognize *him*?

And where were they? Inside the castle, all of them? After the attentiveness Enzo had described, Cullen was surprised they'd leave the site of the first blast so unprotected, with only a handful of guards to keep... watch....

Something *was* wrong, but it wasn't Enzo and Vanek.

Cullen turned, looking behind him into the shadows where Vanek had appeared from. He cast the light from the Ever-Burning Torch toward it, but there was no one there now. Not in those shadows, but somewhere. There was a pulse nearby, a thrum in the air as much as something like an actual heartbeat, building, prowling.

Closing his eyes, Cullen tried to pinpoint the direction it came from. He pivoted as he sought it out, and once he was certain he was looking in the right direction, he opened his eyes again.

He nearly dropped the lantern. Everything had gone muted, like a gray—or violet—cloak covered the courtyard, and everyone in it was frozen.

He spun in a circle to be certain he could still move.

Everyone was frozen but him.

A blur of movement pulled his attention back toward the source of the pulse, the thrum, the presence he'd felt. Whatever it was could still move too. It had been in the depths of a different set of shadows, but now it floated to another like mist, like… shadow itself.

Cullen darted forward from his sentry point to give chase, and it was only then that he realized his outstretched arm holding the lantern was his own black-purple form, and every part of him flickered with hungry tendrils.

The world hadn't frozen. He was in the veil. Not through it, not passed to the other side, wherever that may lead, but in it, traveling where only shadows could tread.

He kept going, unsure how long he would be able to remain here. The presence was moving to another set of shadows. When it was in them, Cullen could almost make out a hulking, winged and horned silhouette, but when it moved from one to the next, it was a shooting star, leaving only a trail of afterimage. If by being in the veil, Cullen moved so much faster than everything else that the world looked still, the speed with which that presence moved must be instantaneous, at least from shadow to shadow.

It was lurking, circling, watching….

The statue!

Cullen ceased his pursuit through the frozen crowd to look as well and couldn't believe all that had happened before he entered the veil. Enzo had already planted the orb. It was mid-explosion. He could see the pulse of flame and first bits of statue blasting away, and it was growing, slowly, but definitely moving, because outside the veil the detonation was happening in a blink.

Enzo and Vanek were halfway across the courtyard. Cullen had completely missed them, since he'd pursued the presence in an arch to the right. He saw now that Enzo was looking at where Cullen should have been waiting, marred by worry and confusion, because Cullen must have vanished right before his eyes.

Eyes… like the ones Cullen felt on him.

The thrum from the presence was growing closer again, and he turned to face it. He stood before a patch of shadows cast by the theater, built into an outcropping of rock taller than the tavern, but with the tavern's bright lights making its shadow long and especially dark.

The presence, the silhouette, was right there, its wings so much more distinct, horns more menacing, and eyes looking at him, as a deep and penetrating voice called his name.

"*Cullen…?*"

The shadows reached out, and Cullen screamed.

A figure knocked into him, toppling him to the ground, and caused his hood to fall back, as the cacophony from the blast drowned out his scream. The world was colored again, normal, moving, and in the instant panic from the explosion, people were running and dangerously close to trampling Cullen.

He could only stare at the shadows, the silhouette gone from view with him no longer in the veil to perceive it, but he could feel it. The presence was still there.

It knew his name.

Then a leg stepped forth from the shadows, solid, with the waver of a long tunic in red and gold brocade, and Cullen's head clanged with such pain, he screamed again.

"Cullen?"

"No!"

He kept his eyes shut against whatever form this creature was taking, because it was a lie, a lie, a *lie*.

"*I love you.*"

"*No!*"

"Cullen!"

He felt around the sides of the Ever-Burning Torch, formed his own shadow claws to strike true, and sliced through where he knew one of the runes magically locked the lightning inside. It burst forth from the lantern in the direction he held it with such blinding brightness that Cullen had to peek, and in the split second that light met shadow, he saw the monster for what it truly was.

A demon made of darkness and light, black and white, and every color between, with claws and fangs like Cullen's own monstrous form but larger. It had horns, wings, and eyes from a nightmare itself like two pinpricks of stars in a night sky… that pleaded for understanding.

Ash….

The creature was thrown backward into the oblivion of the nearby shadows as if the lightning banished it, and the edge of Cullen's memories that had almost surfaced banished with it. He leapt to his feet in search of Enzo, spotting him not far from where he'd last seen him and Vanek, and sprinted to reach him alongside the people fleeing the blast—which was already imploding without a single spray of debris to harm those running in terror.

Vanek was urging Enzo on, trying to drag him out of the courtyard, but Enzo resisted, gesturing toward the empty spot where Cullen had vanished. He wouldn't leave without him, and when he finally lurched his arm from Vanek's grasp, Cullen was upon him.

He descended on Enzo as a great mass of shadow that swallowed him into the darkness, thinking of only one destination that he somehow knew he could reach.

Home.

CHAPTER 9

ONE MOMENT Cullen was diving toward him, the next, he was shadow, descending like a black-purple wave, and then…. Enzo was hitting the floor of his living room with shadow Cullen atop him.

He was so stunned that he barely felt the first caress of hot-cold intensity tingle through him when Cullen stroked his cheek.

"*Are you all right?*" Cullen asked in his echoed voice.

"What happened? Where did you go? Why—?"

The shadows faded from Cullen's form like evaporating rainwater, and Enzo's tongue failed him at having such beauty so close to him. Cullen was just as beautiful in dark shades of midnight, but like this, Enzo was reminded that the fair half-elf was real, not some figment of his imagination or magician's illusion of what the ideal man should look like.

Cullen was slightly heavier in his wholly solid form, as there they were again, hips connected with Enzo pinned.

"Sorry." Cullen sat up, though that did nothing to detach them below the waist, and Enzo resisted the urge to squirm beneath him. "I needed to get us out of there."

An errant spark of blue flickered near Cullen's knee, where he gripped the Ever-Burning Torch that no longer cast light. A deep gouge like a dagger strike blighted the rune on the side of the base facing them. "You used the lantern?"

"I had to. You can fix it, can't you?"

"Of course, don't worry about that. But what happened?"

"There was something… watching you. Watching the square. I think they'd set a trap, waiting for the Ashen to act. I distracted him."

"Him?"

"He…." Cullen cringed, and his form flickered, not becoming his shadow self, but gone completely, like how he'd vanished from the courtyard. Then he was back, weight and all, making Enzo cling to his hips in fear of losing him. "I don't want to remember. I can't. Please… I just want something safe, and strong, and…." His eyes flicked from gazing into the abyss of lost memories to taking in Enzo's face, prompting a hopeful smile in place of his grief. "And *handsome* to be my harbor."

His hands dropped to fan across Enzo's chest. There was poetry in the words, but also denial, deflection. He didn't want to face a truth he didn't think he could shoulder. Enzo understood that, for he'd done the same for years. It was only tonight he'd finally taken responsibility for his birthright and enacted some of the promises he'd made to his younger self, even if done through an act of terror.

But good could come from chaos, couldn't it? And Cullen was allowed to come to terms with his past in his own time. He was wild magic in motion, but he'd done the right thing, the heroic thing, and not only fended off some unknown enemy, but rescued Enzo from the throng and brought them safely home.

Somehow.

Instantly.

The scientist in Enzo wanted to know how, but the man, who longed for something he'd never found in Vanek, gave in to the teasing touch of soft skin on his collarbone as Cullen began to untie his undershirt and tunic.

Shadows returned and poured from him in a similar wave to how he'd enveloped Enzo in the square, only that had been over too quickly for Enzo to feel anything. This caressed his exposed skin and inside his parted clothing like extra hands fondling his body.

Enzo arched his back to get closer.

"I'm sorry," Cullen whispered, still smiling but as if worried his touch might be unwanted. "I don't know if I can hold the shadows back right now."

None of it burned, not in the way the angrier beast had blistered Enzo's skin. When Cullen turned into a midnight sky given shape, the shadows *were* him, made of magic so powerful, they didn't know what else to become, so they cooled and warmed and invigorated as much as their touch grazed an edge of danger like the flat of a knife dragging ever so close to tilting into the blade.

Enzo's fate was at Cullen's whims, but having the most beautiful being he could ever imagine wanting him as a harbor, whether shadow or peach-colored skin, and even if Enzo had only known him for a day, he trusted where those whims might lead.

"Don't hold back, fair Cullen. You are a wonder, a miracle, and we already said what would happen at our return."

Purple fire blazed where Cullen's eyes should be as he succumbed to his shadow self, but he was still Cullen, still with Cullen's visage amidst the darkness-made-flesh. Only the barest prick of fangs or scratch of claws were felt when he gripped Enzo's shoulders and swooped down on him to capture a kiss.

Enzo's gasp was swallowed by Cullen's eager mouth. There was no more threat of Cullen vanishing into nothing, Enzo trusted in that, and though Cullen's weight was lighter like this, the sensations he evoked were more potent than any normal body could hope to cause.

His tongue explored Enzo's with a long enough stretch that it coiled around it, and then coiled again. His hands clung with a grip that pulsed more waves of shadow like rolling mist, expanding with a weight of their own. The tendrils that arched off him were as solid as any other part when he wanted them to be—should he control them at all.

They seemed to writhe and want with minds of their own, wrapping around Enzo's limbs and every exposed bit of skin, and then slithering inside his clothing to caress him all at once. The tendrils were like fingers, but so many more than ten. Several plunged beneath the waistband of his trousers and twisted around his cock.

They were everywhere. They had hold of every part of him. He couldn't move other than to wriggle at their mercy, yet he felt no fear. It was almost too much, that raw power like he was drowning in magic, but whenever it almost burned or frostbit his skin, the pain eased off, leaving only bliss.

Cullen *was* holding back. He had to be. Because when he truly surrendered, he was a beast of the void.

Enzo's member flooded with so much wonderful rushing blood, he felt it harden like steel in the grasp of Cullen's tendrils, and the sudden tightness made him snap from Cullen's mouth with a hiss.

"*Are you all right?*" Cullen echoed.

Enzo laughed, for he would never be all right again. He would never be the same after knowing this man's touch. "I am." He blinked up at the mass of black-purple radiance, undulating with Cullen's face. "But mercy, fair Cullen. If you claim me too much as a harbor... how can I find one in you?"

"*Yes,*" Cullen said with a whisper-wind laugh, and some of the tendrils withdrew.

Lurching upward and rolling to his feet, Enzo used his superior strength to heft Cullen. Shorter of stature or not, and even without the lessened weight, he had him, cradled as close as the remaining shadows clung in turn.

It might have seemed insurmountable to move with churnings of pleasure twisting inside Enzo from every point they connected, but he was determined. He knew what he wanted, and it was such a rare gift for him to be certain of his actions, other than tinkering in solitude. He wasn't as convinced about use of the Dragon's Gland earlier, but with this he had no doubts.

"Come, fair Cullen. There are better places than a cold stone floor."

CULLEN'S BODY pulsed in answer to Enzo's show of strength, as Enzo carried him into the bedchamber as steadily as he'd placed him in the bathtub. Although Cullen felt unraveled with every new tendril that reached a little farther from its source, he also felt connected to every part of Enzo his shadows wrapped around.

Like Enzo's cock, that had felt so delicious in his hold. *Delicious*, like he could taste it, because every part of Cullen's shadows was one in the same. Through them, he could taste, see, and feel everything at once, all the familiar responses of a man, not numbness the way the first eruptions of his shadows had felt to him. Numbness was but a brook to wade through, and on the other shore was bliss.

All he needed was to stay in control, and he could be the part of himself Enzo wanted.

"I don't, um… know how to undress you like this." Enzo's brow furrowed after falling with him onto the bed. "Are your clothes… clothes? Can I remove the tunic and it'll be a tunic again?"

Cullen laughed, his voice a resonant echo like in a cavern. "*Ever the curious one, eh?*"

"Afraid so. And there are wondrous things I long to explore tonight." He was practically caught in a trap of black-purple netting, and the tendrils moved with him when he reached to stroke Cullen's face. Enzo shuddered as if touching Cullen brought him its own pleasure.

"*I can make it easier*," Cullen said, loathe as he was to lose the sensations that Enzo clearly enjoyed. He willed the shadows to leave him, for his skin to be skin, and his attachments on Enzo waned.

"I forgot you were in my clothes...." Enzo's bronze face was already flush, but the sharpest edges of his cheeks turned rosier.

"Like seeing me in things of yours, do you?" Cullen teased. "Ah, but I'd rather you were in something of mine. Is... that the way you like it?" His bravado faltered. "I should have asked."

Enzo's warm eyes shone almost like copper amidst his dark and reddened complexion. "I am glad you asked, fair Cullen, but rest assured, I very much want to make good on our promise."

"That we should do indeed." Bolstered once more, Cullen unclasped his borrowed black cloak, and it fell open beneath him, inviting Enzo to undo the rest.

He'd gotten Enzo's tunic and undershirt off only halfway, leaving the farell's bronze chest with soft thickets of hair exposed from pecs to navel, like some bawdy art in a tavern that would have had a man like him embracing a buxom wench.

Cullen could barely keep his hands off Enzo as in turn Enzo's thick, powerful hands rid him of his clothing. He wanted to trace the gentle points of Enzo's ears. Lick them. Wrap his hands around Enzo's cock with twisting fingers and spiraling shadows to guide it inside him. His darkness was at bay for now, but he could feel it, pulsing like the beat of his heart in wait for its next emergence, like the thrum from....

The presence in the courtyard.

"Skies, you're beautiful...."

Cullen's boots and trousers had been tossed from the bed, his shirt and tunic another layer beneath him, as one of Enzo's meaty hands found Cullen's prick and stroked.

Darkness reclaimed him with a burst of heat, and the clothing melted into the shadows with him, only to return to corporealness with singes.

He worried he might have blistered Enzo too, but the farell looked unscathed, staring at his hand that had snapped away but as if in wonder at the power Cullen held, even if it meant tatters had become of his lent clothing.

With a hungry leer, Enzo thrust one arm beneath Cullen's back to yank him closer. Both gasped at an extra pulse from Cullen's shadows, and Cullen reached for Enzo's ears to thumb them like he'd wanted, while they collided for a deeper and desperate kiss.

Behind Cullen's eyes was the creature from the courtyard.

No.

His tendrils sought Enzo for the harbor he'd been promised. He wanted to be a harbor too. He wanted Enzo inside him. He wanted to forget the memories trying to surface because, surely….

They would only prove the real monster was him.

Moisture pooled in Cullen's eyes, but the shadow tears crystalized and faded where they fell. He willed them away, for he didn't want Enzo to see. There were other better things Cullen remembered, like furtive kisses and caresses in bedchambers. If he couldn't completely tame his shadows, then at least he knew they caused Enzo pleasure more than pain, and he would hold the worst of them back with all he had.

Wedging a hand between them, Cullen found where Enzo's fist stroked his shadow-cock. He halted Enzo's pumps, brought the hand to his mouth, and licked the glistening starlight-like pre-release from Enzo's fingers.

Enzo's eyes darkened, and Cullen licked again, savoring his own taste and the strange feeling of touching anything when he was naught but pure magic. He was raw and untamed, and that held a ring of memory too. No one could tame him. He'd wanted to be free and unrestrained, but oh, how he loved to have Enzo's eyes rake over him with possessive adoration when Cullen sucked two of those girthy fingers into his mouth nearly to the back of his throat.

Enzo whined, with gasps—*moans*—leaving him in rhythm to Cullen sucking the same way he'd swallowed Enzo's cock earlier. Enzo trembled, giving jerky thrusts against Cullen's hip, which was and wasn't solid, with more tendrils arcing outward and delving back into Enzo's trousers.

He was still mostly clothed, while Cullen was naked writhing darkness holding the shape of a man, with a pulsing shadow-cock bobbing upward to graze the remaining ties of Enzo's undershirt. Cullen wanted Enzo's fingers inside him and pulled off, leaving them sopping with a shimmer of saliva that looked equally made of starlight as his come.

"Inspect your sheath, handsome Enzo, so we can garner a proper fit."

Again, Enzo trembled, thighs tightening on either side of Cullen's hips as if to prevent a too-soon release. To aid him, Cullen ceased the restored stroking of his tendrils around Enzo's length, though he didn't remove them from his trousers, leaving them to feather lightly, as he rolled his hips back and spread his thighs for Enzo's perusal.

"I-I... don't think I can," Enzo said with a roughness to his voice that made Cullen's sac ache. "Not like this, I mean! I-I'm just... not sure... where...?"

Cullen chuckled, because he was shadow, after all, but he could oblige. As long as he kept the memories at bay, he could alter how much of the shadows claimed him. And so, with a reining in and will to find balance, he became flesh, but with shadow tendrils spiraling off him, as if they held him in their grasp as much as they held Enzo.

They were like tentacles from a sea creature, reaching when Cullen willed them to and sometimes when he didn't. Existing with them in that half form, Cullen felt what he imagined Enzo did, the cold burn of almost too much that spurred him to want Enzo more.

The first breach of a fingertip made Cullen's head snap back— where the creature still waited in the darkness.

No! Yet there it was—horns, piercing white, but not white eyes, and teeth, so many teeth, all in a black-purple face that *knew him*.

The clothing singed beneath Cullen again, and he hadn't even flickered to full shadow. He needed to stay calm, in control, and opened his eyes to watch the rapture on Enzo's face while pushing in his finger with a smooth envelopment of Cullen's body swallowing him deeper.

"Yes...." Cullen moaned, dropping his head back but without closing his eyes, focusing on how much he loved this feeling.

Even Enzo's lone finger was marvelously thick, with a burn as it thrust inside him that made Cullen's sac tighten with even more aching pleasure. His tendrils flailed, seeking added holds on Enzo with possessive demanding.

"More...," he demanded. "More!"

"Cullen...?"

Quiet! He didn't want the past. The pain. The guilt....

He wanted *this* and rocked his hips to get Enzo to stop being gentle. He didn't need gentle. He needed to be split open, ravaged, taken.

"Cullen...?"

That utterance was real but just as questioning as the one in Cullen's mind, as the twists of Enzo's finger slowed. Cullen couldn't see beneath him, but he could feel the first intrusions of his tendrils, sneaking in around Enzo's finger to aid the stretch.

"You're—"

A howl ripped from Cullen at the intensity of his own shadows slithering inside him to pry him open. "K-k-keep… *ohhhh*…." He trailed off in a wrecked wail, hips rocking madly into the new burn that was fire and ice made rapturous by every drag of Enzo's finger over where the darkness grazed first.

He was fucking himself with thin searing whips of wild magic that could dive inside him deeper than any finger or cock, but oh, he still wanted a cock, Enzo's cock, all that glorious length he'd swallowed and salivated over, and he needed it *now*.

Cullen's shadows snatched Enzo closer with a lunge, taking hold of his trousers and yanking them down his thighs. They nearly tore his undershirt open, and Enzo laughed in apparent wonderment as the shadows took control.

They removed his finger from inside Cullen and gathered his finally freed cock closer. The tendrils coiled all around his throbbing member as they pulled him in, undulating over his drenched tip.

"*Skies*, that's… fuck, Cullen!" Enzo moaned as he was sheathed inside Cullen with the shadows encasing him. Others spread Cullen wider, reached deeper, and Enzo's cock pulsed larger than its natural girth from them covering him. They were everywhere, consuming and claiming all that they touched.

Because he was being swallowed by….

The gemstone.

The darkness.

The void. He was back in the void, black and cavernous and lonely, and he needed something, *anything* to fill the emptiness.

THE WORLD tilted, and, for a moment, everything went black.

Enzo sucked in air like he'd been thrown across his workshop again, but not thrown this time. Flipped.

He was pinned to the bed, bound by tendrils all around his body as Cullen, pure shadow again, hovered over him like a beast before its meal.

"C-Cullen…?"

Every version of him that Enzo had seen shimmered into being, one after the other, fighting for dominance—the larger beast, the shadow-man, the beautiful half-elf with peach-colored skin, even the part of him that could be nothing and nowhere as if gone from existence, all hungry and angry and dangerous… or pleading for salvation in the sparkle of violet eyes.

"*Peace*, fair Cullen," Enzo said, not allowing his voice to quake, for he had to believe his words too. "All will be well. I'm here."

The shadows pulsated, eager tendrils wrapping tighter, as certainty slowly returned to Cullen's eyes. An intense sting of wild magic descended as he resheathed Enzo within him, before he tightened around Enzo with unmistakable flesh at the core of him, too, creating sheer, inescapable ecstasy.

Cullen was all of it—shadow and flesh, fire and ice, man and monster—and Enzo couldn't speak for how gloriously *good* it felt to be inside him.

The bindings holding Enzo's braids together had loosened during the whirlwind, and the strands began to unravel with the first thrust of Cullen riding him and causing his whole body to shift up the bed. Enzo was Cullen's to claim, and oh, he wanted to be, but he had to be certain of who he was with.

"Cullen?"

"*Yes*," Cullen echoed, slowing his thrusts with a delicious roll that brought Enzo in deeper. Then he sank, encasing Enzo with limbs and tendril caresses that made it all too easy for Enzo's mouth to gasp open and invite Cullen's long, searing tongue to claim him too.

The tightness of the tendrils keeping Enzo bound relaxed enough so he could touch back. He held Cullen to him as he thrust up to meet every fervent slam down, certain in the knowledge that this would never be the same with another. It certainly hadn't been like this with Vanek, and not only because Enzo was the one enveloped in the inner embrace of his partner, or because pure wild magic was part of this.

He held on, not fearing the icy burn, and thrust up into what did and did not feel like the tight wet sanctuary he'd envisioned of his first time inside another. Cullen's shadow tendrils were inside him too, opening him wider for Enzo, while enclosing Enzo's cock. *Enclosed* didn't mean cut off from sensation. He could feel Cullen's walls, a slick freshness like ice in winter, the warm embrace of a hot soak, and the pressure of suction as if Cullen was also swallowing Enzo down his throat.

And all while Cullen's true tongue, too long to be normal and better for it, coiled around Enzo's and kissed him hard. The rocking of their hips seemed to go on for ages. Enzo didn't know how. He was certain he'd come after every thrust, yet on they went. The balance they existed in between every element, every probability of what Cullen was, and everything they wanted to share, kept them on the brink.

Then, when Enzo thought he might float forever in decadence, Cullen's constantly moving and exploring tendrils slithered between Enzo's cheeks and gave a long tingling lick across his hole. He spilled, breath lost as he chased the eruption with constant, stuttering thrusts to fill the tendrils and Cullen's hole with every bit of him he could, certain of how hungry they were to be fed.

Cullen's release was magic all its own, like the crushed crystal paint Enzo had made, but warm and slick as it shot across Enzo's stomach. There it seemed to fade like the shadows it came from, leaving only sparkles.

All at once, the fluctuations of Cullen's form solidified to the normal fair half-elf, his shadows expelling from him and Enzo in one great exhale of black-purple mist. With their retreat, he was but a beautiful naked man again impaled upon Enzo.

"Oh... my. That was something." Enzo laughed.

"It certainly was." Cullen carded his fingers through Enzo's hair. "Out of its braiding, your hair is ravishing waves, framing your handsome face like a crown."

Enzo would have been lost for words after such praise, but what stole them first was Cullen's hand cupping his cheek. "Oh!" He clapped one of his own hands over Cullen's, panting from the unexpected zing the connection caused. He couldn't help his curiosity and drew Cullen's hand lower, trailing it down his neck to his chest and feeling as if all his passions might ignite anew.

He certainly felt impassioned, given his cock, sheathed inside Cullen still, pulsed with half-hardness not yet wilted.

"Uh... that sensitive newborn skin you gifted my palms?" Enzo said. "I think you may have gifted it everywhere now. I'm all a tingle."

Cullen flexed his fingers beneath Enzo's hand, and Enzo gasped, proving the theory. "And still half-clothed." Cullen eyed how Enzo had never lost his open tunic, torn-open undershirt, or trousers caught at his knees. "We'll have to remedy that next time."

"As much as part of me thinks there could be an immediate next time, I'm not sure I'd survive it." He chuckled again, but Cullen cringed, like he worried Enzo really had been in danger. "Not seriously! But as good as every touch from you feels, fair Cullen, I'm a bit worn out."

"Me too," Cullen said, rekindling his sweet smile.

Enzo had stuffed him so full, and Cullen had been so open from the help of his shadows, that when Cullen pulled off, the thick release Enzo had spilled oozed out onto the blankets.

No, onto the clothing Cullen had singed with the harsher eruptions of his power. That was lucky because Enzo didn't want to leave the bed. He tore off his own tangled clothes, wiped up the mess between them, and tossed his and Cullen's garments to the floor, leaving a clean bed for them to lounge upon.

"Thank you," Cullen said when they were lying comfortably. With both their heads on the pillows, Enzo's feet were at Cullen's knees, but it was nice being eye-to-eye in the afterglow.

"For our earned boon?" he teased.

"You know what for," Cullen answered more softly, looking haunted, which wasn't what Enzo wanted him to be left with, but he understood there was still so much they didn't know.

"Will you tell me the rest now? What happened? How you brought us here?"

"I... thought it strange the royals were nowhere to be seen after you'd said they were there the night before. Then I realized it was on purpose. They *were* there, or at least one was, watching from the shadows—literally."

"The Shadow King?"

"I saw him. I entered the veil between planes. He uses shadows to travel quickly, but I... *am* shadow, not the same as him, not really. I phased right into the veil without trying, and when I wanted to come here, I knew all I had to do was will it."

"You're more powerful than the Shadow King?" Enzo gawked.

"I don't know about that. But... he knew my name, just like you suspected. And I ran." Cullen cringed again with a waver entering his voice. "I used the lantern on him and ran. The memories *hurt*, Enzo. So much fear and pain and guilt. I... I think I must have done something awful. I think I deserve to have forgotten, to *be* forgotten—"

"Don't say that." Enzo gathered Cullen closer. "I don't believe that. Because I would never want to forget you. And we only just met!" He laughed, pleased to see at least a few of the ghosts behind Cullen's eyes wither. "I swear I'm not usually the type to jump into bed with a beautiful stranger."

Cullen snorted, but then wrinkled his nose, looking sheepish. "Don't feel differently about me now, but… I think I might have been that type a time or two, and even forgot my bed partner's name afterward. Not something I want to repeat now!" He clung to Enzo like he feared he'd be offended.

"Don't feel differently about me, but… it's easy for me to remember the names of my partners. There's only one other besides you."

Cullen's beautiful violet eyes widened and then softened as he grabbed both sides of Enzo's face. That same zing shot through Enzo. Every place Cullen touched now was like knowing touch for the first time, and none more greatly than when Cullen kissed him.

The front door slammed open, tearing their lips apart.

Stomping was heard.

Then Vanek appeared in the bedchamber doorway.

"How did you get here so fast? I blinked and you vanished, and now you're…." His fists clenched at his sides so tightly, they turned red. "Get dressed," he sneered and stomped back out again.

Words couldn't express how angry Enzo was at Vanek's audacity, and he leapt from the bed to get dressed before Cullen could, because a shadow beast tearing Vanek apart was too good for him.

"Vanek, you are not allowed to burst into my home—"

"This isn't over."

Enzo worried Vanek meant what existed between them, only for his friend to finish.

"Tyraag saw to that."

CHAPTER 10

"WHAT ARE you talking about? What happened?" Enzo demanded.

He'd only thrown on his trousers and undershirt, barefoot on the cool stone floor where minutes earlier he and Cullen had landed after a magical blink. Now, he'd burst out of his bedchamber to confront Vanek ahead of Cullen, who *was* under control, but Enzo didn't fool himself into thinking that couldn't change with the right catalyst.

Vanek stood beside the kitchen table and turned his attention from Enzo to behind him with a withering glare. Cullen had found his old clothes to change into, since the borrowed tunic and undershirt were singed and very likely stained on the bedchamber floor.

"Our message was delivered," Vanek said plainly, "painted across the front of the castle behind the crumbled statue by our swiftest mages. *The royal line must topple for the poor to stop suffering.* And with it, we filled the courtyard with scrolls detailing all the wrongs done, all Tyraag and his peers hope to hide from view and pretend isn't happening.

"Those scrolls were burned up by the swiftest *wealthy* mages at Tyraag's command before anyone, including the visiting royals, could see them," Vanek finished with a snarl. "Now he's claiming our actions are by but a handful of dissenters. We need to escalate."

"What?" Enzo dashed toward him with his own fists clenched. "No. I told you I would help you this once, but no more."

"We are running out of time, Enzo. They might… be able to trace the device back to you."

Enzo leaned back on his heels. "One of your riffraff was supposed to recover the orb while creating the message."

"They did." Vanek pulled it from his pocket, but he kept it close, not handing it over like he'd promised. "What we didn't recover was the one I built and used before."

"*Vanek.*"

"The destruction was too great! We weren't able to get to it in time. When they began investigating what happened, they found it."

Enzo felt a cold guilt-ridden chill flood over him, erasing all the good and hopeful shivers he'd felt only minutes prior. "You lied to me."

"I neglected to mention that part."

"Then you already knew you couldn't cause another explosion without me?"

"Yes, I came looking for you last night because I needed the original Dragon's Gland. *Cullen* interrupted my plans. But just my luck you offered it of your own free will this morning."

"And now you are going to give it back," Cullen growled, reminding Enzo of his presence.

"No, I'm not."

Enzo spun, sensing where this might lead, and silently pleaded with Cullen, whose fists were as tightly clenched as either of theirs, but at least they hadn't yet unfurled perilous shadows. He shook his head. As angry as he was with Vanek, he didn't wish him harm, and he couldn't risk Vanek seeing what Cullen was, or a mob of Ashen might show up at his door next, either to destroy the beast or foolishly try to recruit it.

Once he saw Cullen's hands relax and an answering nod was given, Enzo turned back.

"What's your plan? To use it again and again until Tyraag sees reason?"

"To use it again and again until more of the destructive version has been built," Vanek said, proving the worst of Enzo's fears. "It's the only way they'll listen."

At this rate, the whole mountain would cave in on them before long. No help from the leaders of the other kingdoms tending to wounded in camps would mean a thing then. If they survived the carnage, they'd return home and leave the woes of Ruby behind.

Enzo glanced at Cullen again, recalling what he'd said, what he'd experienced in the Royal Square. The Shadow King had been there, keeping watch. They'd set a trap, trying to protect the kingdom where Tyraag was failing. At least for now, they wanted to help.

"Vanek…." Enzo hoped to reason with him once more. "You said it yourself. Tyraag hid the Ashen's grievances even from the visiting royals."

"So it was reported." He shrugged.

"Because they might have believed it. They might have reacted in a way that could help."

"And we'd be under their control instead," Vanek scoffed.

"It doesn't have to mean that."

"Then what would it mean without someone else to step forward?"

Another cold flood of guilt and uncertainty washed over Enzo. He couldn't. Stepping forward now would simply make him a figurehead for a group of anarchists who no one else would believe. That wasn't what he wanted.

Vanek took a slow, measured step forward, bringing him right up to Enzo, as close as they'd been in the square. "If no one will step forward who the highborn might recognize, then *lowborn* like me need to take the throne by force."

"Is that what you'd hoped would happen?"

"Either option works. The former is simply less violent."

No. *Liar.* Enzo would be a banner, a justification for their violence.

Vanek sighed, pocketed the orb again, and turned to go.

"*Enzo.*" Cullen growled in question.

"Let him go. Go!" Enzo barked when Vanek paused at the door. "Take the orb and all that remains of our friendship with it."

Finally, emotion other than bitterness and anger touched Vanek's expression, but whatever sorrow he felt in the finality of this moment, it didn't change his resolve.

"So be it."

THERE HAD been a moment, tangled with Enzo on the bed, when Cullen honestly hadn't been certain of what the beast in him might do. He could have consumed Enzo in a far less enjoyable manner, but instead, he'd found his way out of the void, out of the darkness, and controlled his shadows to give only pleasure.

He would have liked to throw all that aside now and pounce upon the retreating form of Vanek like a hungry hawk.

"He'll attack the castle directly next. The temporary tomb of the king. The other royals." Enzo faced Cullen with a pinch to his handsome brow like all that came next was his burden to bear, his folly, his fault. "Maybe after a day or two of planning, but no longer. And I won't be getting any more notes from the Ashen."

"What should we do?" Cullen approached and took Enzo's hand to hold it between them.

"We?" Enzo smiled up at him. "Cullen, going against Vanek will involve sneaking into the castle to disrupt his plans. It'll be us between two opposing sides, maybe three, with none of them for certain on ours. You'll likely be faced with much more of your past."

Cullen scowled to hear it, though of course he knew. He couldn't champion the cause of a whole kingdoms without personal consequence. "I'm a coward, *was* a coward. That much feels bitterly familiar to admit. If it weren't for you, I might be fleeing the city, the mountains, the Gemstone Kingdoms altogether, anything to be away from the royals who know who I am and what awful things I must have done.

"But then I might also be losing myself to the void inside me, which you alone have proven able to pull me back from. Not that that's the only reason—" Cullen cut himself off, bringing Enzo's fingers to his lips in quick apology. "I enjoy your company, handsome Enzo, so much, and don't yet wish to be out of it, even if I am a hazard to you, full of elemental strangeness."

When Enzo smiled wider, he was the sun again, the glorious dawn sending back the night, haloed by unruly hair free of its braiding. Even his white undershirt seemed brighter without a tunic to mute it. "I'm glad for your company too, fair Cullen." He tugged Cullen to lean down, drawing him in for a soft kiss. "And I think you and all you are has given me an idea."

CULLEN WAS continuously impressed by Enzo, who tried to work as tirelessly as he had the night before, full of inspirations that had him tinkering in his workshop. They'd eaten before the mission, but the diligent inventor still needed sleep, and Cullen eventually pulled him away.

Being in bed again with Enzo reminded Cullen that this was only his second night in the brilliant farell's presence, and only his first getting to share the bed for sleep. The blankets, the air itself, still smelled of their earlier entanglement, with several discarded articles of clothing needing to be laundered tomorrow or thrown. For now, Cullen reveled in the musk and warmth and contentment of Enzo's bedchamber.

By morning, Enzo's legs had found a natural hold around Cullen's waist, as if he'd reached out in his sleep with all four limbs to cling. That made it a pleasant morning indeed, for both woke hard and only too easily succumbed to the natural inclination to rut until their minds were as roused as their bodies. Cullen's shadows stirred only enough to hug Enzo's body close and cause the farell to gasp and lean into every touch.

Again, Cullen hadn't dreamed, at least nothing he remembered, and it had him wondering if he even truly slept. He felt hunger and thirst, and therefore ate and drank, but was it merely memory that he should do any of those things? When he did feel exhaustion, it was different than he thought it must have felt like in his life before.

Was he sleeping or merely succumbing to part of the void?

If it kept his dreams at bay, he didn't mind.

Enzo had many plans the next day—fixing the Ever-Burning Torch being one—but the most important seemed to revolve around the Gemstone Maul, which Cullen had assumed was finished.

"In the sense of its initial use, yes," Enzo explained. "The idea was to craft a smithing hammer capable of imbuing whatever it made with a specific elemental property, but my experiments on you make me think I can be a little more creative."

Cullen helped as best he could, though it was mainly his job to keep an eye on the Looking Glass spell Enzo had put in place. It was simple enough magic, especially using the rune for Reflection. Enzo said it was often used by businesses to keep a lookout for anyone suspicious trying to break in.

A hidden rune was placed on the front door, and another was placed on a mirror that the proprietors could look in to see whichever direction the door's rune pointed. Enzo's door faced Dorff's—a still active member of the Ashen.

A whole day and night passed with no new notes posted, but also no signs of fresh attacks. They had time, but they also knew their time was limited.

Cullen remembered nothing new unless he tried to, so he spent much of that first day trying very hard *not* to remember anything, to focus only on how much he enjoyed being with Enzo. The one exception, in his moments alone, was practicing purposely calling upon his shadows, much as they sometimes frightened him. He needed to believe he could control it.

Especially since, exhausted as they were after a full day of diligence, they sought another messy end before sleep.

The second day went much the same, but when night began to fall, and Enzo assured him he was almost finished with his plans on the maul, Cullen stepped outside to get air and took the mirror for the Looking Glass spell with him.

The people of Ruby were truly ingenious. Homes stacked atop others like Enzo's could be accessed by ladder steps, inset into the stone like the homes themselves. At the second level, Cullen could easily move from the ladder onto a platform where the next home's door was reached. The third and fourth levels were the same. The fifth was the roof, but the ladder went right to it, allowing Cullen to sit on a flat portion of the stone and look out at the city around him.

Most other homes were like this one, stacked domiciles, many taller than Enzo's. A few outcroppings in the mountain looked like larger single homes. Shops of various kinds were the same, some stacked, some that must have been their own caverns once, owned by wealthier shopkeepers.

Dorff's blacksmith shop was the base of another stacked building, and from the roof, Cullen could see its door. He held the mirror close anyway as he watched the city, all built into a single immense cave, large enough to have once housed dragons.

Cullen was certain he'd never been here before waking beside the Ruby gemstone. The sights, while beautiful to him, stirred no sense of memory. There was some familiarity with the crystals used as light sources. He could almost envision a very different kingdom with such crystals and its dark sky dotted by a blanket of stars.

There was a castle on a hill, and the glow of the Amethyst below him in a market square, a beautiful pulsing purple, the same color as Cullen's eyes....

He closed his eyes now, as those memories returned unbidden. None of it felt real when he caught glimpses of places and people or heard distant words. That life was a dream that haunted him, one he didn't think he'd ever been truly happy in.

Was that why he'd done whatever awful things he did? Because he'd been unhappy? What sort of monster did that make him?

This view was better than any in Cullen's mind, even if a glance back at the bow of the horseshoe reminded him that some of the beauty was but a glamour hiding a harsher truth. If he was in those streets, he'd see the cracks. The illusion spell merely filled them in to cover their distortions, but the damage was there.

"How many times did this poor cup break, I wonder, only to be put back together a little weaker than its original form?"

Cullen cringed and closed his eyes again. He was a coward. A *coward*. But so be it.

A coward was better than a monster.

"Enzo, is that you?" a woman's voice was heard.

"Yes, ma'am. Is all well?" he answered, sounding closer to Cullen than she was, like he must be halfway up the ladder steps, about to join Cullen on the roof.

Cullen peered over the edge, and Enzo was indeed climbing back down to the second home's landing, where a dwarven woman peeked out her door.

"I'm sorry to bother you," she said, "but it seems that explosion the other night shook loose some of our lighting crystals. I didn't notice until they started losing power today. Hector's rather afraid of the dark still, you see, and needs light in his room when he sleeps. I don't trust leaving a lit a candle—"

"Say no more. I can't fix them now, I'm afraid, but I have just the thing I can lend young Hector tonight. One moment." Enzo scaled back down to the bottom floor. When he returned from inside his home, it was to hand the woman the Ever-Burning Torch.

"This is too much—" She tried to give it back.

"Nonsense. Neighbors lend each other things all the time. You can return it to me when I've time to fix your crystals. They probably just need new runes behind them drawn or minor adjustments."

"But when you do, I've nothing to pay—"

"No need. I'm happy to do it. An inventor's role is to aid people, after all."

"You are such a sweet man. Thank you."

Cullen smiled at the exchange, not at all surprised, and waited for Enzo to join him—his valiant knight in contrast to Cullen's dark and unknown past.

"All finished," Enzo announced with a ring of jubilance upon climbing onto the roof, as if the task ahead wasn't to thwart the opposing ideals of two dangerous sides—possibly three.

He looked good, in his usual white shirt and basic trousers, but his tunic today was plum instead of red. His sleeves were rolled up, a bit of sweat clinging to his brow, and while his usual braids remained, the half of his hair normally down was loosely tied back, causing wavy strands to fall into his stubbled face. He was beautiful, while also powerful, like a mountain or act of nature, fair and formidable in one.

"It's storming tonight," he said, sitting beside Cullen and leaning against him. They were closer in height like this, but Enzo's legs only stretched so far. "Storms always remind me of my mother."

"Storming?" Cullen looked skyward. "How can you tell?"

"Follow the mirror-lights and rain collectors." Enzo pointed at several visible ones in the distance and traced up their pathways to where the water came from and where the sun and other light reflected. When he got to the very top of the cavern, there was the tiniest opening in the mountain ceiling, angled so that water was seen pouring down the rockface into the collectors, but no rain fell on the city.

They were safe from the storm, but Cullen could see it, the peek of dark sky, the rainfall, and streaks of lightning chasing each other from one cloud to another.

"Some things are difficult to see until you know where to look," Enzo said.

"Like the poorer streets and the Ashen's hidden messages?"

"Yes." Enzo sighed. The mirror rested between them. If its surface hadn't been showing Dorff's door, it might have reflected some of the cavern ceiling and the storm.

As Enzo leaned heavier against Cullen, Cullen dropped his head to meet him and found Enzo's hand to lace their fingers. Enzo fit perfectly in the crook of Cullen's neck.

"You know, I'm the one who told Vanek about that trick with invisible ink and heat."

"Oh?"

"My father used to use it when writing letters to me and my mother."

"He was gone a lot?"

"Yes...."

Like always when Enzo mentioned his father, Cullen sensed there was more to tell, but he didn't push to hear it, not when Enzo was being so understanding about him not wanting to think on his past.

He squeezed Enzo's hand and gazed up with him at the storm, surrounded by glittering crystals in the rockface.

"Even on a stormy night, the crystals are like constellations in a clear sky," Cullen said.

"Only they never move."

"They haven't changed from mining over the years?"

"Some say, because we're so close to the Ruby, the crystals here are more difficult to mine, embedded more deeply. That's why most of the mining is done farther from the city. Others say it's because in the time of the dragons, so much fire and other elemental breath attacks imbued the stone with strange properties." Enzo drew his hand from Cullen's and traced along varied colors in the stone beneath them, where black, pink, and even turquoise could be seen. "It's like obsidian in places, quartz in others. The mixture is what makes it look reddish from afar."

Cullen traced it too, ending with his hand once again atop Enzo's, who peered at him with a radiant smile. "I hadn't noticed. I feel like I'm rather bad at noticing things. Other than how handsome you are, of course." He touched their noses and felt Enzo's shuddery breath on his lips. "That I noticed straight away."

Enzo chuckled with another light puff of air. "I can tell you this much, fair Cullen, whoever you were before, you were definitely a charmer."

That was better than a monster too.

Cullen kissed Enzo before new memories could surface, firm and claiming with the hand over Enzo's lacing their fingers once more. He felt the numbness begin at his hands, the predecessor to shadows unfurling with potent pleasure and intensity to follow. But sweet as it was to hear Enzo whine when the first coils of burning cold took hold of him, this kiss Cullen wanted only to be his, and he tamped the shadows down to keep himself flesh.

Slices of air like steam escaping or sword cuts began in rapid succession, quiet, maybe even dismissive to most ears, but they'd been waiting for this sound.

The loosing of arrows.

They parted and their clasped hands reached for the mirror in tandem. A new note was indeed on Dorff's door.

"I have it," Cullen said. He'd practiced this too. It wasn't as frightening with a goal, and as he'd told Enzo, unlike the Shadow King, he didn't need shadows to accomplish it. The shadows were him.

Fading into the veil, Cullen knew that, to Enzo's eyes, he vanished, but to him, within the violet-haze between worlds, Enzo was like a sculpture. Cullen lightly brushed Enzo's cheek with the backs of his shadow fingers and swore he saw a sparkle in Enzo's eyes in response.

He didn't need to tread slowly the way he'd crossed the Royal Square. He could will himself where he wanted to be, and in a blink, he was there, plucking the note from the blacksmith's door. His touch didn't singe the note, but his mix of icy-hot shadows revealed the hidden message instantly.

Cullen blinked himself back onto the roof beside Enzo and slipped from the veil as easily as he'd slipped in. "I'm afraid it's as we expected." He handed the note to Enzo.

Enzo's lips pursed as he read it. "The Ashen attack tonight."

CHAPTER 11

ENZO HAD never been inside the castle. No one from his part of the city would have been invited to one of the king's personal banquets, least of all an unacknowledged son.

He was getting used to creeping toward the Royal Road at night. He'd worried it might be closed off again, but a couple days had passed since the statue's destruction, and it was open. The guards at the entrance had searched them before permitting them further, but they had no reason to distrust what looked like a smithing hammer. The Royal Square was once again bustling, as if nothing were amiss, despite the empty space where the Dragonbane statue once stood.

There was no medical camp either, Enzo hoped because all who had been there were well enough to have been sent home.

"Anything?" he whispered, as they began to cross the square.

"I don't think so," Cullen said, glancing out from within the hood of his violet cloak. They didn't want to be in black tonight. After all that had happened, Cullen's noble stitching was less conspicuous.

For now, they were not being watched by the shadows or guards and continued at a pace that blended them with the crowd. Cullen couldn't port them directly inside. He'd never been there either that he remembered, and said he needed a direct view or reference point or he didn't know where they'd end up. Which meant, once they were inside, he'd at least be able to port them back out if there was trouble.

They were early compared to when the Ashen would strike. They had to be if they were to stop Vanek. He'd be setting off the next bomb himself and was being let into the castle by a planted kitchen worker. The rest of the Ashen were to do as before, only this time, the message would be larger, the scrolls aplenty—and likely a death count to hammer the point home. Enzo couldn't allow that.

"You said you had a way in," Cullen said as they neared the castle gates, "but how exactly?"

They didn't attempt to enter the gates themselves, which were closed with multiple guards standing watch, but turned left, circling the stone wall, built of connected stalagmites that would have been impossible to climb. Occasional small gaps allowed a view within, but nothing wide enough that even a hand could have passed through.

A glance was all they needed.

"Vanek has his methods. We have ours." Enzo brought them to a stop when the castle wall ended at the cliff face. They were practically invisible back there, tucked away from the shops and bustle, and there was a gap in the wall with a view to an equally unoccupied area of the inner courtyard. "I need you to bring us there. I'll do the rest."

Enzo hadn't had time to appreciate Cullen's power the first time. Now, he saw it coming and tried to catalog every detail—the split second when Cullen became shadow before enveloping him, the darkness that descended, and yet... there was a blink of violet haze and a sense of his breath being stolen, as if time stopped. Then he was elsewhere, with Cullen solidifying before him like a mirage appearing out of the night.

"Spectacular." Enzo marveled at him, enjoying the immediate smile his praise caused, especially when he knew Cullen wasn't completely comfortable with his other self. "Now for a little elemental help."

He drew aside his cloak, revealing the Gemstone Maul attached to his belt. He'd never expected to use it this way, but after all, a hammer could destroy as much as create.

"Before, each side of the hammer's head bore an elemental rune, but not matching the kingdoms like I've made them now, more general as just fire and water and the like." He rotated it so Cullen could see that the runes on each of the longer sides were Sun and Ice now, on the shorter sides Earth and Storm, and on the top was Ash.

"There were different runes on the handle before too," Cullen said. "I didn't recognize them. Several of the same, like... two pitchforks connected?"

"Right, but think if those runes had been separated, one with the tongues of a pitchfork pointed up, the other down."

"Life and Death." Cullen nodded.

"Though in use like that not truly so spectacular. It was simply a way for the hammer to both imbue a weapon with an elemental property and take it away. I've changed those runes to Man because humanity can also mean balance." He moved his hands on the handle to show the M-like symbols. "And I need this hammer to be carefully balanced or risk it exploding in my hands like you did."

Cullen's eyes bulged.

"It'll be fine. I know this will work." Enzo tilted the hammer to show the bottom, where all around where the handle connected to the head were smaller versions of the same five gemstone runes. "You are most powerful with your signature element. It's yours and calls to you, connects with you, like any person with an affinity for one over another. But what makes yours so powerful is that part of each element is in you. A unified circle, like the golden age of the Gemstone Kingdoms centuries past. Like this, each of these individual elements will pack a little more punch than for smithing."

Grinning in excitement, nervous as he was for what awaited them inside the castle, Enzo activated the rune for Ice, causing the head of the hammer to glow blue and emit mist like breath on a cold day. Then he gave it a mighty swing and slammed it into the castle wall.

Frost erupted from the impact point, covering a four- or five-foot radius in what quickly became pure ice. Then, with another swing, Enzo shattered the frozen stone, creating a hole plenty large enough for them to step through.

"Incredible." Cullen gazed on him with an equally triumphant grin.

"Say that again once we've won," Enzo said and climbed through the opening.

He only had a general idea of the castle's layout, but enough that he knew where they needed to end up, even if he wasn't certain about the exact turns or encounters along the way. The first step was hoping he was right that this corner of the castle would be empty.

He put a finger to his lips when Cullen climbed in after him, both tilting their heads to listen for approaching feet or nearby voices. For now, they were clear.

Leading the way, Enzo held the hammer out with the rune deactivated until the next element might be needed. The first thing he noticed was the red glow of the castle's interior, alternating between torches and red crystals along the corridor, reflecting against the reddish, unpainted stone. They had only one direction they could go to start, so forward they went.

In this side hall, the ceiling was low, but once they reached an end that branched left and right, the corridors were taller, with red and gold tapestries lining the walls.

And still no guards.

Enzo motioned for Cullen to follow him left, since right would curve around the castle's perimeter, and they needed to reach its belly. The higher ceilings made their footsteps echo. No—just Enzo's. He couldn't hear Cullen's, either from the half-elf's trim figure or his innate ability to be shadow.

They passed several doors Enzo tried to creep by, and the slow, cautious pace made it easier to notice the differences in each of the tapestries. All had the same colors and simplistic art style in the weaving, but they told a progressing story of how the Dragonbane progenitor banished the last dragon.

The dragon was silvery white in color, and the stitching on its scales sparkled, as if it were made of platinum. It was depicted so large that it would have easily filled up the entire cavern of the Ruby Kingdom. One banner showed it indeed doing so, curled up as if slumbering and surrounded by riches—including the Ruby gemstone snuggled in its grasp like a child's toy.

Another showed Dragonbane facing off against the dragon.

Another showed him riding it, and Enzo didn't think it clear if that meant they had been friends or if it was merely part of a fight.

Another showed Dragonbane backing the dragon toward the Ruby.

Another showed a cave-in between them, cutting the once even larger cavern off from the Ruby that had originally been in its hollow.

Finally, Dragonbane was depicted like the statue once looked, holding his hammer high in claim on the kingdom he would never himself rule.

The end of the story marked the next branch in the corridors, where Enzo could head right or continue forward. Right it had to be to move toward a central point in the castle, but that corridor was dimmer, lit only by crystals, and Enzo couldn't see the end of it.

He hushed Cullen again as he turned down it, pausing at the mouth to activate the rune on the Gemstone Maul for Sun. The hammer's head glowed red like the nearby crystals, and Enzo could feel the heat radiating from it. Far less powerful than how he'd smashed through the wall with Ice, he tapped the head of the hammer on the stone.

Fire licked free as if following a line of oil, causing the first torch it found to ignite, and the flames leapt to another and another all the way down the hall.

No guards there either. Vanek likely picked a time close to when he knew patrols would be light. Again, Enzo motioned Cullen after him, who moved so quietly, it would have been easy to forget his presence, if Enzo wasn't so pleased to have it.

At the end of the hall, they'd need to go left, then right again, bringing them nearer to the grand hall and the throne room.

"Is that brighter? I don't remember lighting those torches," came a voice.

"I didn't light them," came another. "Maybe Roach and Lascaro beat us to it?"

"Why didn't they light the ones at the far end, then?"

Guards. And getting closer. As much as Enzo and Cullen flattened themselves to the wall, that wouldn't hide them once the corner was turned. They could almost see the start of the curve where the guards were coming from, and with a wild idea, Enzo pointed from Cullen to himself to that distant spot and mouthed, *Port us on my signal.*

Cullen's eyes bulged again, but this might be their only chance.

Activating the rune for Earth, Enzo watched the hammer's head turn greenish brown like tree roots, releasing the musky smell of a summer garden.

"You hear something?"

"Weapons ready!"

He arced the arm holding the hammer toward the turn in the hall, propelling several vines to snap like whip lashes, and tripped the guards to topple face-first into the floor.

"The fuck!"

"What'd we trip over?"

Cullen swept over Enzo without needing to be told, and his shadows dropped them around the curve, right at the fallen guards' feet. Calling the vines back into the hammer, Enzo hurried down the hall for the next turn, knowing Cullen was with him.

"What happened?"

"You tripped me!"

"You tripped *me*!"

Enzo would have laughed if it was safe to once they were around the next bend, where thankfully, no other guards waited. They couldn't dawdle. One more left should bring them center.

"You're a genius," Cullen whispered at the side of Enzo's neck.

"Almost like having a mage staff, eh?" Enzo glanced back, but though Cullen smiled, his eyes darkened the way they often did when memory stirred. "Not far now." He patted Cullen's arm.

This final hall was longer, and not all the doors were closed. The first few open ones contained empty rooms, and when they neared one with voices, it was easy for Cullen to port them past it to the other side.

Then that final left was upon them, and one quick peek proved all Enzo's planning was right. The grand hall, the main entrance into the castle, spanned taller than any of the corridors they'd tread so far. It was here that one could truly tell they were inside a mountain. Most of the homes and shops had been built similarly, but this great cavern could have been home to many instead of wasted space.

The lighting was tinted red here too, with only ruby-like crystals, none naturally inset, but in sconces like the torches. The floors were all smooth, pillars meticulously carved to create paragons of kings and warriors past or depictions of the dragon. A more life-like statue of the dragon and fourth size scale—or so it was said—was in the center of the hall, which one had to loop around to get to the staircases leading to the throne room and side rooms around it.

There were guards at the front entrance, facing inward, just as others were on the outside facing the courtyard. Enzo and Cullen simply needed to port to behind the dragon statue, and they'd be invisible.

They did so, but Enzo could tell Cullen seemed shaken every time.

"Does it pain you?" he whispered.

"No? It's just…." He shook his head, urging Enzo on, but Enzo still reached for Cullen and pulled him down for a quick kiss. He knew what it was like to fear one's true self, afraid it would only make reality worse.

Twin staircases led to a large central doorway on a landing with several other open doorways on either side. The way the stairs curved, walking up either would make them visible to the guards, but they needn't use steps.

Cullen ported them again to right in front of the central doorway, and at the end of a long hall as grand as the one they'd left was the Ruby throne. A quite literal statement, for the throne, while carved from stone that reached as tall as the ceiling, had rubies inset every few feet.

Enzo allowed himself to gaze on the throne, imagining what it must have looked like with his father sitting there, but their true destination was the room behind it. He pointed at one of the side doorways since, again, walking there might make them visible, and Cullen ported them within, where they continued out of view.

Here was another corridor, low of ceiling like the first they'd entered, and curving to the right to arch around the throne room. Enzo assumed the other doorway was identical with a curve the opposite way. Living quarters existed beyond, but all they needed was to make it to the central room behind the throne. The antechamber was always where departed royals were kept until burial, where Vanek planned to strike.

They were almost there.

"But, sir, the kings are growing insistent."

"Not to mention the Fairy Queen."

"I don't care about foreign kings and queens or their rowdy *guests*." Tyraag's voice boomed above the others with a drip of derision, as his figure nearly stepped into view down the hall, only to turn and face the men behind him. "We maintain as we have, understood?"

The only place for Cullen to port them back to was where they'd come from.

"We can backtrack," Cullen whispered. "I can—"

"No. We're so close." Enzo readied the hammer, triggering the rune for Storm. The head crackled with white lightning that he prepared to hurl down the hall—

"*Wait*," Cullen hissed, and before Enzo could launch his attack, just as Tyraag began to turn around, Cullen's hands came down on Enzo's shoulders, and the world went violet.

It was like being submerged in a lake on a warm summer day, with everything slowed and still, wavering with a single muted color, and yet, the violet wasn't truly muted, it was… a fairy land. The corridor seemed brighter, clearer, simply painted with amethyst tint and sparkles.

Tyraag faced them, but his frozen gaze couldn't see them.

"It's beautiful…."

ENZO THOUGHT the veil beautiful?

Cullen was glad but also surprised. He'd been so stunned to find himself here the first time, and then frightened when tracking and being confronted by the Shadow King, he hadn't had time to think of this space between worlds as beautiful. He'd been more wary than in wonder, as though he'd seen too long in shades of violet.

"*I suppose it is,*" Cullen said and began to guide Enzo forward. "*But we're not completely out of sync with time. They're moving, just slower than we are.*"

It was unnerving reaching the mostly still advisor and his men, even knowing they couldn't see them while clearly within eyeline as they approached. The hall was wide enough that there was plenty of room to hug the wall and move around them toward the exit.

"Seeing you move through the veil in this form is like the most graceful of acrobats barely touching the ground," Enzo said.

"*I'm behind you. You can barely see me,*" Cullen countered.

"Even a glimpse is enough to think you a dancer."

"*Void beast? Why, he's a void dancer!*"

Cullen shook the memory away.

"I wish we could hear the rest of what he'd been about to say." Enzo nodded at Tyraag.

There was an alcove set into the wall beside the way out, where one of many red crystals in its sconce cast dim light. Cullen wasn't sure why at first, but he brought Enzo into it, his body moving instinctually to tuck them away. He held Enzo closer against him, making them flush with the wall. "I think I can do that too. Hold still in case I'm wrong."

Something familiar as if Cullen had done this before guided his steps, and he was confident they wouldn't be seen as he pulled them just a little bit out of the veil without leaving completely.

"No matter how many times they ask." Tyraag sprang back to normal speed, moving past them, with his guards following. "We say again and again that we have no idea who these Ashen are but presume them petty anarchists looking to capitalize on the king's death. There will be no further postponement of the funeral. Two days is as far as I'm willing to concede, then the burial commences. We must end this so proper mourning can pass before my—*the* coronation."

"Yes, sir."

"Of course, High Advisor."

The voices dimmed, leaving out the other end of the hall, and again, Cullen was struck by how familiar that had been, hidden in plain sight along an alcove while eavesdropping....

He kept them in the veil now that he knew he could and guided them from the alcove into the next area, which spilled them into a wider hall with branching corridors.

"*Do you think he killed the king?*" Cullen asked.

"I don't know." Enzo glanced up at him. "But with two days before the funeral, tradition states it'll only be a week after that before Tyraag takes the throne." He looked forward with a deep sigh. "Vanek could cause a lot of destruction in a week. And worse after.

"Come." He pulled forward, and Cullen kept pace to ensure his hold on Enzo's shoulders. "These should be guest rooms, but a little farther to the right should be an entrance into the antechamber."

Most of the doors were closed, but as they came upon one that was open, even though Cullen knew they shouldn't be visible anymore, he willed them across in a blink.

Which was when he picked up on the voices inside, and his grip on Enzo slackened enough for the farell to move out of his grasp.

"It was him, I swear it," said a deep, penetrating voice.

Ash....

"And *I* swear he's dead," said another voice Cullen recognized— Janskoller. "Sorry to be blunt, but he is. Just a spirit who passed on when Nemirac returned the essences of the gemstones."

"We saw him fade away," Nemirac added.

"Did you? Are you certain? It was him in the courtyard that day. I know it."

"But there's been no sign since," said another deeper voice. "Unless we start going door to door and risk alienating Tyraag into conflict or at least kicking us to the border, we have no proof, not if the lost prince doesn't show himself again."

"But what if these Ashen are involved?" Ashmedai demanded. "What if they've done something to him?"

"I am learning so much from the orb," said yet another voice, young and full of hope. "We'll track these people soon enough, You'll see."

"Cullen?"

Cullen gasped and spun toward the hushed voice behind him. Enzo was a few strides away, blinking past where his eyes should have landed on Cullen, yet staring through him, like he could no longer see him standing there.

He couldn't, because Cullen had let Enzo step from the veil when he lost hold of his shoulders.

His hands returned to Enzo in a blink of willing himself forward, and Enzo was with him again, jumping slightly and then smiling as he looked up at Cullen.

"Are you all right?" he asked.

Cullen nodded and urged Enzo forward.

Not yet. He couldn't face those voices yet.

Their final turn didn't lead to another corridor, but to a deep-set alcove with double doors. A pair of guards stood in front of them, blocking the path to the room they needed. Even without seeing what lay beyond, Cullen believed he could at least bring them to the other side and willed them through it as if passing through the doors directly.

Enzo released a shuddery gasp and stepped from Cullen's hold. They didn't need the veil here, so Cullen left it too, for they were alone.

Save the body of the Ruby King.

The room was small, intimate, likely for storing some of the king's favorite treasures, and as an office of sorts with a desk along one side, a stand for a suit of armor along another, chests filled with riches, and weapons and shields on the walls. But however the room might have looked before now, in the center was a slab of stone like a pedestal where the body of the king lay.

The pedestal was low enough that Enzo could easily view the body by stepping up to it, and so Cullen felt a bit like he towered, seeing the whole of the dead king at once. He wore armor, almost identical to that of the statue they'd toppled, and a glow enveloped the body, a sort of preservation spell that froze the king at the point of death. Enzo said it was tradition during mourning, but once the proper time passed and the body was buried, the spell would be lifted to allow the body to return to the stone.

Surely, seeing the preserved body of anyone recently passed would be difficult, but Cullen thought Enzo especially quiet as he gazed upon it, and a hand reached out almost as if he meant to touch the king, only to recoil with a tremor. He had not expressed before having great love for the Ruby King. He'd expressed very little about him, and Cullen stepped up behind him to gaze more closely and see if there was something he'd missed.

The king had been a handsome dwarf, with ruddy skin, long auburn hair, and a matching full beard. He was broad and thick like a true warrior, though he wouldn't have known war in his time. He was simply built strong like he carried warrior blood, which he did, given the Dragonbane lineage. He almost looked familiar, in face and build, like something in his cheeks that Cullen thought might have been made clearer if he was alive to offer a smile.

The king's arms were clasped atop his stomach, where he held the end of a hammer pointing downward, and it was there, just above his hands, almost hidden by his beard, that Cullen noticed a family crest. If the original Dragonbane had been the one to earn the name by driving out a dragon, then the crest itself hadn't existed yet then, for Cullen didn't remember seeing it on the statue. He had seen it before, however; that he knew immediately.

A shield, with two crossed hammers within, and coiled around the heads and handles of the hammers was an ouroboros like a dragon, with wings outstretched behind each hammer's head.

Like the pendant in Enzo's workshop dubbed *Father's*.

"Enzo—"

"Hurry!" a voice hissed as a different set of double doors burst open and two men entered before shutting them again. "The guards will be—" The man talking cut off as he spotted Cullen and Enzo. "The abyss! Is that Enzo the tinkerer and his pet noble?"

It was Rufus, the same half dwarf, half human whose voice Cullen recognized as the man who'd accosted him outside the Bottom of the Barrell tavern, and who'd been with the ruffians in the alley that first night. He'd been in the courtyard, too, when the statue exploded, a burly man, with blondish brown hair shaved on the sides but with the top long and braided down his back. A chest-length beard was tied together with a bronze bauble, but he was otherwise dressed as a cook tonight.

Just like Vanek, who accompanied him.

"Enzo?" Vanek questioned in equal shock, but his eyes shone with hope. "You changed your mind."

Before Enzo could counter, Rufus snarled and pulled a dagger.

"I really hate it when plans change," he said—and stabbed Vanek between the shoulders.

CHAPTER 12

"VANEK!" ENZO cried, and Cullen felt the world spin and his stomach plummet.

And his hands tingled with numbness.

Rufus wrenched the dagger free of Vanek's back only to grab hold of him and press the blade to his throat, facing Cullen and Enzo, as he began a slow pivot around the antechamber.

"Rufus… w-what…?" Vanek croaked. He was also armed, a short axe revealed on his belt when his tunic shifted, but he hadn't had time to draw it.

"I don't care about your *cause*, Vanek," Rufus scoffed. "At least not more than mine. And you were going to let all this treasure get blown to bits. Don't worry, though. After gathering what I want, I'll still set off the orb. Whether you're caught in the blast is your decision. Which goes for you two as well." His hard eyes shot at them over Vanek's head, and his gaze didn't reveal any hesitation or remorse for his betrayal.

"How do you think you'll get out of here with all this treasure?" Enzo demanded, hands flexing on the handle of the Gemstone Maul, currently dormant but still formidable.

Though not as formidable as Cullen. He could feel the impulse in him to act, pounce, *consume*. He tamped the urges down. He didn't know what would happen if he gave in. But he hated that Enzo was in front of him, closer to the danger.

"I left a path free," Rufus said, continuing to pivot. The pedestal with the deceased king was between them, the most morbid of barriers, which had to be worse for Enzo.

Because he was the king's son.

"Stand down," Cullen warned, wanting to rid Enzo of his scowl that was both for Vanek's plight and his secret loss. The numbness in Cullen's hands was becoming ice-hot intensity, whatever shadows spilling forth from him hidden behind Enzo's back.

"Or what? What do I have to fear from some pretty little elf and Enzo the tinkerer?" Rufus pulled the orb from Vanek's pocket. "Your original, see? In case we needed something extra for our escape. I can use this one to take care of you. Less destruction. The treasure will survive. Then I can gather it all in the chaos and use the other orb to cover my tracks. Bang! Easy getaway. Such a pity some of the Ashen were found in the rubble. Or... you can leave right now."

"Let him go," Enzo snarled in answer.

"Mm, see, most of the Ashen actually love Vanek, and I need time to get out of the mountains. You leave first. I'll leave him alive if he behaves."

"No, you won't," Enzo countered, "because you're a vile creature who cares for no one but yourself."

"Ouch." Rufus laughed. "And what are you? So perfectly caught in the middle of have and have not, you think you're a hero for building a bomb? Or for trying to stop one this time?"

Vanek's eyes shone with understanding that he'd guessed wrong thinking they were here to help the Ashen's mission.

"You're just making yourself feel better," Rufus went on, clearly meaning to goad Enzo into being careless. His next pivot gave a clearer view to him and Vanek around the pedestal, and Cullen saw blood dripping down between where their bodies pressed together.

Vanek's wound was deep and gushing from the harsh stab and yank free of the blade. He'd gone pale, with sweat breaking out on his brow.

"Me, I can admit I'm vile, and I'm fine with that. At least I'll live like a king once I have his treasure." He kicked the side of the slab, and though it didn't disturb the body, the act prompted Enzo to dart forward.

"No!" Cullen grabbed the hammer and swept Enzo behind him before Rufus could get in a lucky kick or swipe with his blade. Instantly, the rune for Ash glowed with such intense light, the room went awash in purple, originating from the hammer's head. Cullen hadn't meant to trigger it, but he felt a surge of communion with the Gemstone Maul as it began to emit the same black-purple shadows as him.

"Anything you try only harms our fearless leader!" Rufus dug the edge of the blade tighter against Vanek's throat.

Cullen didn't care... did he? Why should he care about Vanek, who he'd already wanted to consume several times before now? Vanek hoped to reclaim his place beside Enzo. He was a hindrance, a nuisance, and the cause of so much of Enzo's pain. He *should* be consumed.

And Rufus with him.

"Cullen...."

Again, the hammer brightened, blinding with its violet aura, almost as if to aid the shadows in their growth. The ones spilling from the hammer were at first merely spreading, but they pulled toward Cullen as if magnetized and began to coil around him, joining with the shadows that erupted from his palms and out of every pore.

"The fuck…?" Rufus's hold slackened on his dagger, and Vanek's eyes went wide as they gaped in equal horror.

"*Cullen*," Enzo pleaded.

But he was behind him, behind Cullen where he belonged, safe and protected.

The hammer pulsed again, so bright the shadows looked blacker, with the curling fingers of Cullen's other hand around its shaft. He could feel the darkness all around him now, part of him, in him, and he pulsed too, growing from the shadows' magnitude and the added boost from the hammer's rune.

"What are you?" Rufus gasped and pushed Vanek forward like an offering to stumble back.

What.

What.

He was the void. Hungry and powerful. And here at last was his meal.

"Cullen!"

He slammed the hammer down, propelling shadows across the stone floor, and Vanek toppled. He tossed like someone caught in waves, too weak to stay upright, and the shadows swept him aside. Fine. He could be next. First was the fiend who had dared spew threats at a *god*.

The wave of shadows pinned Rufus to the wall behind him as though he'd been caught in sludge. It oozed over his limbs and any wild thrashes to escape merely caused more shadows to spread across his body. He screamed, for the touch of the shadows visibly burned or iced him, and his eyes were wide from the pain. The dagger melted from his grasp, the Dragon's Gland too, nothing but liquid metal that vanished when it hit the remaining shadows on the floor.

Rufus fought one of his hands free and pulled another dagger that he launched at Cullen like a dart. It too was consumed, even having struck true where Cullen's heart would be if he were flesh. But he wasn't flesh. He was darkness, hunger, and everything feared of the abyss.

"*Monster*!" Rufus wailed. "Help! Help me! Someone—!"

Cullen seized his throat with shadow claws that could have torn his head from his body. But no. That wasn't enough. His claws needn't rend, no more than his fangs. His whole body was a maw meant to devour, and devour he did. He descended upon the man with every desire he'd held back finally let loose, feasting upon the trembling, pathetic spark of life that had tried to defy him.

And there, in the void, for one perfect moment, he wasn't alone, for he heard the death knell scream of the man echo in the dark, again and again, until nothing remained.

Cullen reformed, not as a shadow elf, or even the less man-shaped monster with greater stature, but *greater* than that. He grew, filling twice as much of the antechamber from the shadows he called back to him and the ones from the hammer feeding him more. The hammer was part of him now, like a larger limb extending as a club.

Someone was screaming at him. A name. His name? But all he saw when he turned and found Vanek on the floor, petrified and quaking, with blood oozing beneath him, was another target.

"Cullen!" Enzo entered his field of vision, arms spread wide to guard Vanek behind him. "Please! Stop! You have to stop."

Enzo....

"Voidy...?"

Cullen's attention snapped to the double doors they'd ported through, but it wasn't the guards who'd entered, but a different pair.

Janskoller and his Fairy Prince.

When had they come in? They'd seen him devour Rufus, he could tell that much, for their looks of horror from him to the now empty wall where nothing, not even a scrap of clothing remained, said it all.

"Cullen," Enzo called softly, as the maul was gently pried from his fingers.

He looked forward and... he was shrinking. He was smaller, for Enzo was not as far beneath him as he'd been a moment ago. Enzo's hands were blistering from touching the overcharged hammer, but as soon as it was out of Cullen's grasp, it went dormant again.

"Please." Enzo touched Cullen's arm, and that blistered and burned him too, but still he held fast, pulling Cullen toward Vanek. "We have to go."

"Cullen...?" Nemirac questioned, both him and Janskoller frozen in the doorway.

He was Cullen… wasn't he? He was still the monster, still shadow, but shaped more like himself, a black-purple echo of whoever he'd been.

And he'd consumed someone. Killed them. Erased them entirely….

Trapped between past and present, a monster in all their eyes, surely, he did the one thing he could. He swept over Enzo as asked, over Vanek too, and fled.

Again.

THEY'D SUCCESSFULLY thwarted the Ashen's plans, but Vanek was badly hurt, and now, everything was *fucked*.

They reappeared in Enzo's home in the same positions they'd been in when Cullen descended, with Enzo standing in front of a fallen, bleeding Vanek.

He dropped to his knees beside his friend, and the Gemstone Maul landed with a thud at his hip. Vanek's eyelids were fluttering, threatening that he might lose consciousness. "Stay with me." Enzo patted his cheek. "Stay awake! I can fix this…."

After gently rolling Vanek onto his front to check the wound, Enzo became less certain. The entirety of his white kitchen tunic was red, and the wound gaped as it continued to spill blood.

"I-I… I can fix this…." He tried to press his hands against the wound to stem the flow, but the blood gushed through his fingers.

"Enzo," Cullen called, kneeling with him, still mostly made of shadow.

"G-get that… thing away from me…," Vanek stammered, struggling to right himself and crawl out of reach.

"Wait. He can help," Enzo insisted, trying to hold Vanek still. He'd witnessed Cullen do the one thing neither had wanted to see happen— kill someone with the darkest parts of his power—but he trusted Cullen to aid Vanek now. He didn't doubt the sorrow he saw in Cullen's eyes, even if his own hands were blistered again and stinging.

Cullen brought both hands down, one resting on the wound to replace Enzo's, and the other held Vanek steady on his side with a hand over his heart. When his touch began to heal instead of hurt, Vanek sucked in a breath and shuddered, succumbing to the comfort and what had to be a zing of pleasure to overcome the pain.

Enzo had seen healers close injuries with various salves, runes, and spells, but nothing like this, where wild magic was practically reversing time. Vanek's wound was soon stitched closed without any sign of a scar. Blood still soaked his tunic, but he was able to be laid on his back. He'd need rest. He'd still lost a lot of blood, and Cullen's touch couldn't replenish that.

"Thank you," Enzo said, though his eyes were on Vanek as he removed his own cloak to bunch into a pillow for his friend, not wanting to risk moving him yet.

Cullen's hands grasped Enzo's as soon as Vanek's head was propped. Enzo hissed, but then Cullen healed the same blisters he'd once smoothed before. "Don't thank me," Cullen said, sorrowful still. "Not after I hurt you again."

"*Again*?" Vanek rasped, eyes narrowing despite him not trying to get away.

"It was an accident," Enzo said.

Cullen shook his head, which finally returned to flesh and blood, with peach-colored skin, wavy brown hair, and violet eyes that wouldn't look at Enzo. "That makes it worse, don't you see? I lost control. I couldn't control myself. I couldn't even hear you trying to call me back."

"But you did. You came back to yourself once you saw me."

"*Once* I saw you, but I still hurt you."

"What are you?" Vanek asked with cold suspicion, and Enzo wanted to snap at him—who, not what, *who*. But either way, the answer was the same.

"I don't know. I don't," Cullen persisted when Vanek's gaze turned skeptical. "I know it has something to do with the Amethyst. Who I was. What I've become."

"Amethyst?" Vanek repeated. "Made of shadow.... *Cullen*. You're...?" His eyes widened, and he turned to Enzo. "Don't you realize who he is? Haven't you heard the stories spilling from the Shadow Lands? What caused their curse? He's—"

Enzo pressed his fingers to Vanek's lips, halting the truth, whatever it may be, because he could see how the threat of finally knowing made Cullen wince, and a shimmer of shadows flickered over him like a ripple in a pond. "It doesn't matter. For any of us, all of us, what matters is who we are now and what we do. Please, Vanek." Enzo dropped his fingers from silencing him. "Tell me you know now that your methods are wrong."

"What I know is to be more discerning with my standards," Vanek said, and though it could have been a harsh response, the admission made him chuckle. "Just like you wanted. Maybe I am terrible at reading people. I got plenty wrong about you. And him." He glanced warily at Cullen. "Only you would fall for a void beast from a fairy tale."

"Dancer," Cullen said, and then looked surprised by the phrase, as if saying it tickled another memory.

"Void dancer?" Enzo smiled and wouldn't lose it no matter how much Cullen clung to his guilt. "I like that."

Their eyes met, and Cullen smiled a little too.

Vanek lurched into a sitting position.

"Vanek! You can't—"

"I'm fine. I'll be fine," Vanek contended, offering his arm for Enzo to help him stand. "But I can't stay. I need to check in, see what sort of chatter our presence in the castle causes. This isn't over just because your friend turned out to be myth made real."

"Please." Enzo helped Vanek up as urged but kept hold of his arm to keep him from going. "Give me more time to convince you your methods aren't the way."

"Then what is? Finally admitting the truth of who you are?" Vanek called his bluff.

"I...."

"Maybe he is a better match for you," Vanek added, which Enzo knew was both a brutal and sincere admission, though he didn't understand how. "You saved me, both of you, and for that I'm grateful. I can give you until the coronation before the Ashen make another move, but if it comes down to Tyraag becoming king, your time will be up. We can't spend another generation as the forgotten, Enzo. I won't allow it."

His steps were slow, but not unsteady as he pulled from Enzo's grasp to head for the door.

"What of the orb?" Enzo called. The true Dragon's Gland had melted, but Rufus said another of the destructive kind was in Vanek's pocket.

Vanek didn't deny it. "Find another way, if there is one, and I'll give it to you." He glanced at Cullen again, as if expecting him to counter or demand otherwise, but Cullen remained quiet. "See me to the door, Enzo? Alone?"

Cullen retreated to the workshop to give them privacy, with Enzo already assuming what Vanek's parting words would be.

"You don't want to know who he is, fine, but you can't deny he's dangerous."

"Not to me."

"You admitted he's hurt you before—"

"From a power he's still learning to control—"

"Do you hear yourself?" Vanek hissed. He glanced back toward the workshop, but there was no sign of Cullen trying to eavesdrop. "Why him… and not…?" A reach toward one of Enzo's braids was aborted with the trailing of his words. "I would have had you lead the Ashen with me like the prince you refuse to be."

"I know. But there are some paths in this life where I cannot follow you. I'm sorry."

Vanek nodded with a look of rare resignation and turned once more to go.

Enzo couldn't say for sure if they'd won. They'd bought time, but at what cost? Janskoller and the Fairy Prince had seen them, both clearly knowing Cullen.

Voidy, Janskoller had called him. That made Enzo's lips curl with part of a smile just like void dancer had. There was a good and beautiful side to that creature Enzo had known so intimately, but he couldn't deny the danger, and he wasn't sure of the right answer for facing tomorrow.

When he went to Cullen, having retrieved the Gemstone Maul from the floor, he found him staring at the main worktable, where all that really remained was the pendant.

Of course.

"You saw the crest on him, didn't you? The king?"

Cullen startled, smiling guiltily. "Someone from Ruby probably would have recognized it straight away."

"Yes. And found me out sooner." Enzo sighed, setting the hammer back into place on the table between them.

"A secret Ruby Prince," Cullen said, and for once, it was Enzo who winced.

"All my plans for how things could have been improved for the less fortunate: the Ever-Burning Torch, the Dragon's Gland, this hammer. It's all been used for destruction. I wonder if things could have been different if I'd presented my ideas to my father like I always wanted. Not that it matters anymore."

"Doesn't it?" Cullen questioned. "You could reveal yourself, let the people know a rightful heir exists. That's what Vanek meant, isn't it?"

"I have no proof."

"What of the pendant?"

"They'd say I stole it, a vile member of the Ashen. They'd never believe the king would give the mother of his bastard child a Dragonbane pendant. Unless I could find real proof... but we'd need to go back to the castle." Enzo bristled at the idea after what happened, not least of all having seen his father's body. "We can't. Even if we succeeded and they accepted a farell, a lowborn at that, what would it mean? Me, king? I can't be king. My father was a beloved ruler, even despite everything with the Ashen and the poorer streets. I could never compare to him."

"Ah!" Cullen heaved forward enough that he braced himself on the edge of the table. Tendrils lashed out from his skin like hungry tentacles seeking their next meal, and Enzo hated that he backpedaled to escape them. "D-don't say that. *Don't say that!*"

His violet eyes flashed with the light of his shadow self and then glimmered with tears, which steamed, and yet also turned to ice when they struck his cheeks.

"*Vanek... is right about one thing,*" Cullen said with his echoed voice, "*nothing will change if those in power don't. It could be you if the people on both sides were made to believe in you.*"

"But... I don't know how to lead. What if I made things worse?"

Cullen laughed, and it was a pitiable sound, full of self-contempt and grieving. His form wasn't the larger, ominous one, but his shadows seemed hungry for something, spiraling out more violently as he spoke. "*I think... I was meant to be a leader back home. I didn't want to be shackled by duty, but I was also afraid that I'd fail. And I did. Not by trying, but by refusing to try at all and not facing who I was. I'm....*" He heaved again as if in pain and sobbed harder into the table, shaking like some black-purple spider with too many wriggling legs.

Enzo stepped back toward the table, and it was Cullen who drew back. Enzo approached anyway, circling the table to get behind him.

"*Don't....*" Cullen hunched in on himself when Enzo reached for him. "*I-I don't... remember. I don't remember! But I know I did this to myself. I'm the monster now....*"

"Only if you choose to be." Enzo believed that, because he'd seen Cullen choose to be the brilliant side of his shadow self over the dark and deadly. It amazed him that he could help inspire that choice, but it was still always Cullen who had to make it. "Only if you keep running when faced with who you are. I know I asked it of you this time to save Vanek, but if whatever happened in Amethyst, however those royals know you, whatever you are now, if it all stems from you not thinking you're enough, that you're not good enough or strong enough to be who you were meant to be, please know that you are all those things. You just need to believe it.

"You are good, fair Cullen, and so strong. You… are enough."

With hands still bearing stains of Vanek's blood, Enzo continued to reach, through the flailing shadow tendrils, and right to Cullen's black-purple face. This face was as beautiful to him as the fair-skinned one. It didn't burn or blister him because it didn't want to. Cullen could control it. And when he turned to Enzo, staying hunched if only to keep their statures closer, the tendrils calmed and moved to envelop Enzo, wrapping all around him to bring their heads together with no intent to harm.

The warmth Cullen's shadows caused in Enzo's belly was as tantalizing as ever. Every part of his skin had been hypersensitized by them, like the thrill of a virgin's first touch, the tingle of raw magic, or an unending dream. All magic could be terrible, but that was up to its wielder.

"*I want to believe that.*" Cullen rested his forehead against Enzo's. "*Do you?*"

Enzo knew he wasn't asking if Enzo believed the good he saw in Cullen. He wanted Enzo to believe in himself too.

"*All your ideas to make things better,*" Cullen continued, "*they could be your ideas presented to the people directly, not passed through bureaucracy or shot down by wealthy advisors.*"

"Good intentions don't make a good ruler."

"*No, but trying can when your worst fear is that you'll fail, because it means that what you want more than anything is to help your people.*"

Enzo couldn't help but smile, wrapped in darkness he refused to fear, because after all, shadows couldn't exist without light, and what he saw before him was blinding brilliance. "Sounds like something a leader would say."

Cullen huffed. "*Maybe together we can make enough of a worthy one.*"

"Together?" Enzo grinned, and still had to lean up a little to vie for a kiss.

Cullen flinched.

"Don't turn from me." Enzo held him fast. "You can control this. Like I said, you just need to believe it."

The dark to light fluxes over Cullen's form wavered faster, violet and black at their core but every other color too. His tendrils tightened around Enzo, and Enzo's breath caught. He made sure to lean closer so Cullen would know it was a good kind of gasp.

Carefully, Cullen used his hands, emanating shadows like the rest of him, to trace the tips of his fingers along Enzo's cheeks. He gasped again. Then *again* when Cullen's fingers dug up into his hair. Every touch sang with an edge of potent magic, but controlled, purposeful. Enzo went limp without fear, safe in the hold of the many tendrils around him, and let his head drop back to moan with greater abandon.

"Void dancer…," he said. "Believe every step is under your control, and you'll never be a beast again."

Calm washed over Cullen's expression, and in that moment of euphoria, as peace gave way to sensual intent, the workshop earned a haze of violet.

The veil. Enzo couldn't yet tell if time was slowed, but he felt safe there in that private world. He knew Cullen was hesitant of it, like he expected each pocket of darkness to house a new monster worse than himself.

But he was no monster.

"*Convince me, handsome Enzo*," Cullen's voice echoed in answer to Enzo's thought. "*Dance with me.*"

The table beside them was at Enzo's level, coming up to Cullen's thighs when he wasn't hunched. Even bound by unyielding shadows, Enzo wasn't truly trapped. The tendrils moved with him as Enzo seized Cullen around the waist and hefted him onto the table.

An expulsion of shadows burst all the items from its surface— where they hovered in the air instead of falling to the workshop floor. Frozen in time it was, in a pocket all their own, where nothing and no one could touch them but each other.

Maybe they were hiding again, but they were allowed a few minutes reprieve before everything began to unravel anew. And Cullen, fair Cullen, void dancer, and all Enzo's to enjoy, was beautiful, invigorating shadow, demanding he clamber atop him and claim a deep, possessive kiss.

CHAPTER 13

CULLEN'S TEARS had become like ashes, melted away after freezing into crystals on his cheeks. The memories were closer than ever, as easy for him to touch as stepping into the veil. If he wanted, he could push through the small flutters of familiarity and reach total understanding of his past. Then he'd know, finally, who Cullen of the *Void* truly was.

But not now, not here, not when he was safe in the calmer tides of Enzo's embrace.

It was no great stretch of Cullen's neck to meet Enzo for their kiss, but the shadows helped with an arch of him upward to match every heated tangle. His tongue extended into a long, thinner wisp like his tendrils, and clung to Enzo. The shadows clung too, holding Enzo against him.

A buck of Enzo's hips made Cullen's neck arch, and he saw the haze of the veil around them, dim with monochrome violet covering everything. And yet... blackness hung in the corners, speaking of the void beyond. The depth of those shadows, deeper than his own, like they could swallow everything, called to him with a soft hum. He knew that hum, like whispers and pulses of pure magic.

The Amethyst called him home, and his body hummed in answer.

But no, it wasn't him alone who hummed, communing with familial magic. There was another pulse. Another frequency.

"Touching you feels amazing," Enzo huffed.

Cullen was a black-purple pyre with how he emanated shadows, and Enzo was engulfed within them. To have him against Cullen was the same thrill, on the verge of release before their hips had even begun to rut. "*As does being touched by you,*" Cullen said and took in Enzo's glorious glow.

He was brighter here. Cullen hadn't noticed in the castle, but Enzo was truly like the sun, a bronze god, light in the darkness, all the things Cullen had thought before and more.

Beautiful.

"You're staring." Enzo uttered a shaky chuckle.

"*You're radiant.*" Cullen reached for his face, framing his brilliance between a contrast of dark palms. "In the veil, you glow like embers, your eyes two hot burning coals, like…."

Rubies, he didn't say. He'd always seen Enzo as bronze, but there was a ruby tint to him, as though the gemstone called to him just as the far-off Amethyst called to Cullen.

Magic, pure and untainted, wanted to be free. Not destructive, just free. People tainted it. Like Cullen had. But oh, with Enzo, salvation felt near.

"Your shadows are greedier than you." Enzo chuckled again, and Cullen realized his tendrils were not merely seeking Enzo to caress and entwine but to remove Enzo of his clothes. They were a multitude of limbs, capable of untying cloak, tunic, shirt, and trousers, all at once like a king's attendants. In moments, his thick perfection was bare atop Cullen to feast upon, thicket of chest hair and all.

Cullen's clothing was shadow like the rest of him, but he could traverse great distances in a blink. He need only will himself to be out of them, and they turned to visible cloth beneath his body as a cushion on the worktable.

He wanted the shadows, but without any hint of fangs or clawed fingertips, like he'd managed before when he had Enzo inside him. He wanted only the touch that made Enzo gasp in elation and the aiding tendrils, but with form and definition so Enzo could witness every curve and line of his body, as he was enjoying Enzo's.

"Oh!" Enzo panted like a gasp of pleasure, as what Cullen willed and wanted came into being. "Oh my…." The tendrils, coiling and undulating over Enzo's body, still seemed as though made of black-purple flames, but Cullen's core was becoming flesh—not peach this time but deep purple, contoured and solid.

"Do my greedy shadows have your permission?" Cullen's voice had less echoey resonance but still deep desire. His tendrils dropped the last of Enzo's clothing from the table and returned to graze over the mounds of his rear, spreading his cheeks with promise. "May they enter you?"

Enzo's eyelids fluttered when the first lick of shadow teased his hole. "Yes… but I wish to be inside you again as well."

"They can aid in that too."

Both men erupted, Enzo squeezing his thighs and rocking his hips for their leaking cocks to clash, as Cullen surged up with lips and tongue and shadows clinging. It was a mad kiss with equally mad thrusting, having no true purchase but to rut hard lengths together until the shadows intervened.

They breached Enzo first, lapping across his opening and slithering their tips inside, while more entangled both their cocks and began to pull Enzo toward Cullen's sheath. Further shadows stretched Cullen open as admittance for Enzo's thickened magnificence, coated in Cullen's own essence that eased the way like the slickest of oils.

Enzo's breach inside Cullen ended in a slam forward to sheath him completely, and Cullen howled between their mouths. He slammed his hips up to match. He wanted Enzo deeper, all the way inside him until he burst.

Their kiss never waned, merely turned sideways for breath, then rekindled with tongues twisting. Cullen's shadows moved with and against them, caressing and stretching and *fucking* right with them. They surrounded and engulfed them like the veil, spreading Cullen wider to fill him with Enzo's cock, while just as hungrily stretching Enzo and spiraling inside him to lick his inner walls.

The end neared like an oncoming swell of tide, but not yet—*not yet*. Cullen knew Enzo felt the same, for he wrenched free of their kiss and fucked Cullen deeper but slower to stem it. With ruby-bronze eyes gazing down on Cullen adoringly, Enzo fanned a hand up the length of his dark purple chest.

"How is every version of you more beautiful than the last?"

"You think so?" Cullen grinned.

"Mesmerizing. Stunning." Enzo lifted one of Cullen's dark plum hands and kissed its palm before tonguing his fingers with a worshipful lick. "Your hair, too, is black-violet curls, and all of you shimmers."

"You're the shimmering one. Sunlight… spilling onto my night sky." A sharper thrust made Cullen yelp, and he let it turn into a long, pleading moan. "*Enzo*… spill upon me. In me. Fill me!"

Powerful figure of virility that he was and fucking Cullen harder, Enzo meant to end things another way, it seemed. He seized Cullen by the waist, and with the same show of strength as when he'd thrown him onto the table, he lifted Cullen, right up into his lap to fuck even harder inside him with a deeper impalement.

His knees had to be screaming, but no, no, for the shadows lifted them, cushioning them like a pillowed dais. Cullen's tendrils spiraled from his body, wrapping around Enzo more, *more*, until he had to be black-purple too, utterly enveloped. Yet Cullen felt like the protected one. Enzo had him, safe and claimed, and never once faltered in the force of his hips.

In whatever life Cullen had led before, it was never like this. *Never* like this. He remembered that much clearly.

Not with anyone but Enzo.

EVERY TOUCH from Cullen breached a new world, but this—*this*. Enzo felt like he could do anything. For the first time in his life, he was leading without second-guessing, welcomed, and encouraged to do so by the man he held.

Maybe that was part of it, that Vanek never truly needed him. Everything was always so one-sided, slanted, and ill-fit. But touching Cullen's changed skin, made from a night sky at dusk, was where Enzo belonged, and the shadows that arched across the land as midnight approached were Cullen's limbs greeting him home.

Amethyst eyes sparkled like stars, in a world with that same violet haze. Cullen was a celestial spider in the dark reaching for Enzo's light, and Enzo was happy to give it. To give and *give*, sheathed within Cullen while likewise being spread open.

His insides tingled with the hot-cold spike of wild magic stroking so deep inside his cavities, his entire body felt filled. He couldn't stop thrusting. Harder. *Harder*. The writhing of their bodies was as constant as the wriggling of Cullen's tendrils, gyrating over every exposed part of them—and not so exposed—coating Enzo and stretching him, as he slammed—

He came, and if his vision hadn't already been speckled with stars from gazing upon Cullen, it would have erupted with glimmers from the heavens then.

Cullen clung to his shoulders and kissed him, still rocking on Enzo's spent cock, as Enzo reached between them to find Cullen's. It was likewise wrapped in tendrils, stroking with tight coils, and Enzo added his hand to their efforts.

Cullen gasped, and the desire in his voice made Enzo's gut clench tighter. Extra spurts from his release were still spilling inside Cullen, more and more as he thrust on, like they could wring each other dry until dawn. That's what he wanted, to wring every bit of pleasure and come from Cullen's prick until they wept from the joy of it.

Cullen shot the same stardust between them as their first time, and Enzo was quick to bring his fingers to his mouth to lick the spillage. Cullen tasted like the heavens too.

Even watching the shades of black and purple fade from Cullen's skin was beautiful. The tendrils receded into him as well, lowering them to the table, as their bubble out of time burst.

The Gemstone Maul and Dragonbane pendant clattered to the floor.

"Oops." Cullen chuckled with a crooked smile. "Forgot about that."

"They'll be fine," Enzo assured him, petting Cullen's cheek as he held him close. "And so will you."

Cullen dropped his forehead to Enzo's, taller again by being in his lap. "I want to believe that, to believe in the beauty you see in me."

"All of you is beautiful, fair Cullen. Even being in the veil was like… being inside a gemstone itself."

Cullen winced.

"I know you're afraid of learning the truth, and I swear it won't change anything for me to know who you once were—"

"But I need to remember. I know," Cullen finished. "And I know you believe I can control what I am even without your help, but… not yet. Tonight, I just want to be 'fair Cullen' one more time before I learn the rest."

Enzo stroked his cheek again and nodded.

They disentangled, buzzed and content from what they'd shared. Together, they cleaned the workshop, as well as their bodies in the bath, and snuggled into bed together to sleep, closely entwined like the nights before.

"HAVE A good day now, ma'am," Enzo said after retrieving the Ever-Burning Torch from his neighbor the next morning. Her little boy, Hector, was on her hip, seemingly reticent of losing his new nightlight. Enzo wasn't sure if he'd need the torch for what lay ahead and had gone to fix their crystals early.

"What do we say, Hector?" his mother prompted.

"Tank ooo," the little boy tried with a tighter cling to her waist.

If all went well, perhaps Enzo would be mass producing this lantern sooner than he'd ever imagined.

"Tinkerer!" a voice hissed once he returned to ground level. It was Dorff, hurrying across the street to meet him. He held what appeared to be a new Ashen note, and Enzo glanced back to see one on his own door again as well. "You're closest with Vanek. What's this about holding off on more attacks? There's all these rumors about the attack last night going sideways and Rufus being missing. I didn't even get my own summons for that one. What did I miss?"

He *had* gotten a note last night. Cullen had just stolen it.

At least Vanek clearly hadn't said anything about Enzo and Cullen's roles in what transpired.

"Nothing you need worry about, Dorff," Enzo said. "There are other missions afoot. The cause is not lost."

"You're doing something in secret?" Dorff asked with excitement, and his eyes darted to the Ever-Burning Torch.

"Very secret." Enzo didn't actually know what he'd use the torch for, but he wanted to be as prepared as possible if they were returning to the castle.

A gaggle of young voices made Enzo jump, as several children came running through the street, one of whom was Dorff's daughter. He seemed ready to call after them, only to huff. "Well then. Was not a few days ago those brats were giving my sweet Olive a hard time. Used to call her *Patches*. Now they're all best friends."

Olive had a peppering of splotchy red birthmarks across her face, and Enzo, too, had seen her be the victim of bullying from the neighborhood children. Today, while they ran about, playing some form of tag or keep-away, the others weren't jeering at or picking on Olive, but including her. She had a lovely smile when allowed to wear one.

"Sometimes change merely needs the right push," Enzo said.

"Only those who most often do the pushing are headed this way," a new voice spoke. Jason had a way of sneaking up on people, even with his cane that should have clacked on the stone.

"What's that?" Dorff looked over Jason's shoulder to see what he meant.

Enzo looked too—and castle guards were headed their way.

A lot of them.

"Olive!" Dorff dashed off to gather his daughter, but Enzo had a feeling they weren't coming here for him.

"Did you go and get yourself involved, tinkerer?" Jason grabbed Enzo's elbow.

"Maybe. But I swear, I'm doing all I can to handle things the right way."

"One should hope. But you know what makes a hero in a bard song, don't you?"

Enzo waited for the punchline.

"Who wins to tell the tale." Jason winked and let Enzo go.

Enzo hurried inside. If they were going to win, they had very little time.

He found Cullen in the workshop.

"Are you ready?" Cullen asked.

"No, but we don't have time to be. Guards are coming." Enzo grabbed the pendant, which seemed a silly, sentimental thing, especially since he'd never worn it. He hid it beneath the high collar of his tunic, and it felt cool and comforting against his chest, even if it was a reminder of all he'd been denied.

What he needed it to be was a reminder of what he could become.

"Have you thought of where we'll go?" Cullen glanced nervously toward the front door. "What we should look for?"

Enzo set the Ever-Burning Torch on the table and marched to a wall of shelving filled with tools. Inside a drawer along the bottom were all the letters his father had ever sent. He selected one. "By my father's own hand. He doesn't sign his name and there's no royal seal, but if I can find something in his chambers that does bear the seal and show that the handwritings match, it might be enough for my voice to be heard.

"Not that I know who to tell or—"

"We'll get to that." Cullen went to him and pulled him into his arms, leaning down enough to rest his head atop Enzo's. "First, we find an official letter. Easy."

"And then... for you?" They hadn't discussed how to deal with Cullen's memories or the royals who knew him.

"I—"

Three harsh knocks on the outside door preceded a booming voice announcing, "Enzo the inventor! Open this door by summons of the throne!"

They *were* here for him. They must have traced the first orb back to him like Vanek feared.

"Open up!" the voice boomed again. "Or we'll come in by force!"

Enzo stumbled back. There was too much he needed, too much to think about in too little time. This was his home!

"We need to go." Cullen pulled him back into his arms.

"Wait!" Enzo pushed free once more to grab the Gemstone Maul—just as the front door burst open with a crack of wood splintering from the stone.

Cullen lunged, but Enzo lurched away from him.

"They can't see what you do!" Not when he and Cullen didn't know what the next few minutes might bring.

"Halt! We see you!"

Cullen snatched up the Ever-Burning Torch. "Then I guess you're going to have to fix this again." He scratched out one of the runes and spun as the guards neared the open workshop door, firing the released shock of lightning into their midst.

They blasted backward, and in that moment when none of their eyes were on them, Cullen swept over Enzo like so many times before and vanished with him into the dark.

ENZO'S HEART thundered in the quiet of the room they found themselves in after the din of exploding magic. They were back in the antechamber behind the throne room—the last place Cullen had seen inside the castle.

Enzo's stomach twisted at the thought of seeing his father's body again, but as he peered from Cullen's hold, he found the room mostly empty. The entire pedestal was gone, as was the treasure, leaving barely more than the desk.

"I shouldn't be surprised," Enzo said as he looked around, "given what happened here yesterday."

"Where to now?" Cullen asked.

There was no way back until they found something they could use. "We're close to the king's bedchamber and those of the advisors, Tyraag included, but I'm not sure which one is the right one. I know it has to be a room behind here." Enzo gestured to the back wall, opposite the throne room.

"Let's use the other doors," Cullen suggested, meaning the ones Vanek and Rufus had come through, and held out his hand for Enzo.

Fingers clasped, and Enzo could have pretended they were going for a stroll, until Cullen brought them into the veil. Here again he was in contact with his void dancer, all rippling shadow. He thought of the half-form version Cullen had taken, with tendrils but solid black-violet skin. He liked this malleable version too. He liked it all and held fast to Cullen's ice-hot hand.

Cullen ported them to the other side of the double doors, easily enough as only a small barrier. Outside, they walked more slowly, not knowing what lay ahead. There were no immediate guards, given nothing of value remained in the antechamber, but as soon as they turned left to head deeper into the parts of the castle they'd yet to travel, several guards lined the next hall.

They stood frozen, unable to see Enzo and Cullen.

"This makes trespassing easier, if a bit unsettling," Enzo said as they moved past the multitude of guards. Each seemed to be standing beside a different set of doors, staring blankly forward as time moved at a crawl for them. "I must be right. These are the advisors' chambers, and they increased the watch after last night. But which one is the king's...?"

"*I'd assume the grandest*," Cullen's echoed voice said, and he tugged Enzo to the middle of the hall and a set of double doors with a more ornate frame carved into the stone. He ported them through those doors too, and on the other side was indeed a room built for a king.

It was intimate for something so luxurious. The ceilings were high, the tapestries and furniture elaborate and inlaid with precious stones and metals, but there were also curtains hanging from ceiling corners and as separators throughout the room, creating a cozy atmosphere.

Like the fire burning in the hearth.

"Why have a fire for a man no longer here?" Cullen questioned, shifting out of the veil and releasing Enzo's hand so both could explore.

"Indeed...," Enzo wondered.

The bedding didn't match the rest of the décor. There was a desk that didn't belong either, and an open wardrobe with clothing Enzo knew not to be the style of the king, as if someone else had been moving in.

"Tyraag," he grumbled, recognizing one of the High Advisor's tunics. "The king is not even with the stone yet, and he's been sleeping in my father's bed? He might have already removed most of his things."

"Still worth a look," Cullen comforted, and they moved about the room with curious perusal.

There was a general reddishness to most things, like the rest of the castle, as was Ruby tradition. Red or gold was part of practically everything. Even the stone frame of the bed, all carved, had inlays of gold, and into the headboard was a golden Dragonbane crest with a ruby at its center.

There seemed to be few personal effects left, at least any once belonging to the king. Enzo wondered what had become of his father's body.

"Would Tyraag ever use the royal seal himself?" Cullen asked, having moved to a small bureau beside the bed.

"I don't know why. A new royal line would mean a new crest, a new seal."

"Then this was your father's." He held up a piece of parchment that had clearly once been folded with what was now a broken seal. Cullen closed it as Enzo approached to show the seal as it had been, red wax imprinted with the Dragonbane crest. When he opened it again, the inside looked blank.

"Why seal an empty letter?" Enzo questioned.

They stared at it, Cullen flipping it each way. "Didn't you say your father came up with the method for hidden messages?"

Enzo's eyes widened.

Like with the Ashen's note they stole from Dorff's door, all it took to make the invisible visible again was a quick coil of Cullen's shadows. Familiar handwriting came to life upon the paper, and Cullen gave it to Enzo.

"What does it say?"

Enzo almost couldn't believe it, not only because here was the proof they needed, but because it was a type of proof he never thought he'd hold in his hands. "He... he was...."

"Enzo?"

Enzo's eyes prickled with tears. "He was going to acknowledge me."

CHAPTER 14

ENZARIO DRAGONBANE, *my dear son and heir to the Ruby throne,*

I fear this may come too late, for my health is poor and I have confessed this truth to only one other, my High Advisor, Tyraag Kragvold. It is he who I entrust this letter to now, both begging your forgiveness and seeking an audience with you before my end.

I understand if you will not see me, but please, let me make up to you all my years of neglect by giving you all I ever earned and hoping you will do better with it than I did. I loved your mother as much as my first wife, who died trying to give me an heir. Clara was not the sort of second queen the people could accept, and yet, I was tempted to take her hand and scoff at tradition many times over the years, especially after I learned of your birth.

To change the heart of a kingdom is a wearisome task, but I believed perhaps I could be the one to do it if I had her by my side. Then she died too. I lost my great love for a second time, and I feared the grief was too much to keep my shattered heart together. I could not bear to see you, for all the ways you reminded me of her, and thus I shunned you when you deserved none of my sorrow. You had your own, and I punished you simply for having her face.

I have watched you these many years, kept track of your efforts, your struggles, your creativeness. I would know more of Enzo the inventor. I would hear of it all.

Sometimes I wonder how things might have been different if Clara told me she was ill. I would have denounced my throne to keep her with me. Instead, she died without me ever again looking upon her face. Now, I might die without ever looking upon yours.

You owe me nothing. I owe you more than I can ever give. You are the rightful heir to the Dragonbane throne, and if status and an elven mother be enough to take that from you, then nobles are the true lowborn for thinking something so frivolous matters.

Come, my son, see me, accept your crown and title, and if it also be possible in your heart to forgive an old fool, you would give

me more than I deserve. If not, know only that I am sorry. I love you,
as I loved you mother. I wish I had done better.
    Your father, Amdal Dragonbane, Ruby King, fifth of his line.

CULLEN WAS amazed hearing Enzo tearfully read the letter aloud. Then actual tears struck the paper, turning some of the ink darker from the stains.

"He... he was going to tell the truth." Enzo sniffled, squeezing the handle of the Gemstone Maul in his other hand more tightly. "He was going to acknowledge me and wanted me to see him before he died. Tyraag was supposed to give this to me!" He shook the letter with sudden fury.

"I had a feeling it said something blasphemous like that." Tyraag's voice snapped them from their close huddle. The High Advisor had slipped in from a side door unnoticed. "I suppose I should thank you for finally revealing its contents."

He approached at a slow, unconcerned pace. The dwarves of this kingdom, especially the highborn, carried themselves as though twice Cullen's height, and Tyraag was no exception, commanding the room even being outnumbered and with Enzo wielding the Gemstone Maul.

Cullen felt a surge of the same fury he'd heard in Enzo's voice, urging him once again to consume. He held himself in check for Enzo's sake. This was the Ruby Prince's burden to bear and to decide how things should go.

"You were supposed to give this to me," Enzo said again, shaking the letter toward Tyraag.

"Without reading it? That would have been folly for any advisor when their liege passes a note written from a deathbed." He stopped in front of them, looking at Enzo with scorn, and then up at Cullen in dismissive apathy. "The Fairy Prince and his bard said they chased off grave robbers. Now here you are again."

Chased off...? They'd covered for them. They hadn't told anyone what they saw Cullen do. Not Tyraag anyway.

Which meant he had no idea who or what Cullen was.

"Did you kill him?" Enzo asked with a catch in his voice, more tears close to the surface. "My father? Did you kill him to keep this quiet?" He thrust the letter out once more.

"And to think," Tyraag scoffed, "he would have had a foolish boy like you be the next king. Guards!" he called and snatched the letter from Enzo's hand.

As Tyraag swiftly backed away, Cullen was ready to act, lunge, *kill*, but Enzo held him back, pleading at first with him, and then with Tyraag, not wanting to fight, even as guards stormed in and surrounded them with spears pointed.

"Please… you're ignoring a dying man's wishes," Enzo beseeched. "You're manipulating everything to take the throne."

"I am doing my duty to *protect* this throne," Tyraag snarled. "Have you not heard of the other kingdoms, their rulers, so many of their traditions tossed aside? Their leaders are children or immortal monsters, and you'd have us fall to the same."

"I am the rightful heir!" Enzo cried, and a few of the guards exchanged curious glances.

"He's delusional," Tyraag snapped. "Just another one of the Ashen seeking dissent." Then he tossed the letter into the fire.

"No!" Enzo tried to leap for the hearth, and one of the guards readied to plunge his spear forward—as Cullen made everything freeze.

In the veil, he moved to grab the end of that spear first and pointed it upward, then took hold of Enzo, who sprang back into motion at his touch.

"Cullen!" He gasped at the sudden change in momentum. "The letter!" He tried to leap again, but Cullen held fast, so as not to lose him out of the veil.

"*Everything is still. We can get it.*" He aided Enzo in a more careful maneuvering around the guards. The letter was partially burned already, and as they neared the immobile Tyraag, Cullen's shadows flared in his hatred of him.

"Ah! The flames still burn," Enzo lamented after trying to pull the letter free.

"*I can….*" Cullen trailed off just as he meant to reach into the hearth himself. They weren't alone. Someone else was in the veil. Someone was… approaching from the shadows.

He turned. Which ones? Which shadows? *Where—*

"Cullen!"

The world went multicolored again, and the fire blazed beside them. He'd brought them out of the veil on accident, and Tyraag locked eyes on where they'd moved.

"Seize them!" he cried in anxious worry, and the guards scrambled to change course.

The presence... it was coming.

He was coming.

Cullen grabbed the charred letter, hissing as it singed his flesh, still having hold of Enzo with his other hand, and ported them without thinking. He was running again. He was running. But he couldn't face that presence. He couldn't.

"Where are we? Cullen?" Enzo pulled him from his thoughts, the young farell looking around with the same panic Cullen felt. They were still in the castle, some other hall they'd been in before, as Cullen held a letter half turned to ash all because he'd faltered.

Ash....

"I know this hall. We're not far from the antechamber. Maybe we can find another letter if that one's too illegible. We can't leave." Enzo grabbed Cullen's wrist, probably to not damage the letter further, but a few bits of it sprinkled to the floor anyway. "Please. Don't lose focus now. I have to take responsibility. Somehow, even without proof. This kingdom was meant to be mine, and I can't keep pretending otherwise. My people need me to become the king I doubt I can be."

"It's your doubt that proves how good a king you could be, because what you want more than anything is to see your people happy. You doubt you can do enough, that you can be enough, but that is how I know you will be."

"Cullen!"

He was still coming, homing in on Cullen's presence like Cullen could feel his.

"You are a remarkable man, Cullen. I have no doubts about that because...."

Because....

"No...." Cullen dropped the letter and pulled from Enzo's hold. "Not now... not yet. I can't, I *can't*. Please... I'm so sorry."

"Cullen—" Enzo tried to reclaim him, but the force of Cullen's roar as he burst with shadows propelled Enzo away from him and nearly upset his footing.

"What is going on—" A voice cut short after sounding from behind Cullen, and when he spun, he found what must be the Emerald and Sapphire Kings peering out a doorway, looking stunned by the beast they'd found.

"Jack, it's him…," the Emerald King said, as Jack swept him behind him like a protector.

"Stay back, Reardon. Jan!" Jack called into the room. "Nemirac! Get out here."

Them too. All of them, everyone, and the presence was still nearing, as Cullen felt himself growing into the fanged and clawed monster he'd tried to fight, hungry and furious and so… alone. He needed to consume to fill the void.

Reardon had a youthful glow, pulsing with life. Surely, he'd satisfy the emptiness—

Ice fired at Cullen's shoulder as he reached out a shadowy claw. It stung before sizzling and melting into his darkness. Jack's hand was outstretched from the attack, frost coating his fingertips. The rest of him was flesh and blood, but it seemed some of the Ice King's old powers were still with him.

Interesting.

Cullen swept forward, and Jack readied another blast, only for Janskoller to push out of the room and grab his arm to stop him.

"Wait! He's just…." Janskoller's eyes found Cullen and shot wide. "Really big right now. Got an upgrade, Voidy?"

"Stop!" Nemirac pushed from the room too, farther than the others to get in front of them and brandishing his staff. It seemed plain to Cullen now, for he could picture it bejeweled, once bearing each of the gemstones in its handle beneath the diamond at the top.

What a pretty thing the Fairy Prince was, dark-skinned with silver hair, and eyes that shone gold. The power and life brimming from him was stronger than the others, another being who'd touched wild magic and lived.

He'd satisfy the void too.

"Cullen!"

Sensation rippled across his back, and he reared around with a snarl. Red and orange flames were dissipating from the firebolt Enzo had shot at him using the Gemstone Maul. It glowed crimson from its activated rune, but though the attack had disrupted Cullen's shadows, no mere element could harm him now.

He held out his hand, and the hammer ripped from Enzo's fingers, Sun rune extinguished in exchange for Ash even before Cullen's claws wrapped around its handle. It became shadow once more, his extension to wield, as Enzo gaped, lip trembling in terror.

Stop! A voice cried in Cullen's mind—his voice—but he snarled again and shook it off. He'd leave the farell, but the others called to be devoured.

He turned just as an axe hurled at his head and caught it in his free claws. Janskoller's axe, which melted to nothing like the ice before it and the weapons wielded by Rufus.

"I really liked that axe…," Janskoller grumbled.

Cullen swept forward.

"I didn't mean it!"

"Stop!" Nemirac commanded, but Cullen paid no mind. The Fairy Prince held no sway over him now.

A pulse exploded from the diamond atop the staff, and Cullen met an invisible shield instead of the soft flesh of the mage. He readied the hammer to smash through it with a force of cosmic magic, but on his backswing, he chose another course. Entering the veil, he ported behind them where the shield protected no one.

Fools.

No! His internal voice cried again, loud enough that he faltered. He slipped from the veil, and the others, realizing he'd gone, turned and found him. Reardon was closest now, with nothing to use in his defense save a book clutched in his hands.

They're innocent, please.

They're reminders, the void in him thought back.

Why? Because they're the ones who stood up to lead? Because they chose to rule their kingdoms, chose better paths, and you failed? Are we to consume Enzo too… just for being what we couldn't?

They all still seemed frozen, fearing they'd lost when none could move as quick as Cullen had proven to. But it was Enzo he looked at, farther down the hall, pleading with those bronze eyes. Believing in him. Hoping.

A pulse alerted Cullen that the presence had found him again, that familiar thrum in the air. He felt it right at his back before he even had to turn.

"Cullen."

It wasn't a question this time, or filled with doubt, and when Cullen pivoted to look, he saw shadows down that end of the hall where a large, hulking, winged and horned silhouette stepped out of the darkness to reveal a pale-skinned elf with long black hair.

"CHICKEN? YOUR favorite food is chicken?"

"What's wrong with chicken?"

"It's boring! Everyone likes chicken." Cullen chuckled, rolling onto his front to better see Ashmedai.

They were on the floor in front of the hearth in his father's study. His father's *old* study, since no one used it now. It was one of the smaller rooms in the castle, which was why Cullen loved it, because it helped him forget how large and empty the castle was most days, even if this room was a reminder of his father's loss.

He and Ashmedai had taken cushions and pillows from the furniture and spread them on the rug in front of the fire. Cullen was closest to it, propping his elbows on a pillow to look at Ashmedai beside him, who was lying on his back. They had snacks and wine within reach, no plans in mind other than this, just trying to stay warm when the wind was howling outside from a storm.

Ashmedai was older than him, though by how much Cullen didn't know. He had an agelessness to him that made it difficult to tell. Yet there they were, lounging like school children and sharing stories and favorite things to avoid getting caught in the rain.

"Ah, but I didn't say what kind of chicken." Ashmedai grinned. Sometimes his teeth sparkled almost as if they had points.

"There's only one kind of chicken, Ash."

"But not only one way to prepare it."

"Okay." Cullen hunkered lower, moving his face right above Ashmedai's. "Wow me. What's your favorite?"

"That kind on a stick from the market, red with a sweetness mixed with spice that leaves the tongue burning."

"Fire chicken. That is pretty tasty," Cullen conceded, and they laughed together.

"It is good to see you smiling," Ashmedai said more softly, which had the opposing effect of causing Cullen's smile to drop.

"There hasn't been much to smile about these days."

Ashmedai's brow scrunched as if in realization of the nerve struck, yet he said, "You must miss your father greatly."

"Sometimes I forget he's gone," Cullen admitted. "Or I don't think about him at all. Then, when I do, I feel awful, because what I do think… is how I wish he was here so I didn't have to solve the problem of the kingdom not having a ruler."

"It has a ruler," Ashmedai said.

"No. I mean… look at me. Look at us! Would a king lounge about with a friend on a random afternoon, spread out on a rug like it's a picnic? I'm practically a child."

Ashmedai rolled onto his side to prop up on his arm, bringing their faces closer. "It's my turn to ask a question, isn't it?"

They'd been trading questions for near an hour according to the candle clock on the wall. "I suppose. What do you wish to know about the Amethyst Prince?"

"What are you afraid of?"

Cullen laughed. "Just the usual. The pointy end of a sword, old age, the dark—"

"Cullen."

Suddenly, their closeness seemed suffocating, and all humor dropped like Cullen's smile did once more. "Everything. This castle when it's empty. What the people are thinking. What my father must be thinking, watching from the skies. I am not the man this kingdom needs. I'm not even a shadow of him."

Ashmedai's eyes shimmered as if, for a moment, they held every color instead of none. "You are to me."

The warmth of the fire at Cullen's back, the stillness of the breaths between them as if both were holding them, made the lacking distance between them even more stifling, especially when Ashmedai's eyes dropped to Cullen's lips, and it seemed he meant to lean forward.

Cullen drew up onto his knees. "We should have invited Brax. He's probably wondering what we're up to. You know, I think one of the servants smuggled a cat into a side chamber…."

Ashmedai's brow scrunched again in obvious disappointment and pain before he summoned a false smile and nodded. "Next time, we'll invite Brax."

Never had Cullen been more certain that he wasn't worthy of a crown, and he certainly wasn't worthy of the looks Ashmedai gave him, or the kiss he'd almost stolen. Lovers Cullen could handle, but not love. He'd only ruin anyone who loved him, like he'd ruin the kingdom if it were under his command. He was already being a terrible friend, because he'd let Ash fall for him, when he didn't feel the same and was bound to break his heart.

In the end, he'd done far worse.

WE NEED to forgive ourselves, Cullen heard his own voice, pleading with him like Enzo's eyes. *We need to remember, face it all, let the pain come. It doesn't have to be a void. It doesn't have to be lonely. We just need to accept where we went wrong and strive to be better. We are only the monster we've made of ourselves if we let it continue to be true. Please. Remember.*

It's time to remember.

Cullen keeled forward, seeing only darkness behind his eyes as he clenched them shut—and everything flooded back to him

With no pain following it.

There was pain in the remembrance of wrongs done, but not like he'd feared, not all-encompassing to smother him in their weight. He remembered all of it, the life he'd led, the years squandered, even an endless amount of time in darkness, and a living abyss as a void beast after Nemirac drained the Amethyst and set him loose.

He'd made his own loneliness by not trusting himself and, therefore, had been unable to trust Ashmedai. The one thing he wanted to convey was how truly sorry he was, as he looked up from where he'd fallen onto his knees and his shadows began to evaporate.

ENZO RACED around the others still clustered near the door, as Cullen dropped the Gemstone Maul and fell to his knees. His shadow form was shrinking, leaving only a fair-faced half-elf, crumpled before the approaching figure of the Shadow King.

Enzo hadn't been enough to keep Cullen in control, but it hadn't been Ashmedai that made the difference. Cullen hesitated before then. He'd come back to himself on his own, just like Enzo knew he could.

He meant to step forward and say Cullen's name—

"Cullen," Ashmedai said first and knelt in front of him. His redheaded companion could be seen behind him, keeping his distance with a wary expression. He truly did look like Cullen in some ways. "*Cullen*," the king said again, and when all the shadows had truly faded from Cullen's form, he finished, "do you know who you are?"

Cullen's eyes met Ashmedai's, and though tears stained his face, some disintegrating like ashes, while fresh ones stayed wet on his skin, he sounded... happy when he answered, "Yes." He leapt forward, wrapping his arms around Ashmedai's neck, who looked startled, and then equally elated to hold him. "I'm your friend."

CHAPTER 15

ENZO EASILY could have felt a stab of jealousy from the emotion on Ashmedai's face at hugging Cullen so close and tight, both on their knees. How they knew each other he hadn't yet learned, besides being friends like Cullen had said. But all Enzo felt was relief because Cullen, the true Cullen, had finally found his way home.

"The Amethyst Prince, huh? He looks good not made of shadow," Janskoller said, to which Nemirac elbowed him, no longer wielding his staff like a shield.

Amethyst....

"*What*?" Enzo sputtered, but before anyone could answer, the hug was ending, and as Ashmedai pulled away but kept his hands on Cullen's shoulders, he proved to have been changed, like how Cullen's touch could reveal the truth in many things.

Ashmedai was the one with claws now, pointed tips to his fingernails. His teeth were pointed too, skin pure white instead of peach, and eyes glimmering with white irises upon a sea of black.

"I'm sorry!" He tried to snatch his hands back, but Cullen grasped them, keeping the two in contact, which kept Ashmedai transformed like a creature related to the very beast Cullen could become.

"It's me," Cullen said, bringing Ashmedai's hands together like a shared prayer, "helping you look like the real you. Part of the real you, something I never should have been afraid of. This is still you, Ash, not a monster or a liar or any of the horrible things I said that night."

"But I did lie," Ashmedai challenged.

"You omitted some things in fear of the very reaction I proved to give. I'm sorry." Cullen's voice choked with further tears.

Ashmedai pulled one hand from the clasped prayer and held it to Cullen's cheek, stroking gently with the pad of his thumb to catch the teardrops. There was love there, deep love, but Enzo couldn't truly feel jealous when he knew Cullen was worthy of it.

They helped each other stand, and when they finally released each other, Ashmedai turned elven again. His companion approached from the other end of the hall. He looked curious but cautious as he came into Cullen's view.

"He looks so much like—"

Enzo saw Ashmedai flinch.

"*Brax*," Cullen finished.

"He does," Ashmedai said with a sigh. "It's a long story. This is Levi."

"I remember." Cullen nodded, as Levi came up parallel to Ashmedai. "You were at the Sapphire and Emerald Kings' wedding and in the woods that time. You're…." It was obvious he was putting together that Ashmedai and Levi were a couple, and in that realization, he grabbed Levi's hand and yanked him into a hug too. "Thank you."

Levi changed like Ashmedai had at Cullen's touch, only for him, it meant deep blue skin.

What fascinating creatures these people from the Shadow Lands were.

"Why are you thanking me?" Levi asked.

"Because I love Ash as a friend, but you love him as he deserves."

Whatever jealousy Enzo might have felt faded completely then, and he saw the same relief appear on Levi's face. The three shared a smile when Cullen released Levi, who turned into a normal half-elf again too.

"Voidy!" Janskoller breezed past Enzo to join the trio. When he smacked Cullen's back, the impact lurched him forward, only for Janskoller to seize Cullen around the shoulders and hug him tightly in turn. "All grown up! I mean *Cullen*, of course. And Prince Cullen at that!" He released him with a laugh. "You owe me an axe, though."

Cullen laughed with him.

Prince. He really was the Amethyst Prince from the stories. It hadn't dawned on Enzo, even knowing Cullen was a supposed leader. He hadn't even remembered hearing the lost prince's name before.

"Get over here, Nem!" Janskoller waved the mage closer upon Nemirac's approach and hooked him into a hug too, manhandling them into a group embrace.

There were no magical truths to reveal about Janskoller, but upon contact with Nemirac, Cullen's power revealed Nemirac's skin to glow in places, like blue near his hairline, violet at his wrists—

He struggled out of the others' hold, causing the glow to dim.

"Just leftover magic," Cullen said. "You've nothing to fear."

Nemirac seemed timid, which Enzo thought an uncharacteristic look on the Fairy Prince, who was otherwise quite fierce. "I, um... I—"

"You freed me from my prison inside the Amethyst. Thank you," Cullen said earnestly. Then he smacked Janskoller with equal force to what had been done to him. "And I like Voidy. And void dancer. Plus, my kingdom has no need for a prince when it has a king. You know...." He turned to Ashmedai once more. "I think I was wrong about that teacup. Do you remember, the day my father died?"

Although it was a sad sentiment and Ashmedai's face turned contemplative, Cullen continued with neither sorrow nor regret.

"Sometimes what gets broken and put back together is stronger for it, even if it does show fissures, no matter how many times or how many cracks formed. That was true for me. Maybe for all of us. Certainly for our kingdoms." He turned to encompass them all.

It was then that his eyes met Enzo's, and maybe..., Enzo didn't feel so out of place, because Cullen looked at him like he was the one man in the room who mattered.

"They are *our* kingdoms because this is Enzo Dragonbane, the Ruby Prince."

Those in front of Enzo, and the Sapphire and Emerald Kings behind him, all turned to stare in equal surprise. Maybe he felt a little out of place, with the powerhouses of all five Gemstones Kingdoms around him.

Well, technically not all—

"Here we stand, the monarchs of our lands in a single hall."

As if appearing from the shadows that Ashmedai and Levi had entered from, the Fairy Queen and her Prince Consort added to the gathering. After all, the Fairy Prince was not ruler of his kingdom just yet.

"Mother!" Nemirac scolded. "Where were you? We could have used your help a minute ago."

"Could you have?" she pressed upon joining them, perhaps the most regal among the royals, with her stalwart human husband smiling beside her in equal finery. "Seems things turned out well to me." Her powerful gaze rested upon Cullen, then eventually turned to Enzo with a knowing grin, as if she wouldn't have needed Cullen's pronouncement to know Enzo was a prince.

"Check that way!" barked a distant voice.

Where they clustered was near an opening into another hall, and a guard came barreling down it with a clear line on Enzo.

"Halt!"

He froze, but it wasn't Cullen or any of the powered royals who came to his aid.

Reardon, behind Enzo and beside Jack, dashed toward the opening, waited for the moment when the guard crested it, and clocked him in the face with the tome he'd been holding.

The guard crumpled.

"Reardon!" Jack rushed to him.

"I figured knocking him out was the kinder choice." Reardon shrugged.

"This isn't the best gathering place," Ashmedai stated the obvious, "but I can't move this many people at once."

"I can," Cullen said, and again those assembled looked on in surprise—save maybe the Fairy Queen. "There were guards at Enzo's place, so we'll need somewhere else, but somewhere I've been before."

More guards could be heard closing in, and the one Reardon had downed was groaning with regained consciousness. They needed to move.

And Enzo knew exactly where.

"Bottom of the Barrel."

THE PART of Cullen that might have hated being at the mercy of Vanek and his Ashen no longer mattered when he'd let the weight of so much else fall from his shoulders.

He was the Amethyst Prince, a dreamer, a coward, a man who'd wronged a friend in his panic, and who'd been punished in servitude as a being of shadow to an equally in the wrong prince. Everything came around again in a likewise cycle, until the cycle was broken.

He remembered everything, but he forgave himself for being consumed by the distraction of adventure, for not being ready back then to be king, for jumping to conclusions about Ash and betraying him, for accidentally triggering what became a thousand-year curse. Worse was what he might have done if he hadn't finally been brave enough to face his past. And though he'd found that strength in himself, he knew a large part of getting there had been from Enzo's belief that he could.

He'd brought them into the back room at the Bottom of the Barrel tavern, which was thankfully empty, given the tight fit once they filled it. Enzo rushed out in search of Vanek, wary of the taverngoers learning who'd joined them, but it was soon impossible to keep from spreading that every visiting royal and their companions were amongst the lowborn and eager to hear their side.

Janskoller helped salvage at least two swiped purses before Vanek calmed the crowd and acquiesced to an audience. This conversation couldn't be for all ears, but all in the main portion of the bar, anyone who called themselves Ashen trusted Vanek, and he trusted Enzo.

Cullen did feel jealousy over that, but no shadows or darkness stirred in him. He could control them now, and the only consuming he wanted to do was of the ale in his goblet, courtesy of Sally, the proprietor.

Enzo had reclaimed the Gemstone Maul before they absconded from the castle, but it was Cullen who remembered the burned letter. He kept what remained of it safe in his pocket as they told their tale to the others, huddled tight around the back room's long table.

"I realize all this doesn't excuse the actions of the Ashen," Enzo finished, which made Vanek scowl though not interject, "but they had their reasons. No one will listen to the lowborn, and the Ashen wouldn't want to listen or work with highborns like you unless they could be certain you mean to aid me in reclaiming my throne."

That Vanek looked pleasantly surprised to hear, and Cullen was pleased too. Enzo was a king already where others stumbled.

"We're not *all* highborn," Levi said.

"Far from it!" Janskoller raised his goblet.

"And though my life is different than it once was," Levi went on, "I remember what it was like to be forgotten, to be shunned and considered lesser simply for being too poor to do anything to change my lot."

He had a sweet softspoken way about him. The same had been said of Cullen, but that was merely noble upbringing mixed with charm. He knew what tone and words turned the right heads. Levi was genuine, wholesome even, in a way that seemed to fit what Ashmedai had always deserved in a companion.

Cullen was truly happy for them.

"I believe what Levi means to say," Nemirac interjected, "is that although the ends may not justify the means, we understand the road to the right end is not easy. We've all made mistakes."

"Me certainly included," Cullen huffed, for Enzo had left no part of their story untold, and he wouldn't have wanted him to. "Awful though the man I killed may have been, I wish I hadn't let myself fall so far. So much of the sorrows in my tale are my own doing, because I didn't believe in myself enough to try to be the man I wanted to be." He saw Enzo's brow pinch and added, "I forgive myself, but it's difficult not to dwell on what-ifs."

"If it helps," Jack said, "in my first year as Sapphire King, I became all the things you feared and cursed my kingdom for centuries."

"I didn't get the chance to be king and still cursed mine," Cullen reminded him.

"No." Ashmedai sat straighter. "Brax did. You were merely being the leader I knew you could be and fighting to protect your people."

"But—"

"All is as it was meant to be," Ashmedai insisted. "There is no need to exchange blame. Though none of this would have happened if I hadn't returned to this realm all those years ago."

"Indeed," Mavis, the Fairy Queen, said, calm and unburdened, "none of this would have happened if you and I hadn't returned from where the wild magic folk retreated. It is our fault that after many trials and many mistakes, the Gemstone Kingdoms have been reborn."

Those gathered shared startled glances, as if not having realized how monumental this meeting was until someone said it. Together they made up every kingdom, every walk of life, every race and status, and it all started with wild magic returning to this realm and Cullen foolishly throwing himself between that and his people when he didn't know to trust its intentions.

"Of course, we're not truly united yet," Mavis said. "Our Ruby Prince still needs to be crowned king. How vile is Advisor Kragvold?"

"Not vile," Enzo said, and Vanek gave a snort. "Not truly! Unless he did kill my father. But he said I was foolish, like maybe he wasn't the one who murdered him."

"Um… he wasn't," Reardon said, youngest among them and so far, most quiet. "Besides looking into your orb after the attacks, I also headed the investigation into your father's death. I, um, have some experience with advisors secretly murdering their monarchs and wondered the same thing. But your father wasn't killed prematurely. His death was natural. I am sorry for your loss, but if Tyraag be vile, it's not for being a killer."

"Oh, he be vile," Vanek said, "and though I am grateful the king wasn't murdered, this doesn't change that the best choice for the throne is Enzo, someone between worlds, who understands the poor and forgotten. Tyraag would have the truth buried and the people of Ruby stuck in centuries worth of familiar segregation and ignorance. It has to end."

"I agree," Enzo said, making Vanek look stunned again but then finding a twitch at the corner of his mouth in a smile, "but even with new powerful allies, how can we avoid civil war when we announce my lineage? I don't want that, but I also have no proof any longer to prevent it. The words on the letter my father left me are barely legible, and it'd be far too risky to keep poking about the castle."

"I was thinking about that," Cullen said and drew the letter from his pocket. Even handling it gently, more of it sloughed off into ash, but he'd already revealed the truth of what something should be after it was beyond repair.

He held the letter over the table, and, with a coil of his shadows, its words glowed anew, the smudges cleared, the edges reformed. It was said that Amethyst was the kingdom of illusion and shadow, and sometimes that meant seeing what was hidden, what could be, or what once was. Cullen had never been this adept at magic in his old life, but for all the loneliness and pain being inside the Amethyst caused him, he'd also found himself there. He'd simply needed to fit the pieces back into a whole.

When the letter was as pristine as they'd first found it, even with the seal reformed, he handed it to Enzo, who'd never looked so handsome. Maybe because he sat a little taller and shone with more confidence, finally accepting his regal nature and all he was capable of.

"First," Enzo said, commanding the room as he looked to the others, "you should all get back to the castle. The guards didn't see you with us. Tyraag will blame the encounter on the Ashen if he even mentions it. Let him. After the funeral, we will have much to do, but for now, we need to make it through the king's burial without suspicion and prepare for coronation day."

"That long?" Vanek questioned. "That'll be a week from now."

"I have a plan, but I need to know you're with us."

There would probably always be a part of Cullen who resented the history Vanek and Enzo shared, but when Vanek spared a glance at Cullen, it wasn't filled with the usual challenge.

"To put the proper heir on the throne, who will care about more than highborn ideals...." Vanek scanned the table of royals and their companions and didn't seem as dismissive of them as he might have been before. "That's all I ever wanted. But let's see what the rest of the Ashen have to say. Oh," he addressed Enzo directly, "and I've cleared out quite a bit of the... riffraff if you were wondering." He hopped down from the table to lead them out.

"My coin purse was stolen in the first two minutes," Reardon muttered.

"That's lowborn charm, is all." Janskoller patted his shoulder. "And I got it back for you."

"Did you?"

Janskoller felt about his person and retrieved a coin purse that he handed to Reardon. "Oops. Definitely hadn't meant to keep that." He winked.

Cullen let the others out ahead of him, staying near the mouth of the back room even after they'd filed into the tavern proper. This was Enzo's moment.

"Oy!" Sally shouted above the din, and all muttering hushed as she gestured from the bar to Vanek climbing atop a table with Enzo beside him.

"Now!" Vanek addressed the crowd. "I know we aren't used to catering to royals—"

Jeers and hisses were thrown at all those in finery.

"But! Perhaps there is a good kind of royal after all, and that's one who'll listen to the people. Like Enzo the tinkerer, who in truth is...." He trailed off, waiting for Enzo to announce it.

"The Ruby Prince!" he called proudly and pulled out the Dragonbane pendant from beneath his tunic.

Murmurs filtered through the tavern.

"Prince?" a man sputtered from the bar.

"That's right, Dorff," Enzo said. "Many of you knew my mother, but never the identity of my father. If you need proof, I have it, but I tell you truly, my father was the Ruby King, and he meant to acknowledge me before he died. I never sought a title or wealth. I only wanted to see things become better for the people here. I think I can accomplish that from the throne, but I need the Ashen's help to take it. An inventor's role is to aid people... and so is a king's. Will you accept me as yours?"

A bit more murmuring sounded.

"Well!" Vanek shouted for them to answer.

"I do!" cried an older man, a farell with a cane and floppy cap like Janskoller's, who Enzo seemed surprised to see there.

"As do I!" echoed Dorff.

More and more affirmations rang out, until Vanek called over them, "Three cheers for the Ruby King!"

"Oy, oy, oy!" the tavern erupted.

"You have the Ashen's backing," Vanek said, and Cullen watched him hand Enzo what he knew to be the last of the destructive orbs, just like he'd promised.

IT WAS only one day to wait until the funeral. All were welcome to attend, but few could fit in the tunnels to be at the front and see the king off, for the funeral would be held at the base of the Ruby gemstone.

Cullen and Enzo need not wait in line with others, or even mill about too closely to the snootiest of advisors, nobles, and merchants, for Cullen had been in that cavern before and was able to port them in behind an outcrop. They blended in with a mere step out from behind it.

Enzo had told Cullen that a royal funeral was the only time people were led to and welcomed near the Ruby, for the kings and queens were buried in the surrounding tunnels deeper than where the Ruby rested. Strange to be here for a funeral, he thought, as they stood off to the side, looking down on the Ruby and the pedestal before it that had processed through the tunnels, bearing the Ruby King.

This was where Cullen had been reborn.

He didn't fear the gemstone or its hum like a voice whispering to him, though now he remembered the faint nothingness of his existence trapped inside the Amethyst. It wasn't the stone itself that had had ill-intent but Braxton, the friend who'd betrayed him and Ashmedai both. He'd been there, hiding behind the Amethyst, and corrupted the intentions of Cullen's spell. Knowing now that it had been out of love for Ashmedai, trying to protect him from Cullen, truly broke Cullen's heart. Perhaps Brax might have found love too, if only he'd moved on from his attachment to Ashmedai over the centuries the way Ashmedai had moved on from Cullen.

But Brax was dead now, turned villain by his love not being returned, and Cullen was the one getting a second chance.

"I always feel... calm near the Ruby," Enzo whispered. "Even now...."

"Perhaps because it knows you will use its power wisely," Cullen said.

They wore their hoods low so as not to be recognized by attending guards or Tyraag with the other advisors around the body. The advisors had been the ones to process the body in. If Enzo had been accepted as prince before it was too late, he would have been one of the bearers as well.

The visiting royals and their consorts, co-conspirators playing their roles, were nearer to the body with others of high standing. In some ways, as each of the advisors spoke in turn about the king's greatness and prayers were chorused by all gathered to wish his spirit well into the next realm, it felt as though Cullen had been at his own father's funeral weeks ago. In truth, it had been a thousand years.

"And now," Tyraag spoke as he and the other bearers reclaimed the rods that allowed them to heft the pedestal, "we say goodbye to the Ruby King to make way for the next and return him to the stone."

Cullen took Enzo's hand and slipped them into the veil as easily as taking a breath. With everyone frozen, he ported them past the crowd to in front of the pedestal where none of the bearers blocked Enzo's view. They were at the head, looking down on him at the perfect height for Enzo to press a kiss to his father's forehead.

He squeezed Cullen's hand tighter as he spoke.

"I wish I had known you. I wish Tyraag had been worthy of the trust you put in him to give me that letter. I wish... so many things, Father, but not that I weren't your son. I will do everything in my power to be a king worthy as your successor and greater still if I can.

"May the stone keep you and the skies accept your spirit for whatever adventure the next life brings." He kissed him again, but Cullen wouldn't port them away until Enzo nodded for him to, allowing him the time he needed to simply be there in silence with his lost kin.

Father, Mother, Cullen thought in a silent prayer of his own, *forgive me that I failed, that I could not be this kind of prince or become a king like Enzo. But our lands are in good hands.* He looked at where Ashmedai stood near, able to sense him there in the veil, no doubt, but staying out of it to offer them solitude. Despite all Cullen's regrets, he was truly thankful for who had become king in his stead. *I swear, even not being king, I will strive to better all our kingdoms as best I can.*

When Enzo finally nodded, Cullen ported them back to where they'd been, and time continued for the Ruby King to be processed deeper into the mountain for his final rest.

CHAPTER 16

ENZO HELD the pendant in his palm, gazing upon it, still clasped around his neck. He'd forgotten he was wearing it until trying to sleep last night. He hadn't taken it off even then but slept with his hand clasped around it like this. It had been a restless night, knowing today would be the day he saw his father off.

Dorff had confirmed that he and Cullen couldn't go back to Enzo's home. It was being watched and had been thoroughly ransacked after their exodus. Enzo hated to think of the state of it. Sally had offered him and Cullen one of the tavern's upper inn rooms, which were usually for employees and their families—or for easy marks who hadn't known better than to ask for a room in a place like this.

They were safe, though, for the Ashen were willing to put their backing in Enzo as king.

"Are you okay?" Cullen's voice called softly as he joined Enzo on the roof. It was quieter up here than near the ruckus of the tavern proper. They were higher than on Enzo's roof, and even being farther from the castle, the view was spectacular.

"They'll be burying him in the stone about now," Enzo said.

"For us, we buried our dead in the wood, but then, few from my homeland need to be buried these days. I'd say it seems unfair." Cullen sat close at Enzo's side. "But immortality didn't come without cost to the kingdoms that have it."

"Immortality," Enzo repeated. He could hardly imagine living somewhere where no one aged or got sick. "I don't think I'd want that, even for its boons."

"Some would. Some not. With all five kingdoms unified, I imagine just as many people from immortal lands will move away as those who'll want to go there."

"Even without living forever, people should be able to count on being treated for whatever ailment or injury they're suffering. That's all I want for this kingdom. Peace. Comfort. Confidence in tomorrow."

"And you will give it that. All the world is different now… handsome Enzo." Cullen grinned and took Enzo's hand, while the other still clung to the pendant. "This is the last kingdom to need change. I'm sure your parents would both be proud of what you're striving for."

"As would yours." Enzo squeezed his fingers.

"I don't really remember my mother," Cullen said. "I can almost picture her face, but more so from portraits, and those weren't plentiful. My father didn't like to be reminded of her."

"So seems a common practice."

"If it all goes wrong somehow next week—"

"We're not going into battle—"

"Even so," Cullen pushed on, "I promise to never try to forget you, and ask you to not fear reminders of me. I would rather feel the pain and know I can survive it as long as I have the memories of what was good and beautiful and so very special to me."

Enzo leaned more heavily against Cullen's side, strong emotion choking him, and it took a few moments before he said, "Still a charmer."

Cullen chuckled.

"The Shadow King was never those things for you?"

They hadn't discussed it much, the nature of that relationship, though Enzo had learned the cumulative stories of the other monarchs and their consorts. Cullen and Ashmedai had been the start of all the lands' curses.

"He wasn't the Shadow King then," Cullen said, resting his head atop Enzo's. "He was just Ash, a visiting elf from Diamond, or so I thought. We became fast friends. He was there for me in my darkest hours, after my father died. Honestly, I think I was closer to him in a few short weeks of knowing each other than I ever was with Brax. That made it worse when I realized Ash had feelings for me that I couldn't return.

"Back then, I was afraid to rule, to love, to live. I'd sooner escape up the border cliffside to dream of a life beyond it rather than embrace my responsibilities as prince."

"Perhaps," Enzo said, "but that changes nothing about how… good and beautiful and so very special you are to me. I felt awful, too, that I couldn't love Vanek the way he wanted me to, but I was destined for a different love that spanned centuries to find me."

Cullen's head lifted at the admission, and Enzo felt the weight of violet eyes on him. He lifted his head from Cullen's shoulder to meet them and found untempered joy. "I think you were the one who found me," Cullen said and leaned in for a kiss.

Even chaste, the press of lips made Enzo shiver, and he pushed for more as he let his emotions guide him. The delving of Cullen's tongue went deeper in answer, all the chaos of the days leading up to this one making a simple kiss the greatest amnesty.

Cullen's hand cupped Enzo's cheek, tilting him into a deeper press yet, and a lick of an icy-hot shadow coiled out to stroke Enzo's ear. He gasped.

"You needn't ever fear my shadows again," Cullen whispered.

"I know." Enzo leaned into the caressing tendril and let Cullen see him tremble from enjoyment. "Fear isn't why I gasped."

Cullen leaned in again—when both seemed to sense the weight of new eyes on them at the same time.

They turned, and halfway up the steps to the roof was Janskoller, watching with a gape.

"Now *there* are some mental images that intrigue me," he said and promptly grinned. "Hello, chaps. While I loathe interrupting, and I'm guessing the show you two put on would make an excellent bard song, I believe it's time to discuss just exactly what we're going to do a week from today."

Cullen dejectedly withdrew his hand—and shadows—from Enzo, but Janskoller had reminded Enzo of a larger part of his plan.

"Actually," he said, "speaking of bard songs…."

BIDING THEIR time for a week wasn't easy, but at least Tyraag seemed to believe that Enzo had given up his crusade since he hadn't made himself known or besieged the castle again. Being quiet was better, for it made Tyraag believe he had already won.

They were going to do so much more than simply announce a Ruby Prince existed. They were going to make the people themselves demand Enzo be crowned, just like they had with the Ashen.

"Maybe, with the acceptance of you as heir and prince, the Ruby will reveal its choice of you as well," Mavis said, after their roles had been laid out amongst them.

"What do you mean?" Reardon had asked.

"Your kingdoms lost the knowledge, I suppose," she said, "that the gemstones choose who rule their lands as much as any line or appointment, and the eyes of the rulers take on their patron gemstone's color. You and the Sapphire King are from long lines of succession, your eye colors passed to you from birth, so you never noticed, but when a new line is chosen or voted on, those anointed take on the gemstone's color as well. As do spouses." She looked to her husband, Finn. "Eyes such a clear blue, they're almost white, like the shimmer of a diamond."

He bowed with a loving smile.

"It doesn't affect wild magic folk," Ashmedai explained when questioning looks were given at his, Mavis, and Nemirac's eyes not following the trend. "Enzo likely wasn't passed his father's color because of the secret birth and him not being recognized. But if you announce yourself as king, the Ruby might help us with a final push."

No pressure, Enzo had thought with a lurch in his stomach. He hardly believed he was going to do this, but with the bolstering of so many, including several kings and a queen, he had to stand tall beside them.

Even at half most their heights.

Enzo was still surprised Jason had been among the Ashen in the tavern the night of his pronouncement and again while they were making plans, and asked him, "Weren't you against the Ashen's methods?"

"Sure am. I'm no revolutionary. Just thirsty."

Definitely a bard.

"And it seems that you… are telling this story your way."

WHEN THE day came, 'twas the Forgemaster chosen to lead the coronation. Normally, it would have been the High Advisor, but given Tyraag was the one to be crowned, that would have seemed in poor taste.

"Welcome, all!" the Forgemaster announced.

The octagonal central square hadn't been so packed since the night of the king's death. It seemed even more so, for the people weren't spread out dining at tables or dancing in alleys. They were clustered as close as they could be to the platform framed by an archway of twisted stone, where the advisors gathered to announce the new king.

Naturally, nobles and other highborns were closest, just like at the funeral, with the poorest spilling onto the walkways that led from the square and farther from there into the surrounding streets. Enzo, hooded and hiding his face, was with Janskoller off to the left at a place of honor near the platform, waiting for the appointed time.

Most of the others were with them but spread out around the platform as well. Nemirac was also by Janskoller, Mavis and Finn in front, and Jack and Reardon had the right. Levi was behind the platform, but Ashmedai wasn't with him, not that Tyraag or any of the other advisors took note nor seemed to care about a visiting royal or consort other than to show courtesy to the ones they saw.

Cullen, too, was not amongst them, for his role was to be played farther away. The Ashen, littered throughout the crowd, merely waited for their cues.

"It comes as no great surprise, I am sure," the Forgemaster continued, "that the advisors to the crown have chosen to back the ascension of the Kragvold line to the Ruby throne."

Many in the crowd cheered—though not all.

"The Ruby King himself would have chosen no other, and with him given to the stone a week hence, it is time to officially crown our new ruler. As is tradition, we ask only if there be dissent and reason another be more worthy."

"I have something to say!" Janskoller called, to the shocked snaps of heads from all the advisors and many whispers in the crowd. "Or rather, something to *sing*, if the advisors would bid me leave to commemorate the Ruby King before his crown is passed to another."

Tyraag relaxed from the tight tension that had visibly seized his shoulders.

"I am sure the people of Ruby would never deny the good bard Janskoller a song," the Forgemaster said.

More cheers rang out, far louder than those for Tyraag.

Janskoller ascended the platform with lute in hand, wearing his customary floppy cap, and the cheering and applause continued, until he had to hush them with a wave of his hand. "A simple song, hastily composed, if you'll forgive any poorly constructed rhymes, dear people, but as a lad once from these very mountains, I could not resist immortalizing the lost king with a song I am certain he would want you to hear."

Enzo's gut was a raging storm of nerves. There was no going back now, and he clutched the pendant hidden in his cloak, looking out across the crowd at where he knew Cullen stood sentry on bated breath too.

Then Janskoller began.

THE FIRST strums on the lute made Cullen's heart race faster, as the bard's strong baritone carried from the square all throughout the walkways and streets.

> *"Hail crimson lands*
> *Whose royals sworn*
> *Are tougher than the mountain's strongest stone."*

As his words carried, Levi used illusion magic to display them in giant lettering above the platform, so all could be sure to know what was sung.

The advisors seemed to think it a marvelous trick.

Cullen did too, for it was fitting for a denizen of Amethyst to be gifted such magic, yet Levi had originally been from Emerald, as though the Amethyst had already claimed a piece of him to tie him to his eventual new home.

> *"Your Ruby King*
> *Did die alone*
> *But far from solo in his days of yore."*

"You ready?" Vanek asked, beside Cullen as he too looked out upon the crowd, many of whom were his agents, waiting for their moment.

Cullen looked at him and could not begrudge the leader of the Ashen for perhaps not ever warming to him, but he also accepted his lot, a better man than Cullen sometimes thought he could have been were their positions in Enzo's eyes reversed. "That question is better posted to Enzo, and ready he is. I know he is." Cullen looked again upon the hooded form of Enzo beside the platform.

"Yes," Vanek agreed, "but in no small part because of you."

Cullen glanced again at Vanek, but the farell was looking forward.

"Banes of dragons it was said,
Drove it off to spare its head,
And a yet unending line did dare to tread."

Those lyrics made Tyraag cringe with uncertainty at its meaning. Cullen could see it even from the vast distance separating them while he and Vanek waited at the very ends of the crowd, close to Enzo's home— and to the first few paces that would take one through the glamour hiding the poorest streets from view.

Janskoller grinned wildly as he dove into the second verse, galloping in a dance about the platform as he played and sang. There would be no denying his words' meaning from here, especially as he bowed pointedly to Tyraag.

"A new line called
To rule the mountain,
If true a secret keeper is the right man."

Tyraag jerked forward from the line of advisors, looking up at the words displayed above their heads in large, glowing letters.

"The king did die
Of body failing
But left a way to keep his line prevailing."

"Stop!" Tyraag cried, gesturing for guards around the platform to ascend to his aid. "Stop him! He means to spread lies!"

The first cluster of guards trying to rush the platform found themselves unceremoniously tripping over each other as they slipped upon the sudden appearance of a patch of ice.

Jack and Reardon guarded that side of the platform to prevent more from trying.

Others who sprang into action were quickly confronted by Nemirac brandishing his staff on the left, and the Fairy Queen and her husband guarding the front. No guards seemed bold enough to try taking on a fabled family of immortal *demons*.

> *"Penned a note to make it true*
> *And entrusted for its due*
> *Then recovered from the ashes here for you."*

Janskoller nodded at Enzo, who was permitted onto the platform with letter in hand, held high—which at that moment had copies being passed out amongst the crowd by the Ashen, while Ashmedai watched from the perimeter, shadow jumping as needed to ensure their efforts weren't impeded.

"Lies!" Tyraag cried again, but it was his own peers, the other advisors, who held him back from tackling Janksoller or Enzo, for it seemed they were interested in learning where this led.

Janskoller was never more dazzling than when performing for a crowd, yet he somehow framed Enzo, circling him with his lute, so all eyes were on him when Enzo drew his hood back and held up the Dragonbane pendant alongside the letter.

> *"King lost a queen*
> *And so his heir*
> *But love did stir again in elven fair."*

In addition to the words of the song, Levi formed a giant version of the Dragonbane crest behind the lyrics as a backdrop, so there was no denying what those who couldn't see Enzo's pendant were being shown.

> *"A son was born,*
> *And here he stands*
> *To lead your home in much more able hands."*

The crowd was already murmuring as they read over the copies of the letter being passed around, but all heads snapped up when the dragon from the crest became an illusion of light in motion, forming the outline of a full-sized dragon that flew over their heads from the platform and right toward Cullen and Vanek.

At the cue, Cullen used his power to touch an area of the nearby building where the glamour formed across the street, and his ability to reveal the truth dispelled it completely. As everyone turned to look at the impressive dragon that fizzled into benign sparks, there was no denying the state of the streets beyond, where even more people stood than would have been visible before, those the Ashen had asked to lie in wait, so that no one could deny they existed.

Orphaned children, mothers and fathers in rags, elderly barely able to stand on their own, many who didn't even have homes other than an outcropping in the stone.

> *"For the Ashen have a point,*
> *Those above tend to exploit,*
> *And it's time to ponder well who you anoint."*

"Stop!" Tyraag bellowed, lurching free of the hold of his fellow advisors and rushing Janskoller to seize his lute.

He let Tyraag take it, holding his hands up in mock innocence. The song was already done.

With all that had been revealed, it seemed perhaps some of the wealthier honestly hadn't realized or remembered that slums existed in this kingdom. No paid-off mages were able to act quick enough to reform the glamour, and the murmuring continued, growing into a din far louder than Janskoller's song.

Ashmedai stepped up beside Cullen from out of the shadows.

"Safe?" Cullen asked him.

"Their anger is directed correctly," Ashmedai answered with a smile. "Any guards or mages farther out seem to be just as interested in the letter as others."

As the clamor rose, all eyes were on the platform—on Enzo standing tall with proof of his lineage, while Tyraag looked pathetic beside him, fuming with a stolen lute in hand.

"Is it true?" A well-dressed merchant near the front finally yelled over the din.

The Forgemaster walked past Tyraag to reach Enzo and held out a patient hand to be shown the true letter. Enzo gave it to him, and as it was read, for those who might not have seen a copy yet, Levi displayed its words in place of the lyrics so all could see it clearly.

"I invite any of the other advisors, anyone at all," Enzo addressed the crowd for the first time, "to weigh in on the authenticity of this letter."

"Blasphemous lies!" Tyraag spat.

But the Forgemaster was shaking his head, and when the Master Alchemist joined him, he was quick to announce, "There's no illusion to this. 'Tis the king's handwriting, his seal. And you *knew*, Tyraag?" he asked in accusation.

"He's half-elven!" Tyraag barked in his defense, throwing the lute to the platform floor, which made Janskoller wince and look out at the crowd with a humorous shrug as if it confirmed Tyraag was no good. "From the edge of the slums!" Tyraag tried again when some people laughed and others began to boo. "He's no true heir!"

"Call me a rule-breaker," Janskoller spoke over him, "but I'd say we defer to the people."

A hush fell over the crowd, for now they were being invited to make the decision themselves.

"Then again, it isn't rule-breaking when it's what you asked for," Janskoller added to the advisors. "You know, before you thought anyone had a leg to stand on?"

Tyraag looked ready to intervene, but a female voice cried out from the middle of the populace.

"If you became king, what of the Ashen?"

Perhaps she was a member herself, or someone of higher standing, but it was a question both sides wished to know. The Ashen weren't without guilt, but guilt was shared, and mercy balanced with retribution was one of a leader's most difficult responsibilities.

Cullen didn't envy Enzo having to address it, but he believed in the king Enzo could become. Though Cullen hadn't been able to do the same in his kingdom before his destiny changed, he was content to be in the shadows, supporting another however he could.

"Some of you know me as Enzo the inventor, or tinkerer," Enzo began, taking center stage in front of Tyraag, who looked wild but ineffectual in his defeat. "My own inventions that I had intended to use to help the people of Ruby were corrupted to cause chaos instead—by the Ashen, the source of their explosions."

More muttering arose, for it was accusation and admittance both.

"But!" Enzo demanded their attention. "That happened because unheard voices saw no other way forward, and the only way I saw and pursued another now was because I had help." He nodded in thanks to Janskoller and all those surrounding the platform to keep the guards back, though the guards had long since stopped trying to struggle forward. "None of us, not even the highborn, can accomplish anything without aid from others. We simply need to remember to share our aid with everyone.

"I would pardon the Ashen, just as I would pardon Tyraag for keeping my existence secret." He whirled on Tyraag with what Cullen imagined was a withering look of challenge.

Tyraag had no reply.

"He perhaps truly believed he was protecting the kingdom, but those above should not think it right to hide what they do not wish to see." Enzo turned from Tyraag to face the crowd again, arching an arm outward to indicate the dropped glamour that had hidden the horseshoe streets. "See what your countrymen are going through. We don't need to be divided. Let the other kingdoms be a compass for ours in their striving to accept all, to help everyone, and to unify with us as friends."

Enzo motioned for the other rulers to ascend the platform with him, and it was then that Ashmedai squeezed Cullen's shoulder before disappearing into the shadows to reappear from ones beside Levi so he could ascend as well.

"No kingdoms should have streets so poor that the people barely eat, while others are fat on excess. I do not guilt you for how you were born or what you may have earned," he spoke plainly to the wealthier in the front rows, many of whom Cullen imagined to be scowling, "but a true a leader, a true king, should find a way to aid all his people.

"My father wanted that to be me. But what say you?"

Silence descended again, the Ashen having been asked to wait for others to side with Enzo before they added their own cheers. The crowd was no doubt stunned by so many revelations and a chance to choose when they'd come here assuming their lot chosen for them.

When Tyraag looked ready to attempt to defend himself and sway the people away from Enzo, Ashmedai stepped forward first.

"I was called to be king by my people, a cursed but beautiful people, who put their faith in me when the very nature of them was changed. They chose me because they believed I would put their needs above anything else, and a thousand years since, they still ask me to remain in power. I may doubt my own worth, but I know when I see worthiness in another." Ashmedai faced Enzo and kneeled upon the platform before him.

Levi went forward to kneel as well.

"I was also asked to ascend to my throne by the will of the people," Mavis called, bookending Enzo across from Ashmedai and Levi, with her husband following her. "I see the same," she said and also knelt, with Finn, Nemirac, and Janskoller all mirroring the gesture in her wake.

"We were born into our lines," Jack addressed the crowd next, "but our people chose us anew when we proved our worth."

Reardon took Jack's hand, and together they turned to face Enzo and knelt as one, as Reardon finished, "We invite you all to do the same."

A small huff of disbelief left Vanck, full of awe, which Cullen felt too, watching Enzo, surrounded by the monarchs of the current age, all kneeling before him.

"I am the rightful Ruby King," Enzo called proudly, standing tall in their midst, "but only if all sides of our kingdom unite in naming me so."

A louder gasp than had yet been heard filtered through the crowd, for at this declaration, Enzo's eyes glowed with such pure ruby light, it could be seen from the farthest distance where Cullen and Vanek looked on.

So, too, as the gasp moved through the people like a wave, another wave followed—of everyone from all corners of the square and farther back into the deepest streets, kneeling as the Gemstone monarchs had to swear fealty to their new king.

The Forgemaster, who would have been the one to place the crown upon Tyraag's brow, took it from the case it had been carried in by the Master of Caves and Mines and brought it forward to where Enzo stood. He handed back to Enzo the original letter, and then announced over the quiet square.

"Your Ruby King, as decreed by his predecessor, the advisors, you, the people, and the gemstone itself."

Tyraag could say nothing, and as the other advisors knelt, he eventually did as well.

Enzo bowed his head, and the Forgemaster placed the crown upon it, a replica of the one buried in the stone with Enzo's father, made of gold and rubies, and even pieces of the reddish mountain rock, to an uproar of applause as the people leapt to their feet.

"Thank you," Vanek said from beside Cullen.

"'Twas Enzo's victory," Cullen answered.

"Yes, but we've all won today. Perhaps you most of all." Vanek's gaze was stoic but accepting as he looked up at Cullen. "Love him well, Cullen of the Void," he said and walked off into the crowd.

Of the Void. He'd called himself that once, and he thought, maybe, he liked it. As much as he'd once feared the void, the name befitted this version of him better than "Amethyst Prince" ever had.

And oh, he would love Enzo well indeed. No matter what the future brought, he knew he would, as he met the glow of ruby eyes seeking him across the expanse and smiled.

CHAPTER 17

"NOW, TOMORROW, I'd like to revisit the Gemstone Maul. Its abilities could easily be used offensively, but that was not my intention for it. I'd like to ensure there are strict regulations on who operates it and for what purpose."

Muttering from the advisors concurred—at least to address that next meeting.

"Adjourned," Enzo declared, and the advisors began to disperse, which now included an even number of wealthier and less well-to-do members.

Several previous advisors had stepped down of their own choosing to retire, and Vanek had helped Enzo curate replacements. Seeing as how Vanek was High Advisor now, his counsel made the most sense. Enzo had indeed pardoned Tyraag and allowed him to regain his old seat from years past as Merchant's Guildmaster. Not everyone appreciated the leniency, and Vanek had even warned him against it.

"Wasn't it you who questioned my standards of subordinates?"

"I didn't say I wouldn't be keeping a close eye on him."

Enzo had been king for less than a week, but so much was already in motion. There were plans for an audit of the poorer streets and what could be done to best aid them. All of Enzo's inventions were to be mass produced, such as the Ever-Burning Torch as a light source in the deepest mines, the Dragon's Gland as an imploding explosive, and more he hadn't yet dreamed he could work toward building and putting to use for the people. His days ahead as ruler wouldn't be easy or perfect, but it was a beginning.

He only wore his crown inside the castle, like now. When he walked the streets, his people needn't see him as anything but one of them. He also hadn't taken up residence in the king's bedchamber. Perhaps someday, but most of the castle's rooms had been repurposed into temporary housing for those who had none. Enzo had several construction plans for better utilizing the extravagant space and was content to stay in his original home.

Of course, he did have guards who kept it safe both when he was at home and when he was absent, but so far no one had attempted anything rash at his crowning. He was simply glad no inventions had been destroyed or cherished keepsakes harmed when the place was ransacked.

Another curious and exciting invention in the works was one being offered by the Fairy Queen. It seemed she had a device capable of supporting long-distance travel in a blink, something Ashmedai and Cullen could accomplish on their own but that others could only dream of for the convenience of visiting far-off lands. The hope was that, eventually, all five kingdoms would have a similar device to foster trade and travel.

Which meant much was to be done in the other kingdoms as well.

"The royals are leaving tomorrow, I heard," Vanek said, falling in step with Enzo as they left the council chambers—once one of the smaller bedchambers, for they didn't need a grand space to sit around a table.

"Yes. The Sapphire and Emerald Kings have had their honeymoon and are ready to return home, and the others have their own duties to attend to. Although, I believe Janskoller and Prince Nemirac had their sights on traveling past the Ruby Mountains and adventuring there. But we will see them again. All of them, I hope."

"Of course, there is one other royal," Vanek said softly.

Outside the chamber they exited, Cullen awaited them. He had declined a spot on the council, but just as well, for if he were ever Prince Consort to the Ruby King, it would be in poor taste for him to hold additional power.

"Were you heading back with the Shadow King," Vanek asked him, "to see your home?"

"I would like to see home," Cullen said, "but that is part of what I hoped to do tonight." He held out a hand to Enzo.

Vanek nodded them farewell and continued down the hall. Though there was still some sorrow in him, he was and always would be Enzo's trusted friend.

"Tonight?" Enzo questioned as Cullen squeezed his hand. "You're ready?"

"I am. I don't want to put it off any longer, and this first time home, I want to see it with you. And I know exactly where to start."

ENZO WAS used to Cullen's shadows enveloping him and porting them somewhere far from where they originated. It was always beautiful to him, entering the veil, however brief, before they exited again in a new location. This time, he had to admit, the view when they surfaced from the shadows was like nothing he had ever seen before.

The trees, gnarled and black and without foliage, were stunning, not dead-looking, for the black of their bark shimmered as though covered in stardust. It was night here in the Dark Forest, not because of any curse, but because the sun had set, and stars shimmered above with a perfect half moon amongst them.

A creature flew from one treetop to another in response to Enzo and Cullen disturbing it with their appearance. Or rather, it glided, chirping curiously with eyes that glowed in the dark. Some transformed animal, Enzo imagined. He would have to ask Ashmedai and Levi what it was, for Cullen was not yet familiar with all that had become of his homeland.

"At least, besides the trees and other changed plants, this place remains the same," Cullen said in a somber whisper.

Enzo looked ahead and realized where they were. A graveyard, intimately nestled within the forest. With their hands still clasped, Cullen led them forward toward a pair of particularly grand headstones as if set apart as special. They were special, for there lay the once Amethyst King and Queen.

Cullen was also changed here, into the form he most often took now when succumbing to his powers—with deep purple flesh, not shadows for skin, black-purple hair, violet eyes that glowed, and his tendrils licking out of him like flames from a pyre, tingling where they touched Enzo. His clothes, miraculously, hadn't been burned by the change, but had all become purple and black themselves.

"I've finally traveled, seen the Ruby Kingdom, and I hope to see more," Cullen spoke to his parents. "It would be wrong to say that the adventures ahead of me are worth the cost of your loss, but I do not regret where I find myself now, much as I know I could have handled things better back then.

"This is Enzo, the newly anointed Ruby King." He smiled at Enzo, his fondness pushing through any stirs of pain. "He is going to make great things of the mountain kingdom, just as wondrous things have been made of our home. I will visit again. I promise."

He brought his free hand to his mouth and kissed his fingertips, before placing them on his father and mother's graves in turn. He stood for some time, merely gazing upon them in quiet repose before he turned to Enzo.

"Is this all you wish to see tonight?" Enzo asked.

"Someday I will see the castle, walk the streets, see again some of my people who knew me in my previous life, but not yet. There is, however, one other place I would like to show you."

Again, in a blink, Cullen brought them somewhere new.

Enzo gasped.

"I hear they call it the Black Lake now, but it was the Lilac Lake in my time."

They were in equal solitude as the quiet forest, but here was a calm dark lake that reflected the stars above, surrounded by ravine walls like they were in the heavens themselves instead of on earth.

"I used to climb those rocks, as high as I could, hoping to see the other side. Perhaps now, someday, I can, but not at the expense of my responsibilities, and never again because I feel unworthy to attempt them."

"We can do both," Enzo said. "We can do anything. It's beautiful here."

"Yes, and it was here, mourning my father's loss and a path ahead I didn't want, that I met Ashmedai, and the course of my life changed forever, steering me eventually toward you." Cullen took both of Enzo's hands to hold between them, with the rocks on one side and the gentle rustling of water on the other. "I'll ask only this once, but let me have my doubts in myself one final time. Are you sure you want me, Ruby King, and all the darkness that comes with me?"

Enzo didn't answer with words but let Cullen's hands go to grab the collar of his shirt and tugged him down to his level for a kiss. Only after he felt the first alluring caress of eager shadows did he say, "I would have no other, fair void dancer, for your darkness is a warm embrace, and your light shines there too."

"And I thought you called me the charmer," Cullen teased. He touched a palm to Enzo's cheek. "Your ruby eyes are lovely, handsome Enzo, but do you know what I love more? There's a ring of bronze still circling your pupils because you are king and tinkerer both, and both have my heart." He leaned down once more and kissed Enzo again.

"Kenner! Enough now. It's time for supper, young man."

"Just one splash, Mother, I promise!"

The voices preceded the appearance of a little boy, about ten or eleven.

With horns and scales like some sort of chimera.

Enzo couldn't help how the sight startled him, for though he knew to expect monsters in the Shadow Lands, he'd seen very few examples.

The boy didn't see them, running across the sand and into the surf to splash along the shore. Then his mother appeared from an opening in the rock wall that must lead into the village, and she was scales from head to toe and beautiful in the strangeness of it. A husband and father proved to be with them too, for a minotaur like Enzo had read of in fables appeared next, looping an arm around his wife's waist as they watched the boy kick up sprays of water.

'Twas the parents who noticed Enzo and Cullen several paces down the beach from them and startled more than Enzo had. It couldn't be because Enzo was but a farell and Cullen a purple shadow creature. They would be used to unique-looking people in their homeland, yet their glances seemed for Cullen alone.

"Do you know them?" Enzo turned back to ask.

"I... I think I might." Cullen chuckled in quiet wonder, taking one of Enzo's hands again and squeezing it for support. "But next time." He raised his other hand in greeting, and it was obvious the minotaur was curious and unsure, but recognition made the lizard woman's eyes widen, before she smiled too and raised a hand in kind.

"What now?" Enzo asked.

Cullen engulfed them in shadows just as the boy saw them, an interesting show for him to be sure when they vanished. After the next blink, they were in Enzo's bedchamber, *their* bedchamber, where they fell upon the bed. "Now, handsome Enzo, I intend to make you moan many, many times."

CULLEN DID eventually offer Enzo reprieve from the bedchamber to attend a late dinner with the other royals and their consorts, since it would be their last meal together for some time. They would see each other again, and soon, but there was still some sorrow in their parting the next morning.

Especially with Ashmedai, who pulled Cullen into a crushing embrace.

"Please," he whispered at Cullen's ear, "never be sorry for not loving me."

Cullen's heart lurched, and he hugged Ashmedai harder. "Never be sorry that you did love me. We had our own stories to play out, and while I regret how I reacted to your true form, I am so glad we ended up here. He seems wonderful, Ash," he added in a quieter whisper, releasing Ashmedai and nodding at Levi, who watched them not with jealousy but contentment. "Handsome too." While Cullen more so saw the half of Levi that looked like Brax, he understood that the redhead also shared some similarities to him.

"It would seem I have a… type, as they say," Ashmedai said.

"Me too." Cullen looked then at Enzo talking with Reardon and Jack. Enzo and the Emerald King in particular had formed a fast bond, given Reardon was also a gifted scientist and had only recently been crowned king. Enzo's crown suited him. As did the tight undershirt beneath his sleeveless tunic that showed off the thickness of his biceps.

"Perhaps you'll be a king someday after all," Ashmedai said in playful jest. "Is that where your heart's desire is leading you now?"

"Prince Consort maybe. Reardon and Jack are only both kings because they rule over two kingdoms. Enzo is king here, and it's still early for us, but… it does seem less frightening to imagine ruling beside someone than alone."

"Indeed, it is," Ashmedai said, looking fondly on Levi.

"Then I believe it is someone else's turn to be a Prince Consort before me."

Ashmedai's pale skin in his elven guise blushed very easily.

"Oh, and when you get home, be sure to say hello to Yentriss for me."

"Stop hogging my boy!" Janskoller swept over and hugged Cullen equally tight. "Be good, eh, Voidy? When Nem and I come back through with new bard stories to share, I'll expect some good ones from you too. Best you take more after me than your *mum* anyway."

Nemirac, close at Janskoller's side, smacked him. "It is often better to ignore him," he said, and, perhaps somewhat tentatively, as a less outwardly affectionate man, he hugged Cullen too.

"I don't mind being thought of as a love child to your duo." Cullen chuckled, and Nemirac scoffed and looked away with his own blush, while Janskoller belted a laugh. "But… if this were my old life, *you'd* be in trouble." He poked Janskoller's chest. "I do so enjoy a burly man."

Janskoller sputtered—then oofed when Nemirac smacked him harder. "Wh—? *He* said it!"

"Oh! Actually…." Cullen noticed a pair of men headed into the castle just in time before the others headed out. "Enzo helped me acquire something I owe you, Jan, and it just arrived."

The men were Dorff the blacksmith and Jason the former bard, both Enzo's neighbors. Jason was there to see off Janskoller, as his old mentor, but Dorff carried a newly crafted hand axe. Its handle was curved for an easier grip, double-sided like Janskoller's old one, but one side was larger as the intended front, and the blades were covered in runes Enzo had added to empower it.

"By the skies, for me?" Janskoller marveled at it as the men approached. "Looks even better than yours did, Jason!"

The farell with his cane scoffed. "First you shun me by leaving my offered guest room for the castle, and now more lip? So ungrateful."

"A commission from the new king for Ruby's hometown bard?" Dorff said as he presented the axe to Janskoller. "I couldn't have asked for a better honor."

Janskoller took it and gave a few excited test swings. "Brilliant work, sir! I'll be sure to slice up a few highwaymen just for you. Thanks, Voidy," he added as an aside to Cullen.

"I did melt the other one."

There was still the Fairy Queen and her husband to say goodbye to, as well as Reardon and Jack, who Cullen gladly shook hands with, hoping to know them better someday, but eventually, all were headed home. Ashmedai would be sweeping Levi away by shadow, Janskoller and Nemirac by foot into the mountains, and the others by carriage to their respective kingdoms.

"Do we realize the impact of all this?" Reardon said with clear excitement before their paths parted. "For the first time in a literal thousand years, all five Gemstone Kingdoms are united."

"A better beginning to our parting I could not have said myself," spoke the Fairy Queen. She held the Gemstone Maul, though when she had acquired it clearly even Enzo didn't know, for he straightened with a look of surprise. "What say we make a pact, here and now, upon this clever invention that evokes all our homelands' powers?"

At her words, the rune for Storm, her rune in connection to Diamond, glowed, and the hammer crackled with lightning.

Ashmedai joined her and gripped beneath her hand. The rune for Ash glowed violet and added shadows from Amethyst.

Reardon and Jack went forward together, but Reardon hesitated. "I'm afraid I have no magic, so my rune won't ignite."

"It'll ignite," Mavis said. "We can help with that."

The Sapphire King gripped the maul first, activating Ice and an expulsion of mist. Then, when Reardon, Emerald King, went next, his face lit with excitement at the Earth rune activating at his touch, with vines twining around the maul's head.

The hammer was already a force of nature when Enzo joined the others, shorter among them, but easily able to add his hand to the base of the hammer's handle and activate the Sun rune for Ruby, adding an eruption of flames. In the instant when all five runes and elements were alight, the flurry of power calmed to a single unifying prismatic glow.

"To a new golden age," Mavis announced.

"Gold?" Janskoller called from amidst the others, all just as important as the rulers who led their kingdoms, even if their hands needn't touch the maul to empower it. "I'd say… more like a rainbow."

Cullen liked the sound of that and met Enzo's ruby and bronze eyes with heartfelt affection, while they still reflected the maul's prismatic shimmer.

"Ancient princes back from the dead," Janskoller could be heard as he and Nemirac were first to head out the castle doors, "a kingdom-wide coup, all the gemstones rediscovered, and cursed kingdoms opened that were lost? What's next? Some of that dragon dick I know you're always thinking about."

Nemirac snorted. "If dragons are next, I'll eat your hat."

LATER THAT DAY

THE BLAST was startling, but it only erupted for a moment and then imploded on itself to collect the debris.

"This thing is a godsend," announced the foreman as he approached the pile where one of the newly minted Dragon's Glands, the blasted stone, and the ore they were after could all easily be sifted through.

"More like *king*-sent," chuckled one of the workers.

Mining in the Ruby Mountains had never been easier. They had more workers, too, because the danger was far reduced between their new explosives and light sources. To mine the most coveted of materials, they could go deeper into the mountains than ever before, even past the Ruby gemstone itself.

They were mindful of the catacombs for the dead, but there were many other caverns once thought impossible to excavate in. Now they could, with the hopes of building more homes and resources for those in need.

What the workers didn't realize, nor Enzo, Cullen, nor anyone else safely back home in Ruby or the other kingdoms, was that in a few decades time, or perhaps a century, the mining would reach the last slumbering dragon—his platinum scales already rippling with anticipation within the safety of pleasant dreams.

But that is another story.

Keep reading for an excerpt from
Their Dark Reflections
by Amanda Meuwissen!

CHAPTER 1

SAM KNOCKED on the paneling of the wrought-iron doors, trying to peer through the glass. It was frosted, offering no insight into what lay inside. Mr. Simons's instructions were for him to let himself in, but he still wanted to announce himself.

Hearing no response, Sam tried one of the handles, and it gave way with ease.

"Mr. Si—" He cut off with a gape as he entered. He'd known the house would be impressive from the outside, but this was *Real Housewives* kind of ostentatious, opening into a huge two-story entryway with a grand staircase leading to the second floor.

The décor was antique and modern mixed, with standing radios from the '20s or '30s on either side of the doors, resting atop trendy black-and-white tiles. Two matching art deco tables bookended the staircase in similar fashion, sporting their own vintage radios. This guy must be a collector.

Good. That meant there would be even more worthwhile prizes than what Sam planned to steal.

"Please close the doors behind you, Mr. Coleman," a voice called from the second floor.

Sam obeyed, noticing how the opaqueness of the glass kept out any natural light. The nearby curtains were closed as well, making it harder to blink upward through the dimness and see his host.

Sam had ridden there on his motorcycle to throw off his new "client." Any other professional with his resume would drive something more practical. The bike added a distinctive edge, so that when his skills proved worthy, Mr. Simons would be that much more intrigued by him— and easier to con.

Little good that did when the man couldn't see outside. Sam openly gawking around the foyer like an amateur didn't help either. He was twenty-three, not a child. He needed to act like it.

"Mr. Simons," he said, clearing his throat to start over, "a pleasure to finally meet you in person. I hope you don't mind me parking my motorcycle in the driveway."

"Not at all." He must have seen the bike after all or wasn't that easily surprised. At first, he made a somewhat hazy figure descending the stairs until he was close enough for Sam to see him clearly. "And call me Ed."

Sam nearly gaped again, because *Ed* was not the old rich guy he'd expected.

First, he couldn't have been older than thirty, with well-coifed strawberry-blond hair, green eyes, and a tall, slender frame dressed primly—and maybe a little ridiculously with a sweater vest and bow tie—which all amounted to a nerdy boy-next-door who didn't seem to realize he'd grown up hotter than his wardrobe.

"It's a pleasure to meet you too." Ed smiled warmly and extended his hand.

Hot *and* nice. This wasn't turning out like Sam had planned at all.

"IF I CAN call you Ed, then please, call me Sam."

Attractive *and* well-mannered. This wasn't turning out like Ed had planned at all.

Sam's skills and experience had been listed as housework, groundskeeping, scheduling, even personal finance—everything Ed needed in a temporary assistant. He hadn't expected someone so young, though, or with such a roguish smile.

Ed never realized how much he'd enjoy curls on a man, either, rich black with a few unruly ones falling into eyes that were almost black themselves and easy to get lost in.

Ed had to focus.

"It's cozy in here," Sam said.

"Yes, I keep the house fairly warm, since I tend to run cold. I'm sure you noticed." Ed waved his hand.

"Cold hands, warm heart, right?" Sam flashed a smile again. "Are you an antiquities collector? I couldn't help noticing the radios."

"A little," Ed admitted. "I love theater, but there's something special about purely spoken stories."

"A radio drama fan? That's rare. I enjoy the old oral traditions too." He cocked his head with a stretch to his grin that made Ed forget himself for a moment.

"I-I, um…. W-we should…." He paused to collect himself. "How about I give you a tour, and then we can discuss your schedule?"

"Sounds perfect."

Ed led Sam into the living room that spanned almost one whole side of the house and connected to the back patio that opened to the fenced-in backyard and pool. "I know it's a lot for one man, but I like my space, and I have numerous possessions I don't want to part with."

"I can imagine," Sam said, looking at Ed's framed photographs on the wall. Ed's three favorites were prominent: The Grand Canyon just after sunset, Times Square in 1957, and one of Big Ben first being built, two-thirds to completion. "This last one must be over a hundred years old."

"A hundred and sixty, give or take."

"Famous photographer?"

"Just a family heirloom."

"Must have been a cool family. I take it groundskeeping will include cleaning the pool?" Sam moved to the patio doors and pulled aside the fitted curtains.

"I like to swim at night under the stars," Ed said, holding back in the shadows, "so it can be your last duty of the day."

"You only swim at night?"

"I have photodermatitis and light sensitivity, so the sunlight can be dangerous. That's why I keep the curtains closed."

"I'm sorry." Sam let them fall back into place.

"The tools you'll need are in the pool house, but let me know if anything is missing."

"Stargazer too?" Sam indicated the telescope near the doors.

"Yes, I bring that outside on clear nights. I'm a Pisces myself."

Sam looked at him as if in surprise.

"Not that I take astrology seriously! I just think it's fun. Besides, the stars have their own stories to tell, and how people choose to interpret them can be fascinating, don't you think?"

With his grin creeping up again, Sam sauntered closer to Ed. "Pisces, huh? No wonder you like to swim. I'm a Gemini. What's that say about me?"

Ed felt his face flush as Sam drew closer. "Th-that you're adaptable, curious, witty. You can be the exact person someone needs you to be."

"Lucky you," Sam said. Then, when Ed stood staring like an idiot, he followed with, "For the job."

"Right! You're quite the Renaissance man from your credentials."

"I hope I live up to what you expect of me, Eddie. Can I call you Eddie, or is that too informal?"

Ed could usually read people well, but he didn't often have them in his home for very long. He must be imagining that Sam was flirting. "I don't mind." Although no one *ever* called him Eddie. "Shall we?" Turning swiftly, he continued toward the dining room and kitchen around the other side of the house.

Sam followed. "This Renaissance man can also cook. Did you want—"

"No need," Ed broke in. "I order in all my food and don't eat much. It'd be a waste to have you cook for me. You're welcome to help yourself to anything in the pantry or fridge, though, and since you'll be staying over lunchtime, feel free to make requests."

"I'll take you up on that."

They came around to the staircase again and headed up to the parlor, which Ed considered to be the best place in the house to read, since it looked out over the high ceiling down to the foyer. He still had a book resting beside the armchair where he'd been awaiting Sam's arrival.

"*The Tempest*?" Sam read the title.

"We are such stuff as dreams are made on, and our little life is rounded with a sleep," Ed recited, and then chuckled bashfully when Sam grinned at him. "I, uhh… like to reread classics between new titles."

"Impressive library," Sam said, scanning the bookshelf behind the armchair.

"That's just for what I'm currently reading or about to start. The rest are in the *real* library." Ed motioned for Sam to continue down the hall, enjoying the shock that briefly filled his features.

They passed a bathroom, the office, a guest room, and entered the second guest room that Ed had turned into his library. He'd not only covered every spare inch of wall space with ceiling-high bookshelves, but had placed standing bookshelves in rows like a true library in order to hold everything he owned. He rarely got rid of books and kept adding to his collection.

"*Harry Potter* next to a first edition of *The Canterbury Tales*." Sam sputtered a giddy laugh as he looked around, but then the humor seemed to leave him, and he frowned as he continued scanning.

"What's wrong?"

"There's no order to any of this. Not by title, author, genre."

"I was more concerned with getting them on the shelves."

"Is that how all your organizational attempts pan out?" Sam looked at him with something akin to pity.

"I just don't like the tedium of it," Ed defended.

"I meant no offense." Sam held up a hand and gave a short laugh—hypnotic really, or magical, because it loosened Ed right up again. "Luckily for you, I live for tedious planning. Shall we move to the master bedroom?"

Ed was close to reprimanding Sam for such cheekiness when he realized he meant the *tour*. "Yes! Last stop." He moved swiftly once more to prevent Sam from seeing how red his face had become. He'd avoided real interaction with people for so long, he'd forgotten how to act normally.

Or Sam was just that charming.

The master bedroom was large, with its own bathroom, and housed a four-poster bed and matching dresser, along with a shelf for Ed's cameras—some modern, some antique—but he spent the least of his time in that room. It was mostly only for his safe, set into the wall by the closet.

"You know, people usually put paintings over those," Sam said.

"I will eventually. I just haven't decided which one yet. Besides, I wanted you to see it since you'll be helping me with my finances. It mostly only holds cash and the logins to my offshore accounts on a flash drive. I can't let you have access to any of that or the safe, but you can see printouts of my holdings once we get to that part."

"No problem. That's all I'll need. Do you only collect cameras and photographs or take your own?"

"I take some. Whenever something beautiful catches my attention."

Eager to be out of the bedroom given Sam's effect on him, Ed started to lead them downstairs, but Sam pointed to the pull ladder at the end of the hall.

"That's to the widow's walk."

"May I?"

"Be my guest."

Sam pulled the string to bring the ladder down. The sun spilled into a little pool at the base, which Ed sidestepped with a simple pivot. Once Sam was almost to the top, he turned back.

"I suppose you can't join me, huh?"

"Still a little too bright for me. Go ahead."

Sam nodded and finished the climb. He disappeared for a spell, but then his voice filtered down. "You should bring your telescope up here!"

"I'm not a fan of heights either!" Ed called back. He could never quite get over that sudden feeling of vertigo when he was high up.

Sam returned and carefully replaced the ladder. "No basement?" he asked as they headed to the main level.

"No." At least, not that Sam needed to know about.

"Are you sure you only need me for two weeks?"

"We can play it by ear," Ed said, but he had no intention of extending the contract. Any longer would be too risky. "Shall we plan out your first few days?"

"Absolutely. I'm all yours, Eddie."

Definitely only two weeks.

DEFINITELY NO more than two weeks.

Ed wasn't like the others Sam had conned. Sam considered himself a Robin-Hood-for-hire, targeting rich assholes who had it coming. Granted, he kept all the money for himself, his crew, and his employers, but at least he only stole from bad people.

Until Ed, who didn't seem to have an ounce of badness in him and had no idea who he'd just let into his home.

Sam *Goldman*, not Coleman, who was currently scamming him for every cent in his offshore accounts.

"You got a full tour of the house, know exactly where the safe is and what's in it, and he's lax on security?"

"I even know the model number to the safe."

"Then all you have to do is play it cool for two weeks, and we can make a clean getaway."

"Yep."

"He probably won't even realize he's been robbed for months, with how much he has."

"Yep."

"It'll be the easiest job we've ever pulled off."

"Yeah…."

"You like him, don't you?"

Sam stared at Mim beside him at the table, his best friend and confidant, practically family, who knew him better than anyone—save maybe Gerry, the other member of their "family," who knew him even better from sheer force of will and prying.

Mim was tiny, blond, gorgeous, but packed a mean punch when she wanted to. She was playing with a knife, twirling it around her fingers while they talked, the complete opposite of Gerry.

"Do either of you know what this cord is for?" Gerry called from across the room.

He would have been an imposing man if he wasn't tall, dark, and bumbling more than any other adjectives, a cream puff in the body of a bouncer.

"I mean, it's HDMI to HDMI, which is always useful, but I already packed the other adapters except for what I need for my laptop. Although, since I have the others, I can probably get rid of this one."

"Gerry—"

"Only the moment I do, I just know I'm going to find whatever this goes to and wish I still had it. I better keep it."

"Gerr—"

"Of course, if I do realize I need it later, it's not like it's hard to replace—"

"*Gerry*, will you shut up?" Mim snapped, pulling him into their close-quartered conversation.

They shared the one-room loft. Logan, who owned Lucifer's Rest downstairs, had a soft spot for them, offering free room and board for doing odd jobs and occasionally bartending or waiting tables.

It was meant to only be temporary, but two years ago Sam had finished his twenty-first birthday passed out on that floor.

"There might not even be a payday," Mim said.

"What?" Gerry lumbered over to them, still carrying the cord. "What are you talking about?"

"Sammy's smitten with the target."

"I'm not—"

"Ew." Gerry stopped with a grimace.

"It's not like that. And he isn't some aging sleazeball. This one's different. He's young and handsome and… kind of stutters when he gets flustered."

"He's smitten with you too?" Mim groaned.

"Took to my flirting like he is."

"*Sam.*"

"What? I've flirted to finish a job before."

"Not with someone you like."

Sam fell silent. That was their one rule.

Assholes only.

The three of them had no one else in the world, only each other, grifters since they could fit a hand in someone's pocket. Well, Sam did the pickpocketing, Mim handled muscle, and Gerry was in charge of the technical side. They were criminals, and they enjoyed being criminals, but that didn't mean they hurt good people.

"So that's it?" Gerry said, sinking into the chair at Sam's right. "No big score?"

"I don't know, but I'm not telling the Cramers we're backing out of a retirement-sized payday after only one meeting with this guy. Someone this rich has to have skeletons in his closet. Even if it's also filled with sweater vests and bow ties."

Brock and Celia Cramer, an up-and-coming power couple who'd just moved to Riverside, had come to them with this job. It had seemed like a dream come true when they told them of another transplant, a full-blown whale coming to town and bringing a fortune with him. Sam had never done a job *in* Riverside before—he wasn't an idiot—but this time, they'd be leaving afterward, so it didn't matter. Finally, all the scraping by he and his crew had done over the years would pay off, and they'd never need to con again, at least not to survive.

He couldn't call it quits after one day.

"Aw," Gerry said, bumping Sam's shoulder. "You do like him."

"That isn't a good thing, Gerry. The Cramers are expecting us to finish this job."

"We could always do it anyway, even if Simons is a nice guy," Mim said, picking at her nails with her knife.

Sam and Gerry glared at her.

"Can't blame a gal for trying." She shrugged.

"If Simons is on the level, we'll bow out, but the Cramers swore he was a worthwhile target, so keep packing," Sam told Gerry, "and start working on how to crack that safe. Simons has to be hiding something."

AMANDA MEUWISSEN is a bisexual author with a primary focus on M/M romance. She has a Bachelor of Arts in a personally designed Creative Writing major from St. Olaf College and is an avid consumer of fiction through film, prose, and video games. As the author of LGBT Fantasy #1 Best Seller, *Coming Up for Air*, paranormal romance trilogy, The Incubus Saga, and several other titles through various publishers, Amanda regularly attends local comic conventions for fun and to meet with fans, where she will often be seen in costume as one of her favorite fictional characters. She lives in Minneapolis, Minnesota, with her husband, John, and their cat, Helga, and can be found at www.amandameuwissen.com.

Follow me on BookBub

THE PRINCE
AND THE
ICE KING

A Tale from the Gemstone Kingdoms

AMANDA MEUWISSEN

Tales from the Gemstone Kingdoms: Book One

Every Winter Solstice, the Emerald Kingdom sends the dreaded Ice King a sacrifice—a corrupt soul, a criminal, a deviant, or someone touched by magic. Prince Reardon has always loathed this tradition, partly because he dreams of love with another man instead of a future queen.

Then Reardon's best friend is discovered as a witch and sent to the Frozen Kingdom as tribute.

Reardon sets out to rescue him, willing to battle and kill the Ice King if that's what it takes. But nothing could prepare him for what he finds in the Frozen Kingdom—a cursed land filled with magic... and a camaraderie Reardon has never known. Over this strange, warm community presides the enigmatic Ice King himself, a man his subjects call Jack. A man with skin made of ice, whose very touch can stop a beating heart.

A man Reardon finds himself inexplicably drawn to.

Jack doesn't trust Reardon. But when Reardon begins spending long days with him, vowing to prove himself and break the curse, Jack begins to hope. Can love and forgiveness melt the ice around Jack's heart?

www.dreamspinnerpress.com

STITCHES

A Tale from the Gemstone Kingdoms

AMANDA MEUWISSEN

Tales from the Gemstone Kingdoms: Book Two

Created by the alchemist Braxton, Levi was "born" fully grown and spends his early days learning about the monster-filled kingdom he calls home.

Even though he is just a construct pieced together from cloned parts, Levi longs to fit in with his mythical neighbors, but more than that, he wishes he could say two words to the Shadow King without stuttering.

Ashmedai has been king of what was once the Amethyst Kingdom since it was cursed a thousand years ago. Only he and Braxton know what truly happened the night of the curse, and Ash's secret makes walking among his beloved people painful, so he rarely leaves his castle. However, with Festival Day approaching, Ash wouldn't mind going out more often… if it means seeing more of Levi.

Ash wishes he deserved the longing looks from those strangely familiar violet eyes. He knows no one could love him after learning the truth of the curse. But if anyone can change his mind, it is the sweetly stitched young man who looks at him like he hung the moon.

www.dreamspinnerpress.com

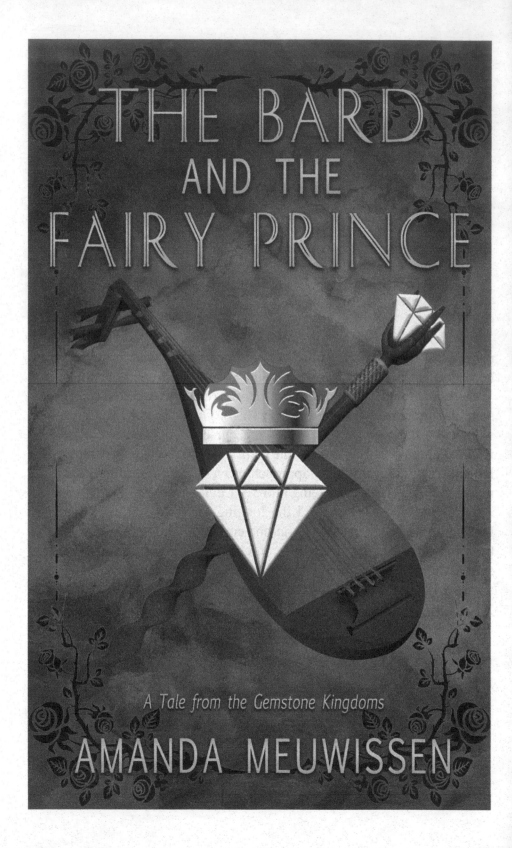

Tales from the Gemstone Kingdoms: Book Three

When Prince Nemirac learns of his heritage, he vows to become the most powerful demon in history. But he can't do it alone.

Feeling betrayed by his parents' lies about his true lineage, Nemirac embarks on a quest to visit all five Gemstone Kingdoms and drain the stones of their power to ascend as a new being. But until he obtains that magic, he's vulnerable.

Enter Janskoller the warrior bard.

Janskoller has just returned to the Gemstone Kingdoms, drawn by stories of broken curses and lands open for travel. He doesn't expect a pretty young mage to hire him as a bodyguard, but it's a good gig for a bard—lots of adventure to fuel his stories, and plenty of travel to spread his fame. Besides, Nemirac's passion and obvious secrets intrigue him. But soon Janskoller realizes the peril of Nemirac's goal—an end that puts the five kingdoms at risk and corrupts Nemirac into a darker, twisted version of the man Janskoller has come to care about. As the two grow closer, can Janskoller convince Nemirac to abandon his pursuit of power in favor of the deeper, more lasting magic of love?

www.dreamspinnerpress.com

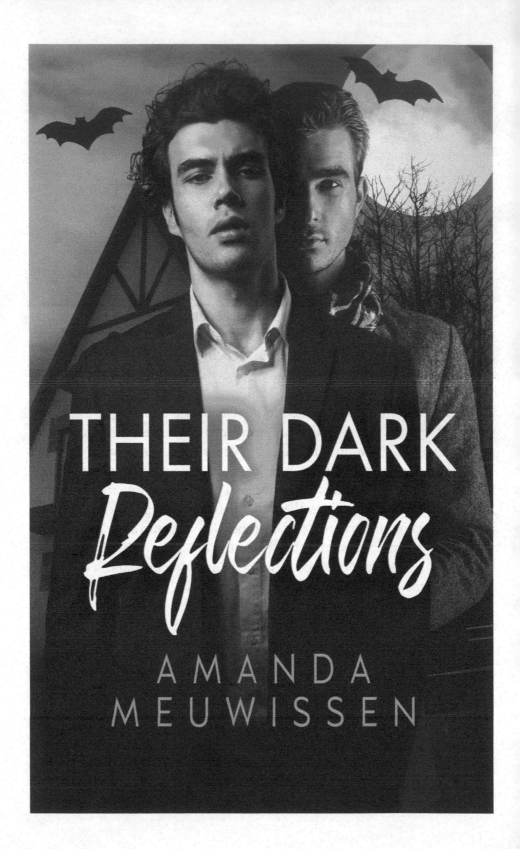

THEIR DARK
Reflections

AMANDA
MEUWISSEN

Personal assistant Sam Coleman can do it all: housekeeping, groundskeeping, bookkeeping. The catch? It's a con.

Ed Simon, his newest millionaire boss, doesn't know Sam Goldman is a Robin Hood for hire who targets rich jerks. Sure, Sam keeps the money for himself, his crew, and his real employers, but at least they only steal from bad people.

Until sweet, fumbling Ed, who doesn't seem to have a single vice. Too bad the people who hired Sam won't let him back out. They want Ed's money, and they'll hurt Sam and his friends to get it.

For years Ed has kept people at arm's length, but Sam's charms wear down his defenses just as he learns their budding relationship was an act. Sam isn't who Ed thought he was, but Ed has a dark secret too: he's a vampire. And someone is framing him for a series of bloody murders.

When the real villains force their hand, Sam and Ed must choose: work together, trust each other, and give in to the feelings growing between them… or let what might have been bleed out like the victims piling at their feet.

www.dreamspinnerpress.com

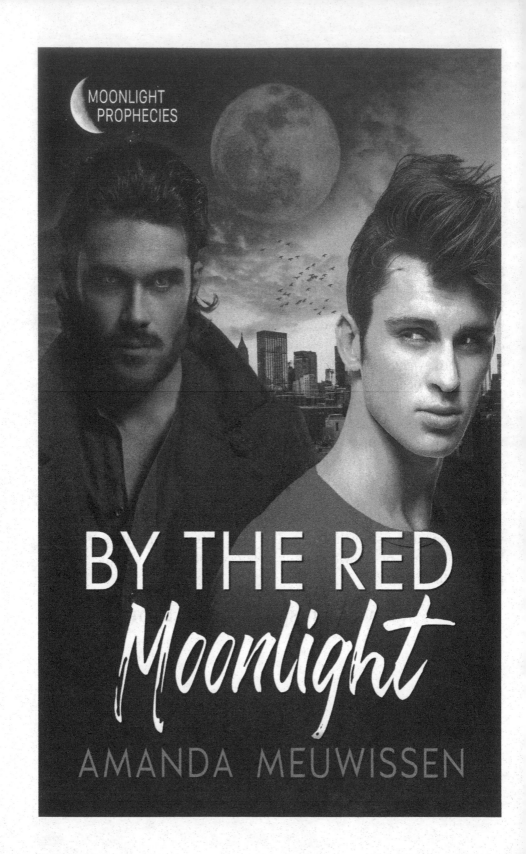

MOONLIGHT
PROPHECIES

BY THE RED
Moonlight

AMANDA MEUWISSEN

Moonlight Prophecies: Book One

Alpha werewolf, crime boss, and secret Seer Bashir Bain is neck-deep in negotiating a marriage of convenience with a neighboring alpha when a tense situation goes from bad to worse. A job applicant at one of Bash's businesses—a guy who was supposed to be a simple ex-cop, ex-con tattoo artist—suddenly turns up undead.

A rogue newborn vampire would have been a big wrench in Bash's plans even without his attraction to the man. After all, new vampires are under their sire's control, and Ethan Lambert doesn't even know who turned him. When Bash spares his life, he opens himself up for mutiny, a broken engagement, and an unexpected—and risky—relationship.

Ethan just wants a fresh start after being released from prison. Before he can get it, he'll need to turn private investigator to find out who sired him and what he wants. And he'd better do it quick, because the moon is full, and according to Bash's prophecy, life and death hang in the balance.

www.dreamspinnerpress.com